Rat

Rat

FERNANDA EBERSTADT

NEW YORK   ALFRED A. KNOPF   2009

THIS IS A BORZOI BOOK
PUBLISHED BY ALFRED A. KNOPF

Library of Congress Cataloging-in-Publication Data
Eberstadt, Fernanda, [date]
Rat / by Fernanda Eberstadt. — 1st ed.
p.   cm.
ISBN 978-0-307-27183-9
1. Teenage girls—Fiction.   2. Single mothers—Fiction.
3. Brothers and sisters—Fiction.   4. Voyages and travels—Fiction.
5. Birth fathers—Fiction.   6. Pyrénées-Orientales (France)—Fiction.
7. London (England)—Fiction.   I. Title.
PS3555.B484R37 2010
813'.54—dc22   2009024849

Manufactured in the United States of America
First Edition

For Maud and Theo

BOOK

One

1

You try calling someone "Daddy" whom you've never met in your life.

Rat has this pad of pink bubble gum–scented stationery with mice on it that's all the rage at her school. Kids will trade a mammoth marble or a jawbreaker just for one page. Rat's got a whole damn pad of it she's just bought with the money her English father's sent her for her birthday. And now she's already wrecked three pages trying to write this damn letter thanking him for the twenty francs he's sent her. First she's ever heard from her father. More money than she's ever had in her life. *Chr papa, mrsi . . . cher Papa, mersi. cher ppa . . .*

You can see Rat's difficulty in the monkish elaborateness with which she is transmogrifying her capital letters, turning the *C* into a snake with a hissing tongue, the *P* into an archer with a bow, the whole set-piece of greeting and gratitude grinding to a halt, firstly, because Rat doesn't know how to write a letter, and secondly, because never having met her father or heard from him before, she hasn't a clue what sort of child he would like her to be.

"Can I see the card again?" Rat asks, hoping for guidance. A picture of a clown sitting on a cake, and on the inside, in English, "To Celia, Happy Birthday, love Daddy" in an anonymously cursive script.

"Where's the envelope? Can I keep the stamp?"

"It came with something else, some bank business. I threw it away," says Vanessa.

"I didn't even know he knew when my birthday was," Rat says, wondering.

"Get back to your letter, girl."

Rat groans. Looks up again, after a moment. "Are you sure it's okay to write him in French?" She knows the answer already.

"Sure, sweetheart, your daddy speaks good French. He went to boarding school in Switzerland."

Rat considers other options, diversionary tactics. "Maybe I should send him a photo, so he knows what I look like." There's a snapshot of herself Rat likes that's tacked up on the living room wall. She's on the boardwalk at Canet Plage, in her Rollerblades, wearing a denim skirt which their neighbor Cristel helped her make from an old pair of jeans. She is unsmiling. She looks tough, challenging, but pretty.

"Sure, sweetheart. Why not?"

"Why don't I just send him the photo and skip the letter?"

Her mother makes as if to swat her on the side of the head, play-angry. "Go on, lazy brat, write."

No need to feel sorry for Rat for having a father she's never met, who only gave up denying she was his when the DNA test proved it. Lots of kids Rat knows are way worse off. There was a story on TV about a man who didn't feed the dogs when his wife went away on vacation, so the dogs ate their toddler.

Besides, hard to see how there'd be room for a man in their lives. Rat and her mother are close as sisters, sometimes twins. Vanessa is so small—child-size, really—they can wear each other's clothes. When one of them has nightmares or there are people staying over or they just happen to feel like snuggling, Vanessa comes to sleep in Rat's bed.

"How're you coming along?" Vanessa asks now.

Rat grimaces, clutches the letter close. "Don't look."

Her mother pushes aside Rat's sheltering hands, and examines the mangled cross-outs.

"You're a real case," she says, fondly. "Here." Vanessa writes out three lines for Rat to copy. "Dear Daddy, Thank you for the birthday money. Love, Celia." Easy-peasy.

Rat tries to summon up the diligence to replicate these lines, but her concentration's shot. She hunches her shoulders, stretches, picks her nose, yawns.

"You finished, sweetheart?"

"I can't do it," Rat grumbles. "I hate writing."

"Just get it done with, Ratkin."

"I can't."

Vanessa reads the letter, folds it, and stashes it in her big patchwork carryall. "Okay? You're finished."

But Rat is hunched, sulky with failure.

Vanessa rumples her daughter's hair, bends down to blow into her ear, to tickle her. No reaction.

"You're done," she repeats. Waves a hand in front of Rat's eyes. "What are you going to do with the money?"

Rat shrugs.

"Come on, grump. Let's go to the beach," Vanessa says. "You can buy me an ice cream. A Magnum."

"No way," says Rat. "I'm not spending my birthday money on an ice cream." But already she's on her feet, searching for her sweatshirt, the bucket in which she collects sea glass and shells.

The thank-you letter that Rat was obliged to write to her father sticks in her mind as an unsettling anomaly in a life otherwise devoid of any such old-fashioned rites of good manners. Or, indeed, of any communications from her English relatives.

Some years later, when it strikes her that a father might come in handy, Rat asks her mother why they've never heard from him again.

And Vanessa, who is in a lousy temper, feeling unappreciated by her now teenage daughter, laughs shortly and says, "Did you really believe that?" There never was any birthday money from Rat's daddy, she explains. It was Vanessa who in the fullness of her heart invented this offering the year Rat moved from preschool to primary and was getting bullied by older kids at recess. "I did it to cheer you up," she says.

Rat is so shocked her normally sharp tongue momentarily fails her. She feels made a fool of. She feels tampered-with, defiled in her innermost sanctuary, the place where she dreams about people who to her waking life are marginal.

"You made me write a letter you were never going to send?"

Vanessa shrugs. "I thought it might help you. You had things you needed to say to your father."

"Like thank you?"

It'll be years before Rat discovers that although her English father doesn't send her birthday presents, he does pay Vanessa child support—a monthly sum which by London standards is probably pretty basic, but which, for the Pyrénées-Orientales, where they live, is royal.

Vanessa is a rich woman, but nobody knows, least of all her daughter. The monthly payments which are intended for Rat's maintenance pile up in a Crédit Agricole account, separate from their regular account, which is always bumping on empty. And meanwhile, Vanessa and Rat live hand to mouth like everybody else they know, off a combination of welfare benefits, undeclared earnings, and gleaning.

To her friends, Vanessa is wide-open generous. The generosity is genuine. Vanessa would give you her only winter coat, and it wouldn't be a game. It's as if she's unconscious of the fact that, unlike her friends and neighbors, she's got serious money in the bank—if she knew, she would buy a new car, instead of rattling around in a broken-down Renault 5. Poverty is also something mental, and Vanessa honestly feels skint.

And Rat, later on when she learns about the child support and thinks it over, doesn't begrudge her mother the money that should logically have been spent switching her to private school after she flunks out of eighth grade because the public high school at Canet is so big and rough that you spend all your mental energy figuring out how not to get beaten up. Or even just taking them on vacation somewhere nice.

Rat doesn't mind, because thanks to Vanessa's teaching, she's learned to fend for herself. Later on, when she meets people who've been born rich, they will seem to her like dogs without a sense of smell. Bank accounts belong to the realm of the unreal. What's real is your quick wits.

Vanessa is a *brocanteuse:* she buys and sells old goods. A natural-born forager, says she. The walls of their apartment are plastered with the kind of things she loves: printed cocktail napkins from a bar in Spain, a leopard-skin carnival mask with gold whiskers, photo spreads from old magazines.

Many of these photographs, laser copied and blown up, are of Rat's English granny, her unknown father's mother, whose name was Celia Kidd. Rat's real name, too, is Celia. She was named after her granny, but everybody except for teachers calls her Rat.

Celia Kidd was a top model in London in the 1960s. There is a black-and-white blowup of her on the kitchen wall from British *Vogue,* a tall slinky girl, slim as an otter, with white skin and enormous eyes, wearing a poncho made of white feathers, and seemingly nothing else. Her gaze is merry and slightly mocking.

Rat's father, Gillem McKane, was her only child.

Rat's favorite photograph is of Celia and Gillem together,

when he was a little boy not much older than Rat. It's a two-page color spread, and it comes from a time when Celia Kidd was married to a British film director.

Celia, older than in her modeling days but still ferociously beautiful, is wearing a brocade fur-trimmed tunic. She is stretched out on the sofa, her long legs dangling over the armrest. Gillem is sprawled on the floor at her feet, drawing a picture. You can't see his face, because he's looking down. But he's got long black hair, and he's wearing a shirt with a frilly collar. In big letters printed along the side of the photograph, it says in English: "Mrs. Harbison's drawing-room is midnight blue, a favorite Empire sofa is upholstered in hot-pink velvet."

Celia and Gillem's lives were so star-studded you would never have thought they would cross with Rat's mother's.

But later on, when Gillem was in his twenties, there was a period when he and his mother used to spend their summers in the Pyrénées-Orientales. They rented a big house on the cliffs above Collioure, which was the village where Vanessa and her parents lived. Celia Kidd would pack the house with her glamorous friends. And for a month in August, Collioure, otherwise rather sedate, would suddenly look as glitzy as Saint-Tropez.

Rat loves hearing the story of how her parents met.

One Saturday night, according to Vanessa, Gillem walked into the nightclub where she and her girlfriends hung out.

"Did you know who he was?" Rat asked.

"Of course. Everybody knew him. Celia's son. He used to ride around town on his motorbike, usually with some drop-dead blonde hanging off the back, who me and my friends'd be doing hexes on—shrivel up and die, you old witch. He was gorgeous. And then that night, it was like, Oh my God, there's Gillem. And he's all by himself!"

"So you asked him to dance . . . ?"

"We danced, we talked. He had this really cute English accent.

I asked him where his girlfriend was, he said she'd gone back to London. I said, Oh, so my voodoo spells worked."

"What did he say?"

"He laughed. Then we danced some more, and he asked me if I'd like to go for a walk on the cliffs."

"What did you say?"

"I said I'd had so much to drink I was scared I'd fall over. And he was like, Don't worry, we'll fall together."

That remark Vanessa thought dead-romantic, but Rat found it a bit too weird, as if her parents might just as easily have died that night, instead of producing her.

"And after that summer, you never saw him again?"

"They stopped coming to Collioure."

"So you never saw him again?"

"Never."

"Wouldn't you like to go find him someday?"

"What for? We do pretty well on our own, don't you think?"

When Rat tries to picture her father, it's never as a grown man, but always as a boy her age, like her friend Jérôme who lives next door, or the Gypsy kids she plays with in the market at Brix. She pictures him the way he looks in the photograph: a boy in a white lace shirt with a mass of tangled black hair falling in his eyes.

Rat imagines showing this boy the treasures she keeps in an old tin lozenge box: bits of sea glass, the china favors she's collected from previous years' Twelfth Night cakes. When she climbs a tree, Gillem is on the branch next to her. She can imagine her father as being this eight-year-old child, but she can't picture him as a grown man. Can't picture him eating supper at Vanessa's kitchen table, or driving Rat to school in the morning, or coming to kiss her goodnight. Can't imagine him doing any of the things fathers do on a Sunday afternoon: trimming the hedge, or tinkering with the car, or playing *pétanque* with the neighbors, or yelling at you to clean up your room.

. . .

The first time she is conscious of seeing her mother—whom she'd thought as much a part of herself as the scar on her forehead or her broken front tooth—judged by a stranger's eyes.

Vanessa is taking Rat and the neighbors' kids to the beach. To get to the beach from their place, you have to cross a highway. It's not a megahighway—there are only two lanes—but it's the kind of dead-straight, flat-as-a-pancake, five-kilometer stretch where drivers like to pretend they're practicing for the Paris–Dakar. There's a culvert that runs under the highway, which is where you are supposed to cross, but after it's rained, the tunnel goes knee-deep in black mud. So Vanessa has made the kids scramble up the embankment, and now is urging them across the road.

There's nothing hurried about Rat's mother's approach: she is strolling right into the threat of fast traffic, willing any oncoming cars to halt. Solenne, who is little more than a toddler, Vanessa is gripping firmly by the hand. Rat and Solenne's big sister, Emilie, are following closely, like chicks with the mother hen, hesitant, then scrambling in jerky moves to safety.

Only Jérôme is left behind. Vanessa yells at Jérôme to move his butt, but he has frozen. Remains stock-still by the far side of the road, seemingly unable to budge. It's obvious neither he nor Vanessa is going to make a move, so finally Rat goes darting back and grabs him. Jérôme's a year older than she is, but sometimes he just spazzes out. On the near lane, there's a gap in the traffic, but on the far side, as they cross, there's a van heading right for them.

You'd never think a machine could be sarcastic, but the lordly last-minuteness with which this van grinds to a halt exudes contempt. When they are safely across, Rat's mama smacks Jérôme's skinny butt. "When I say come, you come."

The driver's window's down. He's watching the spectacle with an air of disbelief. Then he leans out his window and says, "Lady, it isn't your son who deserves the spanking."

Vanessa's eggshell skin stains red with anger. "*Connard!*" she shouts back. Her words are lost in the engine's departing roar.

Rat picks up Jérôme's towel and bathing suit, but her head's on fire. She's burning from the shock of seeing her mother as others might see her. Vanessa has done something demonstrably dangerous, and she's been scolded like a child for it!

"What an asshole," Vanessa says, once they reach the beach. "What is it about people they can't mind their own business, they have to stand over you, nya nya nya all the time?"

Rat doesn't answer.

Vanessa takes her own sweet time choosing the perfect patch of sand, not too far from the water, not too damp, unrolling their mats and securing them with rocks. Jérôme and his sisters are already waist-deep in the sea.

When she's done, she strips down to her bikini bottom and stretches out delicately on her mat. And only then notices that her daughter is still standing.

"What's wrong?"

"*What?!*"

"What's biting you?"

Finally Rat says it. "Mama, that was dangerous what you made us do. And why did you have to spank Jérôme?"

There's an unspoken etiquette that's been breached: unless you're a teacher, you don't smack other people's children.

Vanessa sits up, bare tits bobbling, instantly furious. "Look, whose side are you on, anyway? All my life people have been standing over me, telling me what to do, snipping at me for even breathing. You think it's easy, lugging four sniveling brats to the beach? Would you rather be back at the house, broiling? Enjoy yourself. Relax, have a swim, live it up a little. And leave me the fuck alone. Okay?"

Rat sits down beside her, chastened. "You're going to get burnt on your shoulders."

She rubs the suntan lotion across her mother's back, all the way down to the butterfly tattoo nestled at the base of her spine, just above the two dimples on her buttocks.

She braids her mother's hair, which is henna-red, but she has nothing to tie it with, and little coils and tendrils keep escaping. She tries to fasten it with a strand of seaweed, but the seaweed breaks.

"Yuck," says Vanessa. "Horrible kid. Vile brat," but her tone is affectionate now, and she rolls over and rubs her nose against Rat's in an Eskimo kiss.

"Do you love your little Vanilla-do? Tell me you love me."

"Yes, I love you, Mama."

"I love you too, my little Ratkin. Don't you forget that, I love you, love you, love you."

Rat's mother is exquisite. She has a tiny heart-shaped freckled face with a pointed chin, and huge eyes like a cat's. Beside her, Rat feels raw-boned, gawky. She lies down beside her mother, so that she can peek into Vanessa's eyes which are deep-river dappled. Her cat's eyes change color, from green-brown-gray to brown to green again, depending on her mood.

Rat knows the language of those eyes. Brown when Vanessa's sad (worried about a friend who's sick, or a boyfriend she's broken up with). Gray when she's angry (a fight with Mémé Catherine, Rat's French granny, or with the landlord who won't fix the drain). Green when her favorite song comes on the radio, or when she's dancing around the house, parading some crushed-velvet scarf or feather boa she's found for nothing in the market.

"You're so beautiful; you should have been an actress," Rat says. "You'd have been a superstar."

"Yeah," says her mother drily. "Story of my life, one long string of should-have-beens."

And Rat feels doubly bad, because she knows if it weren't for her, Vanessa could have been any one of those things she dreamed of—artist, actress, singer, fashion designer.

Because Vanessa's missed so many chances on Rat's account, she feels extra guilty for giving her mother a hard time. When Rat grows up, she's going to buy the two of them a big house with a walk-in closet, and a bathroom with a full-size bathtub and mirror walls and vanity lights with a dimmer. She's going to take Vanessa to Venice and Africa and the Greek Islands, all the places she loves to read about, and she's going to bring her breakfast in bed every morning.

Rat isn't easy. That's what Vanessa tells her friends, she isn't easy. Other times, she says, "You're the love of my life."

2

Summer evening. The sky is pale blue, but already an egg-yolk moon is hovering above the still, mirrored sea. The rising moon is orange with harvest dust.

Rat and Jérôme have been building a fort in the long dune grass of Saint Féliu Plage. Rat wishes they could spend the night, but Jérôme's supposed to be home by nine.

Their fort is an observation post, positioned to spy on the tourists having dinner at Chez Ernest. It's Saturday evening, and the beachside restaurant's terrace is flush with elegant blonde women, glittering with makeup and jewelry. Tanned men. Vacationers who speak in the hard clipped accents of the North. Jérôme calls them all "Parisians." *"Parisien, tête de chien, Parigot, tête de veau."* Behind the restaurant, big cars with out-of-state license plates—Bordeaux, Toulouse. There is even a Mercedes-Benz with a Belgian plate.

Some of the grown-ups Rat recognizes as local—pals of Ernest and his wife—the local men are beefier than the "Parisians." They talk about rugby and boats and how much things cost. I paid *deux mille balles* for this, he paid *dix mille balles* for that. Normal things—the grown-up's equivalent of the way kids boast at school.

The "Parisians" are a race apart. It grates on Rat, how cosseted their children are. In the day, they are slathered in suntan lotion and made to wear hats so their skin won't burn. On the beach, they wear sandals so their feet won't get cut by broken glass. As soon the sun goes down, their mothers ease them into hooded sweaters, knitted cardigans.

Sometimes one of the bolder kids will approach Rat and Jérôme and ask, "Do you want to play?" but they have evidently been trained to stay within their parents' eyeshot, and if you suggest venturing further—into the dunes, or up on the bunker—they get nervous. Once she and Jérôme played with a boy who started teasing them about the way they spoke—"Why do you say 'de-meng' for *'demain'*?"—and only shut up when Rat pinned him to the ground and threatened to pour sand down his throat.

Tonight Rat and Jérôme find themselves spying on two kids who are swinging in Chez Ernest's hammock. The little girl is trying forcibly to eject her big brother. She pushes at his low-swinging bottom, encased in hammock netting, but she can't budge him. Failing, she runs back to the restaurant, bawling for their mother.

The mother intervenes.

The boy, sighing theatrically, surrenders his place to the little girl. Swings her as high as the hammock will go, and, as soon as their mother is out of sight, turns it upside down, depositing his sister hard in the sand. "You go running to Mama once more, and I'm going to take the biggest hairiest spider I can find, and put it in your bed tonight."

Rat and Jérôme by now are losing interest.

"We should go home," says Jérôme, reluctantly.

"Not yet. We need to check first that the enemy's not approaching by sea." That's their signal to head for the bunker.

The bunker is a cement block, just out of sight of Chez Ernest, built by the Germans towards the end of the war in readiness for an Allied landing on this stretch of Mediterranean. There are hundreds of bunkers up and down the coast. Originally this one was sand-colored, but now it is so solidly spray-painted in graffiti—dark blue, red, yellow—that it looks like one big tattoo.

There's a room inside where the German gunners would have hidden, and where today older kids go to smoke pot and kiss, but it's dank and dark, and it gives Rat the creeps. Even when her friends dare her to crawl inside, she goes only with reluctance. Later on, after a girl from Fitou is raped in it, the municipality cements the entrance shut, and it becomes like a Pharaonic pyramid that holds a curse.

The bunker is oddly configured, shaped like a turnover, with one side not sheer but sharply slanting. Rat and Jérôme like to scale its cliff face. When you get to the top, you can see the entire coast, from the white limestone crags of the Corbières down south to the dark-green wall of the Albères, the Pyrenean foothills that mark the Spanish frontier. In between, is a harsh blazing Mediterranean flatland of marsh, delta, bulrushes, sandy plain.

This plain is Rat's home. Its blistering sun is her sun, its thistles and parched hummocks and reeds are the only vegetation she knows. Occasionally she's been up into the mountains—to the market at Brix, or camping in the Cerdagne. But for the most part, Rat's world is flat and tricornered, bound by three markers: the beach, where they also buy their groceries; the village, where she goes to school; and home.

Rat's territory isn't big—it's one kilometer from her house to the sea, and another kilometer to the village—but within it, she has abounding freedom.

A gang of children from Chez Ernest have followed her and Jérôme to the bunker. A man calls, and three of them disappear, leaving only a tall towheaded boy. A boy without brothers or sisters, who belongs to nobody visible.

"What are you doing?" the boy wants to know.

Neither she nor Jérôme bothers to reply.

"How did you get up there?"

Jérôme and Rat slide down the bunker and scramble up again, down and up, heedless, just to show him how easy it is.

He watches them. "Should I take my sandals off?"

They don't answer.

He starts to climb, but his jellies get in his way. He stops to unfasten them. Holds them in his hand, as if he intends to carry his sandals with him. Finally drops them back down as timorously as if they might explode.

Crawls higher, clumsily, painfully. Then stops, spread-eagled, just where the angle gets sheer and there are no more bumps in the cement for finger- or toe-holds.

Jérôme and Rat peer down at him.

The kid's trying to make it look as if he's just taking a leisurely break in his climb, pausing to enjoy the view, but they can see he's paralyzed with fright.

"I'm stuck," he says, finally. "What do I do now?"

"What do you want to do, go up or down? You might as well come up, you're almost here."

"I can't. I'm scared."

They watch with genuine puzzlement. Jérôme's sister Solenne's only three years old, and she can scamper up the side of the bunker like a monkey. This kid's way bigger than they are. They've never heard of anybody's getting stuck. Either you're too little to do it, or you do it.

Jérôme climbs down, and helps him back to the bottom. The boy's legs are trembling so hard he can hardly stand. They wait for him to go away but instead, he stays. Sits himself down in the thistly sand, looking up at them. Rat lobs a piece of loose rubble at him to make him go away.

"Leave him alone," says Jérôme.

"Is he a moron or what?"

"Leave him."

Rat hates what happens to her coast in the summer. All her secret places that are empty year-round are suddenly overrun by tourists. For two, three months you can't move because the roads are bumper-to-bumper with trailers driven by Scandinavians who don't know where they're going. Her favorite beach becomes a nudist camp. And every weekend there are brawls between the Parisians and the local boys, usually over some girl.

"Did you hear what happened to Enzo and Marina?"

"What?"

Enzo and Marina's mother's having a romance with a Dutch windsurfer she met at the Sol y Mar. An older guy with a dog. Rich, apparently.

"She's gone off with him. Just disappeared. Marina came home the other day, nobody there, no note, nothing. She'd disappeared with him, like that," says Rat.

Jérôme whistles. "So who's looking after them?"

"I don't know. Their dad's handicapped. He had some horrible accident that's left him practically a vegetable."

"So what's gonna happen?"

"I dunno. I guess they're gonna go into Care. That's what Cristel says. They're waiting to see if their grandmother will take 'em, but if not, it's Care."

"*Putain*," says Jérôme, sobered.

"Care" is the menace that hangs over the more precarious players in Rat's world. Every kid who isn't actually stuck to some family unit with Super Glue can in theory be taken into Care. If the teacher notices you're coming to school with no socks in the winter and hungry as a wolf by lunchtime, if her requests for a meeting with your parents go unanswered too long, it's Care that sooner or later is going to come knocking at the door, wondering, Who actually is this child's legal guardian?

Of all the kids she knows in what the teachers call "fragile situations," only Florian is brazen enough to say, "Fine, let them put me in a Home. That way at least I'd get three square meals."

"That boy's still down there. Why don't I chuck another rock at him?"

"Nah. Let him be."

"I don't like him spying on us."

The fairy lights strung along the trellises of Chez Ernest are twinkling red-green-white. The sky has turned a dark neon blue.

A lady in a sarong comes out onto the patio of Chez Ernest. She calls, "César! *Cou-cou!* Cé-sar!"

"She's lost her dog," guesses Jérôme. But Rat knows from the way the blond boy below them goes invisible, sinking down into himself, that it's him she's calling. The lady's beautiful, but her son isn't.

"Is that your name, César?"

The boy doesn't answer.

"César, isn't that a dog's name? I thought she was calling her dog."

The lady has been joined on the beach by a man. Together they look around, and finally spot the boy. The man heads over towards his son, then catches sight of Rat and Jérôme, who are peering over the edge of the bunker.

"*Tiens,*" the man says, laughing. He is wearing a black shirt and white jeans. "Come eat. Didn't you hear your mother calling?"

He flicks his chin up at the bunker. "What's that?"

"It's a German bunker," says Rat.

"Oh really?"

"The Nazis built them during the war."

Her desire to impress is so fierce it's like a pain in her chest. "Do you want to see me jump from the top?"

"No, I don't, thank you."

"Your son doesn't climb very well," she says.

"He's a city kid."

"Paris?"

"No, actually we live in London."

Rat's heart pounds. For one crazy moment, she thinks, This is my father. He's come back to find me. "You speak good French," she says, testing.

He laughs. "I am French; I just work in London."

Rat still stares, reluctant to give up. Maybe he just doesn't want to say it. "I've been to London. Lots of times. My daddy lives there," she pursues. "He's a city kid, too."

"Oh really?"

"My daddy's English."

The man smiles condescendingly. "Do you speak English?"

"*Yes. Very much.* His name's Gillem McKane. Do you know him?"

"It's a big city. César, dinnertime."

"When I go to stay with him, he drives me around in his red Ferrari. He lives in a great big house next to Buckingham Palace. You don't know him?"

"Sorry . . . It's a big city. César, dinner."

"Everybody knows him. My granny was a top model," she insists. "I go to stay with them every vacation."

"Really? Come on, César. We're eating. When your mother calls, you come the first time."

"Why did you name him César? Isn't that a dog's name?"

"Not really. It's the name of a man who built bunkers on this coast long before the Germans."

Rat rolls her eyes at him for thinking she's so moronic she's never heard of the Romans, but he's not looking at her anymore. César shakes himself as if awoken from a dream and crouches down to fasten his jellies.

"Say good-bye to your pals," says the man. César casts them a glance of unexpectedly intense hatred and says nothing.

"You got the time, mister?" Jérôme shouts, when they're almost out of hearing.

The answer's inaudible. Rat and Jérôme watch the man and boy saunter through the long grass back to the restaurant. The man slings a casually proprietary arm around César's shoulder. Rat feels hungry just thinking about the dinner that's waiting for them. They serve good food at Chez Ernest, though not good enough to warrant the prices.

"We should be heading home," says Jérôme. "It must be way past nine."

It's late enough so even Vanessa will start worrying, but Rat's not ready yet to tear herself away from the night sea, the flamenco music coming from the restaurant, the sound of laughter. The sky is navy blue and the moon's casting a pale yellow moonpath across the water.

Between here and home, there's the highway underpass to cross, which is spooky even in the daytime. You never know who you might meet in there, or whether your bicycle's going to get mired midway in mud, a double nuisance for Rat, who is barefoot.

"I still think César's a stupid name," she says.

"It's a good thing he didn't want to see you jump off the top, you would have broke your fucking leg," says Jérôme.

They both laugh. Rat leans over the straight side and spits. "Don't you find it a bit stupid, César?"

"Is it true your daddy has a Ferrari?"

"Yeah. Like Michel's." Michel owns the catamaran company where Jérôme's father is manager. "A red convertible Ferrari. That's the kind my daddy has."

"That's not a Ferrari, jerk-head, that's a BMW," says Jérôme, affectionately.

That night, safely home, Vanessa says Rat can come sleep in her bed.

Rat, drifting off to sleep to the sound of the television, pictures the man in white trousers being her father, his loose lordly arm around her shoulder. But it's too strange to imagine herself on the other side of the looking glass. If she too became a "city kid," would she forget how to climb the bunker, would she fight over whose turn it was to swing in the hammock, would she suddenly get scared of spiders?

"Vanessa," she says.

"What, sweetie?"

"Do you think someday we could go meet my dad?"

No answer.

"Why don't we call him up and ask if we could go see him?"

"In London?"

"Why not?"

Her mother laughs.

"Why don't we?" Rat insists.

"Your father's an odd guy. He's kind of a hermit," Vanessa says finally.

"What's that?"

"He doesn't see anybody. He doesn't answer the phone, he doesn't answer his letters."

"That's pretty weird."

"Oh, I guess he got sick of people swarming around him just because his mother was famous."

"That sounds nutty," says Rat, grumpily. A father who doesn't answer the phone doesn't sound half as good as a father who drives a red Ferrari.

. . .

Rat and her mother, and Jérôme's family, too, live at Mas Cargol, just outside Saint Féliu.

Fifty years ago, Mas Cargol would have been a working farm with orchards, arable land, pasturage for sheep. Today, the farmhouse and its outbuildings have all been converted into apartments, and the surrounding fields into an industrial zone of garages and warehouses. All that's left of the Mas's agricultural past is a garden and some cherry trees gone wild.

There are six households living at Mas Cargol. Certain neighbors Rat leaves alone—an elderly couple who have a gift shop at Canet Plage and a Yorkshire terrier called Cuddles who likes to bite your ankles; an ambulance driver who works the night shift and yells if you make too much noise in the daytime. Most of them, though, are her friends—Cristel, who works at the town hall; Laurent, who has his carpentry workshop in the courtyard.

The Cabreras, Jérôme's family, live in half of the farmhouse. The other half belongs to Monsieur Bordon, an elderly doctor from Toulouse who only comes there in the summer, and who owns a couple more apartments in the Mas, including Rat and Vanessa's.

Rat and Vanessa's apartment is in the old *cave* where they used to make wine. It's small but cozy. There's a living room, with a kitchenette at one end, two tiny bedrooms, and a shower. They have a backyard where you can sit and eat when the Tramontane isn't blowing, and a shed where Vanessa stores her flea-market goods.

Vanessa dreams of one day living in a house big enough for a bathtub and a proper closet; she complains about how whenever it rains, the living room floods, and the toilet backs up. But Rat wouldn't want to live anywhere else in the world.

Nine months a year, Rat and Jérôme and the littler kids run wild, making themselves amusement-park rides out of the rusty threshers, rotting cart wheels, and old wine barrels that still sit in the courtyard. They build tree houses in the cedar tree at the bottom of the garden, they collect pinecones and smash them open to extract the tiny yellow pine nuts, they hunt for frogs in the irrigation canal that runs down to the sea.

In the short winter months, or when the Tramontane's too bitter, life moves indoors. They watch cartoons, they play on Jérôme's father's computer, Rat pesters Vanessa to take her to the library to get more comic books. She hunts for kindling for the stove, stealing fruit crates from the back of the superette at Saint Féliu Plage. At night, when it's cold, she climbs into her mother's bed and the two of them cuddle under Vanessa's quilt, and fall asleep watching old movies on TV.

Then when the days begin to get longer, Rat and the other kids are back outside again, stealing cherries from the orchard, collecting snails, hunting for wild asparagus, reclaiming their old forts and hiding places.

If it weren't for school, Rat's life would be close to perfect. But once she goes through those gates each morning—pried away from her mother's wiry arms—she enters this alien universe where people call her "Celia" and she doesn't understand what's expected of her, how to draw a spiral or distinguish a verb from a noun.

In this world, Jérôme can't help her. They overlap in the playground or the cafeteria, but the tacit understanding is that at school they don't fraternize: at recess, Jérôme plays football with the boys, and she plays hopscotch or skip-rope with the girls.

As soon as Rat's old enough, she will leave school and then she'll do as she likes. Maybe she'll work with animals. She saw this woman on television who ran a shelter for birds of prey that had been burnt by perching on electrical wires. That wouldn't be such bad work, as work goes.

·   ·   ·

Rat loves to hear the story of how Celia Kidd, her father's mother, got discovered. According to Vanessa, who read it in a magazine, it all began one afternooon, when Rat's granny, then eighteen years old and fresh from an expensive boarding school, was strolling along Kensington High Street.

Suddenly this small dark man with a face like a water rat tapped her on the shoulder, all out of breath—he'd been chasing her for miles—and said, "Excuse me, darling, I'd like to take your picture."

"What did she say?"

"She said, 'Tell me another one.' "

"What do you mean?"

"Well, that's a line nasty older men tend to feed girls when they want to get up their skirts. If anybody ever comes up to you and says he'd like to take your picture, well, you say, You'll have to discuss it with my agent."

"So what'd Celia say?"

"She said, 'Sorry, I can't. I'm late for lunch with my aunt.' "

"And what'd he say?"

"He said, 'How about after lunch, then?' "

"And?"

"And that was that. In no time flat, your granny's picture was appearing in every glossy magazine in the United Kingdom. And perfume-makers were saying, I want her to be a spokesman for my perfume, and movie directors were saying, Can she act, I think she'd be just brilliant in the next James Bond, and music producers were saying, Can she dance, I think she might do a number with the Rolling Stones . . ."

"Cool."

"That's not what her parents thought."

"What did they think?"

"Well, they were upper-class snobs who thought it was a disgrace to have their daughter's picture in the papers, especially in miniskirts up to her crotch."

"So what did they do?"

"What could they do? It was a bit too late, because by that time she'd left home, and was living with the photographer, who was teaching her how to eat with chopsticks and not cough when you smoke a joint, and fashion magazines were flying them all around the world so he could photograph her on the Pyramids or on beaches in Tahiti."

Rat chuckled. "Did she marry the photographer?"

"No, she never married the photographer. She married Gillem's daddy—your grandfather—who was this megarich Canadian, and later on she married this gay filmmaker, but she never married the photographer. They stayed good friends, though."

"Did she ever meet me?"

"You? No. Your own daddy never met you."

"Do you think she'd like me if she met me?"

Vanessa flicks the briefest of glances sideways at Rat. "Not if you had chocolate smeared all over your face."

"No, seriously."

"Seriously? Sure. You're gorgeous. You're a gorgeous girl. One gorgeous girl likes another. Besides, you've got her long, long legs. Those Kidd legs."

"I do?"

"Well, you don't get 'em from your half-pint mama, that's for sure."

3

They are rattling along the coastal road, on their way to the flea market at Brix.

It's not yet dawn, with a crescent moon and a couple of silver-bright stars in the sky. You have to get to the market early—five thirty, six—to make sure you get a good place.

The Tramontane is hurtling their van from side to side. It feels like a hurricane. The Pyrénées-Orientales is the Command Center of winds. Here they all congregate, quarrel, barter, and rule. There are said to be 119 different winds in the Pyrénées-Orientales. (If you could sell wind we'd be rich, people used to say in the days before the foothills got sown with rows of gigantic new wind turbines, without bringing a marked improvement to anybody's fortunes.)

Rat knows the names of only a few of them. There's the Narbonnaise from the north, there's the Vent d'Espagne from the south, the Marin, a clammy east wind from the sea that encloses you in a gray-white fog for weeks on end. And then there's the infamous Tramontane, a harsh howling broom from the northwest that sweeps the clouds from the sky and turns their court-yard into a dust-bowl cyclone, their apartment into a sandpit. When the Tramontane's blowing, you eat, breathe, pee dust, you go to bed with dust up your nose, and awaken with your head screaming. Other people hate it, but Rat doesn't mind.

The Tramontane is Rat's wind. When Rat first started school and didn't have any friends, Vanessa used to ask her whom she'd played with that day. And Rat would reply, "I played with the wind."

"Which wind?" asked Vanessa, laughing.

"Ours." Ours was the Tramontane.

Looking out the back window, as you rise onto the plateau of Château-Roussillon, you catch a last glimpse of the sea and the gray lagoon of Saint-Cyprien, chopped and churning with white-caps. Out Rat's window, there are fields of artichoke, their long coarse serrated leaves olive-gray. Underneath, the fruits are purplish bruise–colored.

Approaching Perpignan, artichoke fields and vineyards give way to malls. The shops have grills over their windows.

Mist clings in the hollows of land, dark gray clouds engulf the Albères.

Vanessa takes the low road through Perpignan, alongside the river Têt. There's a tiny shantytown of cardboard boxes and fruit-crate shelters down by the river. A trio of homeless men are huddled by a campfire, and another one fishing, and just below the waste-treatment plant, a blue heron stands lonely in the mid-dle of the river.

As they head up into the hills, the land gets drier. Nurseries, greenhouses, market gardens give way to limestone crags. Gar-rigues. The only vegetation in these hills is stunted live oaks and yellow broom. Bandit-land. Wild West.

It was Vanessa's old boyfriend Max who started Vanessa on the *brocantes*. Max had a Volkswagen van that he'd take door-to-door, asking people if they had anything to get rid of—burnt-out pots, stacks of LPs, sofas with the springs gone. On Wednesdays, he and Rat would go to the town dump to see what they could salvage. People throw away wonderful things: one time Rat found an old-fashioned manual typewriter in mint condition, once you got the *e* unstuck. On weekends, they'd work the yard sales. Then they'd resell what they'd found at the bigger markets.

Rat loved Max. He was Swiss, but he hated Switzerland. He was the most generous person Rat ever met. Once he gave her a little gold heart that was a locket, and another time, he brought her back from Switzerland an old horn penknife with a folding fork and spoon.

Last summer, he took them all on a trip to Morocco, along with Vanessa's friend Souad and Souad's son, Morgan. They went in Max's van. They drove down to the southern tip of Spain and then they took a ferry across the Strait of Gibraltar, and camped on a beach outside Tangier.

It was the most fun Rat had ever had in her life.

At first she hadn't been too pleased about Souad and Morgan's horning in on their adventure, but Max had explained to her that Souad was sick and when you're sick, you need cheering up even more than at normal times. Which was typical of Max: he had the saddest face you ever saw, but he wanted everybody else to be happy.

Vanessa was pretty sweet on Max, too, but his indecisiveness drove her nuts. When he spent the night, sometimes the next morning Rat would find him in Vanessa's bed, sometimes he'd be sleeping on the sofa, and sometimes in the van. Eventually, Max decided he was definitely the gay end of bisexual. He'd fallen in love with a doctor who was home on leave from Réunion, and when the doctor's vacation was over, Max moved to Réunion with him.

When he left France, Max sold Vanessa his van for almost nothing. She'd been working the *brocantes* with him for a couple of years by then, and she had a knack for it, Max said: it was a good way of life for someone who was resourceful and independent-minded. Way better than waitressing. Besides, it was one of the few jobs where a single mother could bring along her kid: bung Rat in the van with a lollipop and a stack of old comics, and she'd be happy all day.

As *brocante* country went, the Pyrénées-Orientales had good pickings. Not for antiques, but for the almost-new. The coast was full of condo developments, where people were always moving in and out. End of June, when lots of landlords kicked out their year-round tenants to cash in on summer rentals, it was a gold mine. Suddenly, faced with a car trunk that wouldn't close, people were a little more willing to get rid of an old cassette player or a carton of their kids' outgrown ski clothes.

Upcountry was more primitive: plummier prizes, but harder to dislodge. You'd go into a bar and chat up the regulars, you'd look at the announcements in the *tabac*, see who'd died and who was selling, but you had to proceed on tiptoe. Vanessa was always hoping to chance on some old pack rat who was moving into a retirement home, and wondering what to do with sixty years' worth of TV guides and jam jars. Once she and Max had heard about a man who'd just inherited his great-uncle's farm. They'd followed this dirt track all the way up to some godforsaken shack in the Aspres, and guess what happened? The guy set his dog on them! In some people's minds, a *brocanteur* is just a sharkier kind of thief.

For the most part, though, it was pleasant work. Vanessa sometimes called it fishing, sometimes foraging. If Vanessa had her choice, she'd be high-end, someone who dealt in lace night-dresses and china teacups, not someone who got dogs sicced on her, but the Pyrénées-Orientales was a poor, bargain-basement end of the country—hot Siberia, joked Vanessa—and you took what you could get.

Clear road now, and the rising sun is just beginning to tinge the dark gray mountains and hilltop villages with gold.

Rat feels cozy in the van, just her and Vanessa. It's her favorite place to talk, an enclosed realm of parallel daydreaming, where she can get her mother to slow down and answer all the questions, tell the stories she's usually too busy for. In the van, you're safe, everybody who's in it is strapped tight, there to stay. If it were up to Rat, they'd live in it full-time, sleep there every night, the way they did in Morocco.

"Mama? Will you tell me a story?" She makes her voice deliberately babylike, entreating.

"What kind of story?"

"A story from your childhood."

"What childhood?" Vanessa retorts. "*You* have a childhood; I never had one."

Vanessa was an army brat. She'd grown up all over France and Germany, wherever her father was posted. They never lived anywhere more than three years. When her father left the military, they moved to a condo in Collioure which Vanessa's parents had bought for their retirement. Vanessa's older sister was already married by then, and Vanessa was a teenager. It was her first real home.

"What was Mémé Catherine like when you and Marie-Christine were kids?" Rat asks. Hesitantly, because they don't speak to Rat's French granny anymore.

When Rat was little, she used to spend almost every weekend at Mémé Catherine's. Mémé Catherine lived in a complex of identical houses called Les Glycines at the top of Collioure. From the end of Mémé Catherine's street, you could see the harbor, flanked by a church built from the rocks, whose clock tower was an old lighthouse. The coast of Collioure wasn't flat and sandy, like Saint Féliu, but sheer jagged cliffs and tiny coves, where the rock was dark gray schist.

Mémé Catherine was a gardener: Rat remembers the gaudy magenta of the bougainvillea that climbed her garden wall, the more sedate lavender of the wisteria over the doorway. The garden was pocket-size, but it had everything: lettuces, tomatoes, strawberries, melon; carrots and potatoes in the winter. Even a quince tree. When Mémé Catherine sent Rat home, it was always with a carton full of vegetables and homemade preserves. "Oh fuck," Vanessa would groan. "Not another jar of fucking quince jelly!"

Rat's room at Mémé Catherine's was a bare cubicle with tile floors. Over the dresser, a crucifix decorated with dried Palm Sunday fronds, and a picture of Baby Jesus and the Virgin Mary. It used to be Vanessa's room, but any trace of Rat's mother—the batik spreads and incense cones, the rock 'n' roll posters, or torn pages from fashion magazines with which Vanessa invested any lair that was hers—had been expunged. Only the window giving on to a side alley, through which Vanessa says she used to escape for nocturnal sorties, bore a kind of negative witness to Rat's mother.

Mémé Catherine always called Rat Celia, and Vanessa by her real name, which was Agathe. ("Can you believe she named me after a martyr who got her tits sliced off? How castrating is *that?*") Mémé Catherine was pretty, with a pale freckled heart-shaped face, like Vanessa's, and fair hair faded to gray. She was smiling, but strict. If she did something for you, you said thank you, and then she showed you how to do it for yourself.

Rat used to help Mémé Catherine with the housework. They mopped the floors; they beat the carpets out the window; they hung up the wash. In the morning, Mémé Catherine would send Rat down the hill to the baker, where she picked up an extra loaf for Mémé Catherine's neighbor, Madame Brunet, who was crippled, and a newspaper for Monsieur Oms.

To her neighbors, Rat realized, Mémé Catherine was not a grandmother, but a strong vigorous young woman.

In the afternoons, Mémé Catherine would take her down to the sea for a swim, and Saturday evening, after Mass, her grandmother ironed while Rat watched TV. There are certain smells—the toasty smell of ironed cotton, the ecclesiastical reek of melting candle wax—that remind Rat of her grandmother with an inexplicable mixture of comfort and unease, as if there were a heaven after all, but not for you.

In Rat's recollections, it's always summer in Mémé Catherine's house, the rooms dark because the shutters are closed to keep in the cool. The house is more exposed to the Tramontane than Mas Cargol: there is a little hook to latch open each door and window, so it doesn't slam in the wind.

Whenever they pass Collioure, Rat tries to catch a glimpse of Mémé Catherine's housing complex. She wonders what Mémé Catherine and Vanessa would do if they met by accident. Would they stare right through each other? Would Mémé Catherine even recognize Rat? Would she think Rat had turned out to be a bad seed like her mother?

"Mémé Catherine? She was a typical military wife. Never a day sick, no complaints allowed. Unfailingly cheerful. Me, I hate cheerful—it just stinks of suppressed rage." Vanessa mimics Mémé Catherine's bright tones. "'So we're moving again? Wonderful! I always wanted to live on an army base in the middle of fucking Alsace. Girls, pack your bags. No back talk.' Our dad came first, second, and third. I couldn't stand her hypocrisy. There was this whole world out there, some of it very ugly and miserable, some of it very exciting, and all your energies were spent pretending it didn't exist. The only thing that counted was what the neighbors—the other army wives—did. It made me swear, I'm never living in a ghetto, not a middle-class ghetto, at least. I'd rather be poor than uptight." After a moment, she says, "I'm sure glad I don't have to eat that bitch's jams and pickles anymore."

They laugh, but Rat feels disloyal.

"And your daddy?"

"Never home. Kind of jokey, but the kind of jokey that has a little hint of menace, like, Don't joke back or you'll get a smacking. I asked him what he did once, when I was really little. He said, I'm a zookeeper. He showed me this big set of keys, he said, Just for now, you can keep the keys, but if you lose them, the animals will starve, and then there'll be hell to pay. I went boasting to the other kids at school, I said, My daddy's a zookeeper, he gave me the keys that keep the lions and tigers locked up. They laughed at me, You liar, your daddy's a soldier just like ours. He was badly hoping for a son, both times. Girls he just couldn't get his head around. Of course he lived like a pasha. I remember my uncle coming to stay and Daddy offering him a drink, Mémé Catherine was out; well, it turned out Daddy didn't have a clue where she kept the cocktail glasses. He couldn't even find a can of peanuts! Tonton François was laughing, saying, You can order a battalion of grown men to lay down their lives for you, and you don't know where the glasses are in your own house?"

"Did he like me?"

Vanessa raises her eyebrows. "He died before you were born. Dropped dead of a heart attack two years after he retired, to your granny's intense relief. Course that didn't stop her saying to me, when you came along, The only mercy is your poor father's not alive."

"I guess nobody was too happy about me being born," ventures Rat.

Her mother's eyes are on the road.

"I was," she says, finally. Her tone is so brusquely definitive, so quelling of any doubt, that it brings the conversation to a close.

The morning mist is already burning off. Where the sun hasn't reached, it's still chilly, but you can tell it's going to be a hot day.

After Vanessa's paid her vendor's fee and been assigned her space, they stop by the bar in the market square to warm up before unloading their wares.

Vanessa orders a *grand crème* for herself and a hot chocolate for Rat. They stand at the counter, Rat balancing on the foot rail. There are two men in blue overalls turned white with plaster dust, drinking coffee and shots of brandy, and an elderly North African man in a wool watch cap and tweed jacket who looks at everybody with shining black eyes. When Rat meets his gaze, they both nod hello.

Rat slips a couple of sugar cubes into her pocket when Vanessa isn't looking.

"I saw you," says a voice at her back. Rat swirls around to find William grinning at her. William's short, with a walrus mustache and a compact belly. He and Josiane are *brocanteurs* from Elne. Rat and William, and then William and Vanessa, exchange kisses.

"Still no shoes, huh?" says William, jerking a head towards Rat.

"Frankly, it's not worth the fight. She's a savage, what can I do? The most annoying part is, she's never a day sick."

"What's your teacher say when you show up barefoot?"

Rat wriggles, uncomfortable. "I wear shoes to school. And when I take them off at recess, she says, Put your shoes back on. That's why I don't like to go."

William stares at her a moment, then turns to Vanessa. "Hey-ho, my girl. I've got something for you."

They follow William to his van, where Josiane's unloading, and he hauls out a carton of magazines. Twelve years of *Paris Match*es, '84 to '96. Complete set. Mint condition.

"Nice," Vanessa says appreciatively. Rat watches her mother whisk through them, counting, checking there are no pages missing.

"How much?"

"I'll give 'em to you for what I got 'em for. Soon as I saw them, I thought, Vanessa."

He names the price. Rat can tell Vanessa knows he's added a little, but she agrees.

"I'll pay you at the end of the day, okay? You're a gem,

William. Josiane, your man's a gem. If you ever get tired of him, you can pass him on to me."

"How much will you pay me for him?" Josiane winks at Rat.

"He looks pretty used."

"A wreck," pronounces William. "After seventeen years with that old witch, I'm a wreck."

"It's not seventeen. Is it really seventeen? William, you can't count."

"You should have seen me when I was a spring chicken. Before she got to plucking me, before she wrang my neck." William does a little dance, clicking his feet like a rooster chasing a hen, to show how perky he used to be. They all laugh, except for Josiane, who's still trying to puzzle out how long she and William have been together.

The *brocanteurs* are like one big family. People look out for one another. Everybody knows Vanessa's crazy about old magazines. Fashion magazines, movie magazines, people magazines. She'll read anything: rock stars' bouts in rehab, television anchormen's beach houses, celebrity funerals. What she likes best is reading about the old stars from her childhood, and their children— Chiara Mastroianni, Charlotte Gainsbourg, Julie Depardieu. When the lead singer of Noir Désir murdered Jean-Louis Trintignant's daughter in a hotel room, that was Vanessa's kind of story. Some people might call it morbid, but Vanessa says it's just human.

The sky is naked blue now, sun overhead. It's shaping up into a scorching day. Vanessa wears a straw hat and dark glasses, but even so, over the course of the morning, Rat can almost see her mother's freckles multiplying, merging into a sea of rosy brown. Rat tries counting them, before they disappear.

"Buzz off," says Vanessa, fondly.

"I love your freckles," says Rat. "Let me see the ones on your arms. Tell me about the time you painted your face with stain remover to make them disappear."

"Shush. It wasn't stain remover, it was Wite-Out. Buzz off, I'm working."

People mill around, picking up objects, putting them down again, circling. When somebody comes to your stall, you can't help getting your hopes up. Vanessa knows all the habitual customers—who's likely actually to buy something, who's just whiling away a Sunday morning. There are a number of foreigners who have vacation homes in the hills around Brix. The foreigners are always nosing around for something picturesque, something typically "French"—straw hats to hang on their wall, enameled coffeepots. There's one Danish lady who's crazy about yellow. Anything yellow, she'll buy it.

That's the fancy end of the Brix market. The rest is much like the village's year-round population: rough. Arabs and Gypsies selling bits of cable, dial telephones, ancient radios, homeless-looking people offering old clothes-pegs, school notebooks that have already been written in, roller skates with a wheel missing.

Vanessa chats with the couple at the neighboring stall.

Rat sits by her mother, reading a *Lucky Luke*.

A man and a woman stop to look at Vanessa's wares. Rat's seen them before; they must live in Brix. The woman's German, but she speaks French perfectly. Today she's wearing a long batik skirt that leaves her belly bare, revealing a ring in her navel. She has two more rings in her nose, including a big gold hoop.

Her boyfriend is tall. He leans back as he stands, rolling on his hips. He's always in black, with high-heeled cowboy boots and a thick studded belt, even in the summer. Rat catches Vanessa giving him an oblique once-over.

She nudges her mother. "Cut it out." She hates it when her mother checks out guys.

"*What?*" Vanessa, all-innocent.

"You know."

The woman picks up an enamel jade-green colander, shows it to her boyfriend.

He makes a face. "You need a colander?"

He has a surprisingly high voice for such a tall man. It makes him seem more vulnerable.

"Why not?"

"Look—it's rusty."

"It's pretty. I like the green." Her German accent is tiny, almost imperceptible, but it accentuates her air of unworldliness. Rat wishes she had a foreign accent, too, so people would always be trying to guess where she came from.

"A rusty colander is pretty?" The man in black is playing to Vanessa, clowning it up for a laugh. "How much?" he asks her.

"All the prices are marked," says Vanessa, who's gone back to reading her magazine. You'd never have thought half a minute ago she'd been checking out the guy's broad shoulders, the nice way his jeans ride low on his slim hips. He looks a little like Max. Vanessa's always drawn to tall guys.

"I saw. But how much *really*?" His tone's flirtatious, insistent.

Vanessa finally looks up. "What do you mean, *really*? Is this a course in metaphysics?" She laughs, addressing herself to the woman. "I don't deal in real/unreal, I deal in things. The colander is *really* eight euros."

He lowers his dark glasses, looks down at her, narrowing his eyes in exaggerated surprise. "Eight euros for a rusty colander? You could get a new one for less."

"So get one," shrugs Vanessa.

"I like it—it's cute," says his girlfriend. She fumbles in a drawstring purse that's tied to her skirts, produces a crumpled red bill.

Rat wraps the colander in newspaper for her; Vanessa finds the change.

The girl moves on, but the cowboy dawdles.

"I haven't seen you two ladies here before, have I? Do you do the market every week?" he asks.

Vanessa makes a noncommittal face. "When I think of it."

"Where're you from?"

Vanessa nods her head back towards the coast.

Her rudeness is a form of flirtation.

"From the sea? I could tell you were mermaids," he says.

She laughs, uncomfortable. "You're dreaming."

"I like dreaming. Don't you?"

Vanessa shrugs. "Depends what you have to wake to. Yes, ma'am? Can I help you?"

There's a lady who wants to tell her that the record in the sleeve of the Enrico Macias album isn't Enrico Macias, it's some rumba group. The man in black—Johnny Cash, they call him later—moves on.

"Why were you rude to him?" asks Rat.

"Was I? I wasn't rude. I don't know—I get sick of people always trying to chisel you down."

Rat's surprised because usually her mother can bargain the hind legs off an Armenian rug merchant.

The morning is long and languid. Rat gets bored, but even the boredom is pleasant. When she finishes reading her *Lucky Luke*, and leafing through her mother's magazines, she wanders off into the backstreets. There's a small square with a fountain where Gypsy women and children hang out. The mothers are even younger than Vanessa, but they wear long black skirts. They speak a strange kind of Catalan. Lots of the old people in Saint Féliu still speak Catalan, and Rat can understand a bit. But just when she thinks she's ferreted out a word or two of Gypsy chatter, the women, as if sensing her interest, dive into something high-speed and utterly impenetrable.

The girls are playing in the dried-up fountain. There are four or five of them, the oldest about Rat's age. None of them Rat recognizes from previous excursions.

"Is Sephora around?"

"No."

"Is she coming back soon?"

"She's off with her aunt."

"Oh. Do you want to play?"

They look at Rat's bare feet and look at each other and giggle. Finally, the oldest one answers. "What do you want to play?"

"What games do you like? Wolf?"

The Gypsy girls don't know Wolf, so they end up doing clapping games. Rat knows some clapping songs they don't know, they know some rhythms and moves she doesn't. She teaches the girls a clapping song whose words are always verging on obscene, before veering clear. Every time she says the almost-swear word, the girls giggle and hide their faces in each other's shoulders, although to Rat, the language is pretty mild.

Later on, people will tell her she shouldn't play with Gypsies, the way they tell her not to hitchhike alone or not to let a dog lick her on the face, but she doesn't pay much attention to what people tell her to do or not to do.

When the mothers call the girls for lunch, Rat wanders back to the market square. She passes the bar where they had breakfast. The man in black is sitting at an outside table with a couple of other men. His German girlfriend isn't with him anymore. The men are drinking pastis. She lingers just a second too long, and he spots her.

"Hey, barefoot," he says. "Where you going?"

Rat shrugs. "Nowhere special."

"Your mom lets you run around town on your own?"

Rat's insulted. "I can look after myself. I've been going around on my own for years. Everybody knows me."

She glances fiercely at the waiter who is bringing them another round, and he nods in confirmation.

"No doubt," says the man in black, and his companions chuckle not altogether pleasantly. "You look thirsty. What would you like, a syrup?"

Rat is mollified. She lets him order her a grenadine. She drinks it in one go, and then fishes for a couple of ice cubes from the bucket on his table and crunches them.

"Don't you know you shouldn't chew ice?" says the man. "It fucks up your teeth."

"My teeth are already fucked up," says Rat, putting down the glass and walking off.

The man says something she doesn't catch, and she hears them all laughing.

Back at her mother's stall, somebody's just agreed on a price for the giraffe lamp Vanessa picked up in Alénya. Rat means to tell Vanessa about the grenadine. She's not supposed to accept things from strangers, especially not male strangers, but sometimes she forgets.

When they get back home late that afternoon, Rat and Vanessa stack the cartons of unsold goods in the shed. The take was pretty piddling, once you subtract the mileage. Less than Vanessa clears when she helps out at the Sol y Mar. But it was fun being up in the mountains for the day. Coming back down to the plain, the neon-blazing malls and fast-food chains feel hot and dirty.

Rat fans her mother with a broken-spanned fan she found in the parking lot behind the market.

Vanessa yawns and stretches luxuriantly. "I'm going to have a long cool shower, and then I'm going to read my magazines. Bliss."

In the event, the blissful evening gets spoiled, because Souad's boss calls to tell Vanessa that Souad's back in intensive care, and that's the first time Rat remembers hearing her mother cry, but not the last.

Morgan's mother, Souad, was Vanessa's best friend.

Afterwards, it will be hard for Rat to disentangle her memories of Souad well from Souad dying, hard to picture her other than how she looked the last couple of months, curled up on the hospice bed, blackened skin shriveled tight across her body, and eye sockets gaping.

Vanessa and Souad had struck up acquaintance outside the preschool in Saint Féliu. This was when Jérôme's mother had gone back to her nursing job full-time, and Vanessa was taking care of Solenne while Marielle was at work. Souad's son, Morgan, was in the same starter class of Touts Petits as Solenne.

Saint Féliu wasn't a friendly village. Most of the school parents didn't bother to say hello, even though you'd been waiting outside the gates together day after day for years.

One day Vanessa said to Rat, "There's another mother at the preschool I like the look of," and when she pointed her out, Rat was surprised. The woman was tall and gaunt as a man, with a great head of frizzy red hair and a hollow, haunted face.

"What do you like about her?" Rat had asked, and Vanessa replied, "Her face looks lived-in."

Eventually, the two women started chatting, cracking jokes about the other mothers, and before you knew it, when Rat came home from school, Souad would be hunched over a cup of coffee in the kitchen, chain-smoking these long skinny cigarillos that made her breath stink. And her little boy would be sitting under the plane tree in the courtyard, silent, just staring at you with baleful black eyes.

Souad definitely made enough noise for two. She had this way of saying quite aggressive, confrontational things in order to cut through all the preliminary stages of getting to know someone. When she was talking to you, she would grab your arm, and follow you everywhere, even into the bathroom, till she'd finished her story. And when she got to the punch line, she'd clutch you even harder and throw her head back in a loud harsh guffaw, so that you saw the roof of her mouth. Rat didn't like her much at first, but later on, she could sympathize with her.

Souad worked at the Sol y Mar campground.

When the warm weather came, she used to invite Vanessa and the kids over for the day to swim. Some of the campgrounds at the beach were said to be dirty or unsavory, but this one, Sol y Mar, was run by the ex-mayor of Crussols, a decent guy who had put money and care into the place. Souad and Morgan lived there year-round, in a snug little trailer of which Rat was frankly jealous.

And the ex-mayor had done everything correctly, on the books, so that later on, when Souad was too sick to work, she got full pay.

Rat and Jérôme could spend hours cavorting in the campground pool, splashing each other with cannonballs, while Solenne with her water wings squealed with joy at the shallow end. But when you asked Souad's son, Morgan, if he wanted to come into the water, he shook his head. Ask him twice, and he'd go into full retreat, taking himself off into the shade of a eucalyptus tree. "That's a real child of the Mediterranean for you," laughed Vanessa. "You spend your whole life by the sea, but you'd never dream of actually getting wet."

Vanessa had a kind of crush on Souad; there wasn't any other word for it. She found Souad's background intensely romantic—her early childhood in the Algerian hinterland; the three-room shack in the north of France where she'd lived with her parents and eight siblings, till the government found them an apartment in the projects ("Running water, central heating: the Ritz!" Souad laughed); the arranged marriage to an older cousin who beat her; her years on the street, after her family renounced her for leaving her husband.

"That's what your mama and I have in common," Souad told Rat. "We've each had to make our own way in the world. It's not easy to cut yourself off from your family, never to be able to cry on your mother or your older sister's shoulder. Be good to your mama; she struts around like a fighter, but she's soft as butter inside."

Souad was always telling people how she and Vanessa were alike, single mothers too independent to settle down. Morgan's father? "Gone with the wind," she joked.

Souad didn't drink, but she loved to dance. Saturday nights, she would take Vanessa off to the Fandango at Canet Plage or to hear live bands in Perpignan.

Morgan would get dragged along, too, but after the first couple of times, Rat refused to go again. It was smoky in those clubs, the noise hurt her ears, the strobe lights hurt her eyes, and she hated the way men and women with bad breath bent down and tried to fake-dance with her.

"I'm not coming," she said. "I'm old enough to stay home alone."

By that point, Rat could light the stove, cook herself some pasta. She felt capable enough to run a country single-handed. If she had a problem, she could always go to Jérôme's parents— Jean-Luc and Marielle never went out at night, she concluded pointedly.

Vanessa and Souad laughed at her.

"She's such a priss," Vanessa complained.

"She doesn't like me," said Souad.

"She's jealous, she's used to having me to herself."

"Don't worry, kid, I won't be around forever," Souad told Rat.

"Don't say that." There was a clutch of panic in Vanessa's voice.

"It's true, isn't it?" Souad gave her loud barking laugh.

Rat knew that Souad was HIV. What was HIV? It was something people joked about, it was in the air. One day Florian boasted to a bunch of kids after school, I'm HIV, the way he might have said, I'm a vampire, and at first you didn't believe him, and then you weren't so sure.

Souad you were sure. She was taking these homeopathic cures that were supposed to keep the beast at bay, she said, but then she got this thick drowning cough that wouldn't stop, and when she became too weak to get out of bed, Vanessa took her straight to the emergency room.

Morgan stayed at their place while his mother was in the hospital.

On the face of it, the kid didn't have much charm. Not that he was bad-looking: he was a wiry little boy, with caramel-colored skin and a head of dark gold curls, and big eyes a bottomless black. He might have been cute, if he weren't such a zombie.

When you put food in front of Morgan, he ate it. Even if it was something disgusting like squid, he polished his plate, then went and laid it in the kitchen sink. He wasn't like Solenne or like Cristel's godson who were always pestering you to put on a DVD or push them on the swing or let them play on Jérôme's father's computer. Morgan just sat there like a lump.

At first the other children would ask him if he wanted to come play, but he never did. All he wanted to do was sit in a corner or under the plane tree, clutching some nothing little trinket—a Bugs Bunny key chain from a cereal box, a minipuzzle—that he didn't want to share with anybody else. He was a hoarder, that kid. And the other children, having got nowhere trying to be friendly to Morgan, let him be.

The first time Souad was in intensive care, Vanessa's van was being repaired. It took almost an hour, and two buses, to get to the hospital. Every day after school, Vanessa would take Morgan and Rat to visit Souad. Rat dreaded those interminable bus rides through the northern suburbs of Perpignan, across the river Têt, and then winding along Bas Vernet and Moyen Vernet and Haut Vernet past the stadium to the hospital.

She'd look out the window at the projects where Gypsy women in black sat on the sidewalk, men in black talked in clusters. Little girls playing hopscotch. Storefront churches with signs painted by hand, Life and Light, Eternal Salvation. All Rat could think was how much she'd rather be playing hopscotch in the street than going to the hospital, where Souad lay in a ward full of dead-looking people in printed shrouds.

It was late winter, and the mimosas were in bloom, their flowers toxic yellow. Once when they were waiting for the bus, Vanessa had taken Rat's horn penknife and started hacking away at a mimosa bush by the side of the road. The other ladies at the bus stop clucked disapprovingly.

"Stop it, Mama," Rat begged.

Vanessa was cheerily unconscious. "It'll bring a little color to Souad's bedside." There wasn't much besides mimosa that was in bloom in February, she pointed out.

For years afterwards, when Rat saw mimosas, she got this mean flashback to green corridors and death.

Home. Home. Home. All afternoon Rat's been longing to get home, bottling it up to tell her mother. Angélique's mother lets her off by the mailbox, and Rat goes storming up the drive.

That morning, Marie-Jo had posted an announcement on the classroom door that head lice were back, and could everybody's parents please check their children's heads. At recess, Océane had come up to Rat and started teasing her, saying she was the one who had started the lice.

Océane was new in their class. She had been held back from the year before, so she was bigger than the other kids, and snottier. "Elodie"—that's the girl Rat shares a desk with—"says your hair's crawling with lice."

Elodie, whom Rat had thought was her friend, refused to meet her eyes. Rat was genuinely puzzled. Every year, there were periodic waves of head lice. You didn't exactly regard it as a gift from Santa, but there'd never been a stigma to it, either.

"I don't have lice, you fat bitch," she retorted. "Go look at your own greasy head." And she'd shoved Océane in the chest, with both hands, hard. It takes a certain amount of force to make a fat girl topple.

It was just Rat's luck that Marie-Jo, who was sitting with the other teachers in the sun, had witnessed only this last part of the exchange. Which meant that it was Rat, and Rat alone, who got detention.

Rat can't decide which makes her more furious, the injustice of the one-sided punishment or Elodie's telling mean lies about her. Already in her head, she's telling her mother, "I'm never going back to school again. That's that, and you can't make me."

As she comes around the corner of the drive, Rat sees that Vanessa's van is gone. She bursts into the house. Nobody home. No note on the table. To Rat, skilled at scouting the signals of human presence, there's no sign that somebody's just nipped down to the corner for a pint of milk and is coming back soon. The stove is cold; the kitchen table clean. She almost wants to cry from disappointment, so instead she kicks the wall hard, practices her swear words. Then she makes herself a *tartine*, and goes around to see Laurent, who's in his workshop.

It's already dark when Rat hears the rumble of the van's engine. She rushes out into the courtyard to meet Vanessa. The need to unload her grievances, to press herself tight against her mother's skinny body and be comforted, is as urgent as a bursting bladder.

Her mother opens the van door.

"Mama!" cries Rat.

Vanessa looks grim. "Help me unload the groceries" is all she says.

It's only then that Rat sees Morgan, who is sitting in his child seat in the back. Morgan doesn't even look up to acknowledge she's there. Rat reaches past him to grab one of the shopping bags. "Why can't Morgan do something to help, for once?" she wonders aloud.

Back in the house, she watches her mother put away a six-pack of long-life milk, packets of frozen lasagna.

"Did you remember to get me some more Coco Pops?" she asks, reproachfully.

Vanessa doesn't answer. She rips opens a container of fish fingers, lights the stove, turns on the grill.

"I hate fish. You know I hate fish."

"Next time you do the shopping, okay? It's not fish. It's fish fingers."

"I didn't know where you were, when I got home," Rat complains.

"Lay the table, will you?"

"How many places?"

"Three, of course."

"He's staying?"

Vanessa shoots her daughter a killer glare.

After dinner, when Morgan's asleep in Rat's bed (Rat, Vanessa says, can sleep with her), Rat speaks up.

"How long's he staying this time? You know, you could ask me for once, before you offer somebody my bed." Her voice is louder, more belligerent than she intended.

Vanessa bends down to pour herself a glass of wine from the *vrac*, and starts rolling a cigarette. She doesn't answer.

"So Souad's back in the hospital? I thought she was getting better."

"She was. Now she's not."

"Why's he have to stay with us every time?" It seems to Rat proof of Morgan's absolute worthlessness that there is nobody to claim him, nobody in the whole wide world who wants him. "Doesn't he have a granny or granddaddy who can take him?"

Vanessa sits down at the table. Rat notices for the first time that her mother's eyes are red. "Look, I'm beat, and the last thing I need is trouble from you," she says. "Souad's dying, do you understand? They're talking about moving her into a hospice."

"What's that?"

"A place where they don't try to make you better anymore, they just try to ease the pain. The least I can do is take in Morgan. She would do the same, if it were me. You know that, don't you? So don't be such a selfish brat."

But Rat won't let it go. All she can think about is how she never gets her mother to herself anymore, how this kid is always sitting there like a spider in the corner, silently taking up all her mother's attention. She can't even remember the last time they did something fun together, just the two of them. And now Vanessa seems to be saying this is not just an occasional ordeal but the new reality.

"I don't want Morgan living with us forever. It's not our fault Souad was a prostitute."

The word hangs in the suddenly terrifying silence. "WHAT-DID-I-HEAR-YOU-SAY?" her mother hisses.

Rat doesn't dare repeat it.

"What's a prostitute, Rat? What do you think a prostitute is?"

"I know what it is. I know she caught AIDS from sleeping with truckers at the border."

Vanessa's on her feet now, leaning across the table. For a moment, Rat thinks her mother's going to smack her. She's angrier than Rat has ever seen her. "What kind of trash talk have you been listening to? You want to make out we're living in a universe where innocent people get punished with horrible diseases just for doing what it's in our own human nature to do? Listen to me, girl. You have something mean to say, you say it to me in your own words, you don't come sneak-repeating gossip bored mothers tell each other in the village."

"That's not where I heard it," mumbles Rat. In any case, it's not Souad's past or current profession that's the point; it's Rat's right to be consulted before her own mother decides to take in somebody else's child.

Vanessa glares at her. "Souad is a beautiful soul, a big brave woman who's fighting for her life, who wants the best for her kid, just like I do."

Rat subsides, grumbling. "Where's he gonna sleep long-term? I'm damned if he's gonna spend the rest of his life in my bed."

"I'm going to get Laurent to make a little mezzanine for him, a sleeping loft." Vanessa indicates where it will go. "We'll take out the kitchen cupboard, and eat against that wall, instead."

It's true: the apartment is small, but its ceilings are high.

"Where're you gonna get the money?"

"Monsieur Bordon will pay."

Rat looks skeptical.

"He will," Vanessa insists. "If we convert this place to a three-bedroom, he can up the rent. Doesn't make any difference to us—we get extra benefits all around, with a second kid."

So her mother has it all worked out. Never again will it be just the two of them.

"Mama?" It comes out in a tremulous little voice.

"Yes, my girl?"

"Mama, I don't want to go back to school anymore."

"Tell me about it, my girl."

Rat tells. And Vanessa, being Vanessa—that is, in every way divinely unpredictable—listens to her story of betrayal and injustice, and is outraged in all the right places, and proud that Rat stood up for herself against Océane. Then she hauls Rat under the light, runs her fingers through her hair, and says, "But you know? That fat bitch was right. You do have lice again."

Rat groans.

"And you know what else? I'm too dead-beat to do a thing about it. Go round to Marielle after school tomorrow and see if she'll do the treatment for you."

In the end, of course, the sleeping loft goes in Rat's room, and it's Rat who sleeps above, with a ladder to go up and down, while Morgan sleeps on a mattress on the floor.

That mezzanine—Rat's getting her own private bear's lair, which no grown-up can be bothered to climb up to—is definitely the best thing that came out of Souad's dying.

Dinner at the Cabreras'. The kids are plumped in a heap on the sofa, watching *Peter Pan*. Solenne, head on Jérôme's shoulder, is almost asleep. Jérôme's eyes are glazed and his thumb has slipped into his mouth. Jérôme has almost been shamed out of thumb-sucking, except when he watches a movie.

At the table, the grown-ups talk, and Rat, who's already seen the film a million times, off-and-on listens. Vanessa is telling Marielle and Jean-Luc and Cristel about the judge who is in charge of Morgan, now that he's become a ward of the state, and the bureaucratic hell she's having to go through to become his legal guardian. They go on to discuss Souad's debts and assets. Jean-Luc thinks he's found someone who'll buy her car for enough money to pay off what she still owes on it. Vanessa's sold Souad's furniture, it wasn't much, but it helped cover the funeral.

Rat's switched back to the movie, but when she sees Vanessa shooting a glance her way, she pricks up her ears.

"She's being such a piss pot," Vanessa's complaining. "She just doesn't seem to get it the boy doesn't have anybody but us."

"It's normal, if she's a bit jealous," says Cristel.

"It's not normal if—"

"It's scary for her," Marielle says, suddenly.

"Huh?"

"Well, think about it. Here's another only child of a single mother, no family to speak of. If Souad dies, that means you could die, too. A child doesn't want to have to consider that possibility."

Vanessa obviously doesn't like that answer. "I couldn't believe my ears when I heard her calling Souad a whore—she sounded just like my fucking mother. I thought, Here we go again, one more hard-hearted sanctimonious fire-and-brimstone bitch in the family! You know what the judge said? He said, Madame, you're a saint. I'd like to see the look on my mother's face if she heard that. Madame, you are a saint."

Rat's had enough. "I'm not jealous," she says, loudly enough to break into the flow of the grown-ups' conversation. "And you're not a saint."

There is a surprised silence for a moment, then the grown-ups burst out laughing. She gets up in a huff, disentangling herself from the other children's sleepy limbs, and stomps back to her house to bed.

Hard to say when Rat started to come round to the kid. It was gradual.

There was a spell, just after Souad died, when Rat used to awaken in the night to find the kitchen ablaze with light, and go out to find Morgan sitting in his usual chair at the kitchen table, just as if it were breakfast time.

"What do you want, Morgan? It's the middle of the night. You hungry?" She's never asked him anything this nice in years.

He doesn't answer.

"Go back to bed."

When he doesn't budge, she finally goes and gets him a handful of cookies, a mug of water.

"Eat and go back to bed."

It was Rat who figured out he was scared of the dark, and got Jean-Luc to rewire the little moon-and-star lamp they'd found in the dump and fix it up with a twenty-watt bulb.

Not that she liked Morgan. More that she had a sense of order that was rudimentary but still more intact than her mother's, at this particular moment. For it was as if Vanessa, having gone through the trials required to adopt Morgan, was now sunk in her own private mourning for her friend, a state that rendered her uncharacteristically slow and myopic. If Rat noticed that Morgan had been wearing the same socks for a week or that his toes were gray with dirt, it got to her.

"Vanessa, the kid's dirty."

But niggling little things like hygiene weren't registering with her mother, so eventually Rat would have to give him a shower herself. And because Morgan, it turned out, had his own sense of order, and besides, didn't like anybody seeing him naked, soon all she had to do was dispatch him to the bathroom and he'd emerge if not clean, at least wet. This made her feel they were basically on the same side.

Over time, Rat began to notice things about Morgan. Things that singled him out from other people's younger siblings—not that he was her kin.

She caught herself bragging about his bravery. At school

they'd be talking about snakes and Rat would tell about the time Solenne and her cousin found a giant grass snake (big as your waist) in the water barrel, and how Morgan had fetched a garden hoe and hacked the snake in two without saying a word. And Rat, who had heard this story from Solenne, had been way too impressed to tell Morgan what she begins to teach him later, that there's no need to kill an animal that's harmless, that if you go around killing everything that scares you, the world becomes a prison.

When Morgan finally starts talking, she discovers that his imagination is dark, fearsome, vindictive, that he's never forgotten a mean look anyone gave him, that for him the world is full of traps, of enemies waiting to humiliate him, cheat him of what's his. That every time they venture as far as the field behind Mas Cargol, he's genuinely expecting a lion to spring from behind a rock and devour them. That his bravery is the braver for coming from a bottomless pit of fear.

The first time Rat succeeds in making Morgan crack up laughing—a torrent of helpless squeals that erupt from him, till he falls off his chair and rolls around the floor, clutching his stomach—she's proud as if he were her own born son.

5

Of course, that wasn't the last she and Vanessa saw of Johnny Cash, the man in black who wanted to know if they were mermaids. Even if the coastal plain and hill country were two different worlds, the Pyrénées-Orientales were still small enough so everyone turned up again eventually. There was nowhere else to go. Drift any farther and you were in Spain.

Rat was eleven the next time they met.

She had started junior high six weeks earlier. She'd moved from village school in Saint Féliu, where she'd been with the same kids since kindergarten, to junior high at Canet. The junior high's real name was Victor Hugo, but it was known as the Bronx.

There were twelve hundred students, most of whom looked to be on steroids, and she was now among the youngest. You had to go through metal detectors to make sure nobody was carrying weapons. There was a different teacher now for every subject, in a different building, and there were gangs looking out to torture you on the walkways in between.

This was how junior high worked: protection. If you wanted to survive the first year, you needed some older friend or sibling watching your back. Sometimes protection involved nothing more strenuous than being told that East-Pak floral-pattern knapsacks were hot, whereas knapsacks on wheels spelled social death. But more often it meant being warned about hidden land mines, such as Mickael Garcia, an annoying little runt in your class who looked harmless enough, but turned out to have two older brothers and an uncle who were all itching to break your legs if you ever looked cross-eyed at him.

Rat had Jérôme, who was okay at helping you avoid a fight, but useless when it actually came to one.

As for the schoolwork, it was like this computer game that had suddenly blipped from Level One to Ultra-Plus Advanced. Rat couldn't understand a word her teachers told her, but everybody else seemed to follow just fine.

It wasn't only Rat's brain that was betraying her. Seemingly over the course of one summer, she'd grown from being this little kitten who could still curl up in impossibly small hiding places into a tall angular person, all elbows and moods. She felt furious that she could no longer run around topless, wearing only a pair of cutoff jeans, that her nipples were starting in the most painful way to swell and her hips to burst through the seams of her shorts. Furious that Jérôme, sixteen months her senior and three inches shorter, was still as free as a dog. And she wasn't. Partly because adults now treated her differently, in a manner that seemed, to her newly raw-skinned sense of self, somewhere between mockery and reproach.

One day, when her and Vanessa's favorite song of the moment came on the radio, Rat grabbed her mother and danced her around the room until Vanessa stopped, pulled free, and said, with a strange look on her face, "You know, Flea-bite, it's time you started using deodorant." And Rat realized that that acrid animal smell was her.

It was off and on, this adolescence business. Some weeks she'd be back to playing Ninjas with Jérôme, helping him reconstruct their fort after the winter's ravages. And then suddenly Laurent would make some stupid joke about Rat's half-baked tits, and when Vanessa joined in the laughter, Rat would stalk back to her house, slamming the front door so hard a pane of glass broke.

Now Rat craved locks on doors, the bathroom to herself, a full-length mirror in which to study these disturbing changes.

Her mother didn't have a clue. For Vanessa, it was always about her: a loyalty test. Were you her little Ratkin or weren't you? Did you realize she'd had a lousy day, and needed mint tea and a back rub, or were you a selfish brat? Rat was still jealous of her mother's attentions, still needed Vanessa's love, but in a warier, more combative sort of way: love not as baby talk and butterfly kisses and sleepy limbs entwined, but as a hard backboard against which to slam your grievances. Wide-awake love, challenging, that would answer all her whys. For the first time in ages, Rat found herself wishing she had a father.

And Johnny Cash, who could sniff trouble a mile away, arrived as if by accident in the middle of this low-level turmoil. His German girlfriend had just dumped him, and he was lost. This was how he came into their lives, as this wounded, humbled person Vanessa took under her wing. The second person she brought into their house, only this time it broke them.

October. The summer sun has lost its fire. In the mornings now, the grass is wet with dew. The figs on the Cabreras' fig tree are wizened on the outside, their insides the syrupy purple marmalade Rat loves.

The *vendange* is done. One weekend they go up to Château-Roussillon and take all the grapes the harvesters have missed. When you go past the Cave Coopérative in Saint Féliu, you almost faint from the fumes of fermenting grapes.

Hunting season has begun, and at dawn now, you awaken to

the sound of gunshots, dogs' excited yelps. On weekends, Rat makes Morgan wear his Day-Glo orange sweatshirt so he doesn't get mistaken for a rabbit. The hunters are supposed to stay a hundred and fifty meters from people's houses, but you're always finding men in camouflage wandering through your backyard with their shotguns cocked, spent cartridges in the garden.

The beaches are empty, except for windsurfers in wet suits. Chez Ernest is boarded shut for the season. Its owners are trying to decide whether to spend the winter in Martinique or Mauritius.

Wednesday afternoon. A dancing, flickering blue-and-gold autumn day. Rat and Vanessa have come to Perpignan on a shopping expedition: Rat needs a pair of gym shoes. It would be quicker and cheaper to pick up a pair at Intermarché in Canet, but Vanessa doesn't believe in chain stores. Rat should just feel lucky her mom hasn't got it into her head to find her a used pair of sneakers at Secours Catholique, or the flea market at the place Cassanyes, which is where most of Rat's clothes come from, except for the hand-me-downs from Jérôme's big sister, Emilie. Rat actually prefers the place Cassanyes since Emilie tends to go in for hot-pink capri pants and turquoise halter tops.

Vanessa's feeling expansive. They've come to town, and she wants to get her money's worth. She parks the van up on the Place Rigaud, so they can borrow some CDs from the *médiathèque.* Then they stop by the health-food store to see if they have gingerroot, except the health-food store has moved, which reminds Vanessa that she wanted to sign up for acting classes at the storefront theater on the rue Main de Fer. (Rat refrains from saying that to her own way of thinking, Vanessa doesn't need drama school, she needs un–drama school.) Everything Vanessa wants to do, she swears will only take a second, but Rat's sick of tramping around town.

"I thought we were here to buy me sneakers," she points out.

"All in good time, my girl." Vanessa slips her arm around Rat's waist. "Look, we're in the big city. Bright lights, beautiful people. Enjoy it." Not often they get an outing, just the two of them, Morgan parked with Laurent for the afternoon.

"I'd kinda like to get back home." Jérôme has this new computer game where you each pick a character and give her a job and a house and a life. Jérôme likes managing the family budget; Rat likes arranging the furniture.

"Look where we are," Vanessa says. "The shoe store's right around the corner."

They are standing in a tiny square tucked in an angle just behind the big shopping streets. It's called the place des Orfèvres—a hidden place Rat's never noticed before. The square's centerpiece is a medieval fountain crowned by three frogs, out of whose mouths the water flows. The frogs are made of the same local marble that paves the downtown sidewalks and arcades—an orange-purplish marble with white streaks. They are square-cut, childishly rough, like grotesques on a cloister pillar.

Rat goes over to dip a finger in the fountain—an instinctive good-luck gesture. Rat's outgrown most of those loserish sort of tics that other kids tease you for, but she still retains a few. Running water is always magic. Marielle has a friend who's a water-diviner. The word for "water-diviner" is almost the same as the word for "witch."

There's a man sitting on the bench by the fountain. He has a dog on a leash. The dog's some kind of Border collie: speckled black-and-white, low to the ground. Its eyes are motley: one light brown, the other an eerie pale blue. It doesn't look especially sociable, but Rat doesn't mind. She loves animals. She's young enough still and maybe vain enough to think she can stick her head in a crocodile's mouth with impunity.

Rat bends down to stroke the dog, and it utters a low warning growl. For years afterwards, she will think, If only I hadn't gone over and patted that dog, our lives would have been so different.

Its owner speaks. "Girl, you should never touch a dog you don't know."

The dog glances briefly at the man as if he's been maligned, and looks away again. But Rat's recognized the high-pitched, slightly nasal voice. She's like that. By now, she knows not to let on, mostly. People tend to think you're some kind of stalker if you tell them, I saw you at a bus stop three years ago; you were wearing a red hat.

He is rougher, more down-and-out than when Rat last saw him. His black jeans and T-shirt have faded to the color of rust and it smells as if he's been sleeping in them for a while.

"Your daughter's very trusting," the man says to Vanessa.

"Hummmph," grunts Vanessa. "Only with animals."

And now he recognizes them.

"Don't I know you from somewhere?" Takes a moment to place them. "Didn't you used to live up in Brix?"

"We go to Brix from time to time," Vanessa admits.

"I remember who you are—you're the market ladies."

"How's the colander?" Rat rejoins.

"The colander was fine." He smiles a ragged sort of thin-lipped smile. "But that woman you sold me—remember, with the little ring-thingy in her nose for leading her by?—she turned out to be a real piece of shit."

Rat is disturbed by this way of talking. He's drunk, she decides. She tries to catch her mother's eye. "Mama, we should get going," she says. "It's getting late."

But Vanessa just looks at her with a dazed expression, and says nothing.

The man in black finishes rolling himself a cigarette. He offers it to Vanessa, who hesitates, says no, then says yes. Rat starts to remind her mother that she's quit, but stops herself.

He lights Vanessa's cigarette, then starts rolling another for himself.

"Some people forget that smoking is a sociable activity. Passing the peace pipe," he says.

The guy's definitely bombed, Rat decides. "Mama, are we going shoe shopping, or are we . . . "

"Let your mama finish her *clope* in peace," says Johnny Cash.

Rat ignores him. "Mama . . ."

"You go on ahead. You start looking," Vanessa says. "I'll catch up with you in a moment."

Johnny Cash's real name was Thierry. He came from the north, near the Belgian border. This is the story he told Vanessa, when he first moved in with them, him and his mean snarly collie, Vesuvio, who almost succeeded in making Rat beware of dogs.

His father was a town surveyor. Every week or so, after work, his father used to go out drinking with a couple of colleagues, and when he came home, he would beat Thierry silly. His mother and sisters, Thierry maintained, were the worst of all, because they looked on and did nothing.

His entire childhood Thierry could never remember anybody's kissing him or putting him to bed or saying a kind word. Even at school, the teachers said he was useless.

When he was sixteen, Thierry realized he was bigger than his father, and if he didn't get out he was going to kill him. He moved in with the carpenter he'd been apprenticed to, but the carpenter made a pass at him, so he left. Went to live on a commune, where he learned to tend a kitchen garden and to cook for thirty people. Later, he'd trained as a youth counselor, helping kids with problems. This, Thierry felt, was his true vocation. After he came down south, he worked a few summers at a camp above Brix for teen delinquents, but he'd fallen out with the director, a fat-assed bureaucrat who wasn't interested in the kids, but only in his own comfort.

For the first year or so Thierry lived with them, he and Vanessa seemed genuinely in love. He was an attractive man, physically. Even Rat could tell, and grown-ups didn't hold much interest for her. He was long-limbed and so tall Vanessa barely came up to his chest. He had glossy black hair and curly black eyelashes and by afternoon, his cheeks and chin had a blackish sheen, too.

His brown eyes sparkled like a sunlit stream, giving him a somewhat deceptive air of vivacity. (When he was drunk or had smoked too much dope, they went little and bloodshot, which better expressed his true character, to Rat's way of thinking.)

He would stare at Rat's mother with those light brown eyes, as if he wanted to eat her up. And she stared back, scarcely breathing, her cheeks flushed pink.

Rat had never seen her mother so into anybody before, or anybody into her mother, and the experience was unsettling. At night, Rat blasted the radio in the bedroom so she and Morgan couldn't hear the noises coming from Vanessa's room. Rat didn't understand why copulation sounded so much like murder, but it made her grateful to be a kid for a while longer.

Because Vanessa was so happy—because everybody said she hadn't been this happy since Souad died—Rat wanted to keep an open mind about Thierry.

He definitely brought some order to their home. He mended the broken windowpane on the front door, and installed a new showerhead in the shower.

Thierry's biggest project was the backyard, which he reorganized with one corner for a laundry line, another for an outdoor table and chairs, and at the far end, a kennel for Vesuvio. The second winter of Thierry's moving in, he planted a little kitchen garden, so they could eat their own vegetables.

He was a good cook. For him, cooking was a form of self-respect, a way of being a family, and it bugged him that Vanessa would just open a can of stew or shove a frozen pizza in the microwave. When Thierry cooked dinner, there would be a roast chicken or a couscous, salad from the garden. Once he even baked bread. Rat hadn't tasted homemade bread since Mémé Catherine. When Rat told Thierry his bread tasted great "if you liked sawdust," he sulked for about a week, and never baked again. He was thin-skinned, for someone who'd had such a rough life.

Thierry always told you how much he loved kids, but it was a dark harassing sort of love. Whatever task Thierry had set himself, he'd try to draft Rat and Morgan and the Cabreras into an auxiliary workforce. His way of nagging you to help, or carping that you'd done it wrong, set everybody on edge. Invariably, by the time they were finished the afternoon's project, all the kids would be seething.

Thierry had his favorites and his antifavorites. Rat, he soon concluded, was a spoiled brat with all her mother's failings and none of her strong points, and Jérôme he had a peculiar sort of grudge against, but Morgan he thought was the sort of boy he himself had been: a clever sensitive kid crying out for a man's care. There was something odd about the way he always took Morgan's side against the women, even when there was no fight to pick.

One harrowing period, Thierry got it into his head that Morgan was dyslexic, presumably because he himself had been, and that no one was attending to his problem. In the evenings, he tried to make Morgan read aloud and do special exercises. When Morgan's teacher complained that he was coming to school dead-exhausted and that anyway he could read just fine, Thierry threatened to yank Morgan out of the system and homeschool him.

Vanessa had been obliged to get Thierry to back off and leave Morgan's education alone.

Later on, Rat could look back and see how Thierry had disintegrated over the years he lived with them: how all his initial domestic enthusiasms, his projects to make himself a workshop in the shed, or to keep hens so they could have fresh eggs, or even to sublet the apartment so they could all go live in Guadeloupe, had fizzled out, giving way to a corrosive apathy.

One day, he pulled a muscle in his back helping Vanessa move a dresser, and from then on, he barely left the house. When Rat and Morgan got back from school in the afternoons, Thierry would still be asleep in bed, or maybe sitting on the front stoop in an old kimono of Vanessa's, smoking a joint and drinking pastis.

Rat and Morgan tried not to talk too much about Thierry when they were on their own, because they were stuck with him and it would only make it worse, but when he was drinking, they tended to stay over at the Cabreras'.

One time, when Thierry didn't know Rat was home, she overheard him pestering Morgan in a way that seriously spooked her.

He'd found a tick in Vesuvio's fur, and he wanted Morgan to hold the dog still while he extracted it with the tweezers. But Morgan was completely phobic about Vesuvio, and rightly so. Every time he tried to hold Vesuvio's collar, the dog would crane round and try to bite him, and Thierry would curse at him for letting go.

"Why are you so scared of Vesuvio, my darling?" Thierry asked, now in his softest, most cajoling voice. "Vesuvio wouldn't hurt a fly, you know that, don't you? You're too big to be scared of dogs. You're a big boy now, Momo. You know that, don't you?"

Morgan said nothing.

"Have you got a sweetheart yet, Momo? Which of the little girls at school is your sweetheart? Is it Solenne? No? Have you been with a girl yet, or are you and your friends still playing with each other's *zizis* in the back alley?"

And then his voice got suddenly sharp. "Don't let the fucking dog *go,* do you hear me?"

"He's biting me!" Morgan shouted back, equally furious, and came storming into their bedroom, slamming the door.

Thierry followed him, but when he saw Rat was there, he said only, "There's to be no slamming of doors in this house, do you hear me?" and left.

"What was he saying, about you and girls and shit?" Rat asked Morgan when he'd gone.

Morgan was lying on his bed, scowling. "I don't know."

"Has he talked to you that way before?"

"No."

"Well, tell me if he tries it again. It's not right."

Funny, Thierry's knack for poisoning goodwill. When he first moved in, the neighbors were thrilled Vanessa had a proper boyfriend at last. Everybody'd loved Max and they knew how sad Vanessa had been since he was gone. Jean-Luc and Laurent would invite Thierry to join them at *pétanque,* or Cristel would ask him along on her monthly trip across the Spanish border to load up on cheap cigarettes and gasoline. But after a while, people were barely speaking to him.

The turning point was one evening at Marielle and Jean-Luc's.

Dinners at the Cabreras' were festive. Jean-Luc liked to mix his own music—he'd put on some combo of Tuareg blues, New Wave tango, birdsong—and after dinner, he'd open a bottle of eau-de-vie made by his brother-in-law in the Auvergne. Liquor that had been concocted in the same spirit as Marielle baked her cherry tart. Something homemade, to be enjoyed together. But that wasn't how Thierry drank. It grated on him being another man's guest, and he drank as if you were trying to cheat him with your liquor, and when he was half drunk, he needled and sniped, and when he was three-quarters drunk, he ranted.

The conversation had turned to politics. Jean-Luc and Marielle, like Vanessa, were old-fashioned leftists, but Thierry on this particular evening decided to take the side of the entrepreneurial classes. He told them how France was going to the dogs, because nobody was willing to work anymore. French people were lazy, and the immigrants they let in were even lazier.

America was smart, he said, they let in Asians who knew how to bust their asses to succeed, whereas France only let in Arabs and Africans, who saw themselves as victims of colonialism. You can't run a country on guilt and apologies, he said. People get tired of bowing and scraping in their own country, saying Sorry, sorry, and when they've had it, they'll vote for a strong leader who'll clean house.

At first, the other grown-ups tried deflecting Thierry by teasing, but he wasn't teasable, so then they started talking among themselves, chatting about the new administrator at the clinic where Marielle worked or the sailboat Michel, Jean-Luc's boss, had just bought. Until finally Thierry, pissed off that nobody was listening, picked up Jean-Luc's bottle of eau-de-vie and the box of chocolates Vanessa had brought, and walked out of the Cabreras' house, without a word. When Vanessa and Rat and Morgan got home later that evening, he was passed out on the living room sofa, melted chocolate all over the cushions.

And now when Thierry and Jean-Luc crossed paths in the courtyard, they barely nodded.

But Vanessa was unflappable. She was in love with this man, she told Marielle, even if he wasn't always easy. He'd been badly hurt in his life, an abused child who'd never known a parent's love, and if it weren't for them—meaning Vanessa and Rat and Morgan and the Cabreras and even Laurent and Cristel—he'd be lost.

You have no idea how sweet he can be, how tender, how thoughtful, she said. He's just like a little boy, so remorseful when you show him he's been an asshole. He says and does those things to shock you, but he doesn't mean it, he's just trying to get a reaction, it goes back to childhood when his father wouldn't acknowledge Thierry's existence except to whack him.

Marielle seemed unconvinced. "Look, it's really not your job to make up for someone's unhappy childhood. And it's not possible, anyway." Silence, then she asked, abruptly, "You're not still thinking of having another baby?"

Rat, who'd thus far been pretending to be busy doing her homework, now swung around, outraged. "Mama! A *baby*? With that creep? You *mustn't*."

Vanessa laughed. "I'm *thinking*," she said. "I'm allowed to think. Course, when a guy's downed half a bottle of pastis, baby-making tends to remain in the realm of thought."

Middle of the night. A bitter howling night.

Rat is curled up in her bed, knees hiked to her chin, hands tucked between her thighs to keep warm.

This winter, Rat's finally decorated her sleeping loft the way she always wanted to. For years, she'd had this dream of making herself a kind of Oriental tent, so she could be completely private and enclosed. Then one day, Vanessa brought her back from the market an enormous orange-and-purple-patchwork Indian spread with tiny mirrored sequins, and they hung it from hooks on the ceiling like mosquito netting.

Inside is just big enough for Rat's mattress and her bedside lamp, which casts a cozy golden light. If you look at Rat's loft from the outside, when the light's on, it looks like a glowing jack-o'-lantern.

On the wall she's taped a galaxy of photographs—snapshots of her and Max and Morgan on the beach outside Tangier; of Vanessa and Aunt Marie-Christine as children at a ski resort, perched on the slope in their snowsuits and goggles; a blown-up photocopy of Celia Kidd from the old black-and-white *Vogue*, big boppy mascara-gummed eyes, wearing the white-feather poncho, and seemingly nothing else. Pages torn from more recent fashion magazines.

These are Rat's household deities.

When Rat was younger, she believed in gods—the water nymphs whom the ancient Celts used to worship at the hot springs above Brix, or Artemis, who had the man who saw her naked turned into a stag and ripped apart by his own hounds. Even Jesus—not Mémé Catherine's blue-eyed babe, but Max's Jesus, who taught you not to judge and not to set too much store by worldly things. Now all she believes in is finding somewhere quiet in your own head.

Below, she can hear the soft rumble of Morgan's sleeping breath. It's the only safe sound to hang on to, like a match flicker you need to keep alight.

Normally at this hour of the night you might hear the owls hooting from their nest in the hollow plane tree. Or farmyard dogs barking, first one, and then all the others. Or distant trucks rattling back and forth to Spain. Night sounds, lonely but not unpleasant.

Tonight all she can hear is the shouts from her mother's bedroom, voices ugly with anger, recrimination. Rat tries to plug her ear holes with spitball Kleenex, but it doesn't keep the sounds out.

Occasionally she can make out a word or phrase: Money. Lies. Money again. Most of what Vanessa and Thierry fight about is money.

The shouting is louder and angrier than usual. It seems as if it will never stop. Suddenly, Thierry's voice, right outside their bedroom door: "Is that what you want, bitch, is that what you want? If that's what you want, watch out, because you might just get it." And Vanessa, mocking, shrill, "No, it's what *you* want."

There's a loud slam, a kind of thud, a crash like a chair being knocked over onto the tiled floor, and a little scream from her mother. Then the sound of Thierry shouting, and another scream. A thud. And silence.

It's not as if Rat doesn't have troubles of her own to keep her awake at night. Prime among them, the fact that she's flunking school. Madame Renaud keeps sending home notes to Vanessa asking her to come in and discuss the problem, but Vanessa is too busy to go see her. Rat doesn't think she could bear repeating a grade. Aside from having to hear all the same boring teachers explain the same boring things all over again, she's already two feet taller than the kids in her own year.

Rat is thinking about how Marie Trintignant was murdered by her boyfriend Bernard Cantat. She was filming a movie in eastern Europe, and Cantat came to visit her. He murdered her in her hotel room during a drunken fight. He said he didn't mean to, she was laying into him and he lost his temper. He said he thought she'd passed out drunk, but by the morning, she was dead. Marie Trintignant had young children, too.

Rat is holding her breath, listening for noise. But there's silence. Maybe they've made up, or maybe they've gone to sleep. But maybe her mother's dead.

"Morgan?"

No answer.

Only the catlike purr of her brother's sleeping breath.

Rat creeps down from her loft, opens the door, and, heart thumping way too fast, ventures out into the living room. Empty, except for the usual chaos of leftover dinner. Does she dare go into Vanessa's bedroom? The door is slightly ajar. She peeks through, heart pounding hard.

Her mother and Thierry lie in bed, seemingly asleep. Thierry is sprawled wide, snoring, Vanessa curled up with her back to him. Breathing. Alive.

Instead of feeling relieved, Rat's just plain furious. Isn't it mothers who are supposed to be worried about their teenaged daughters' getting themselves killed?

She climbs back up into her sleeping loft.

Try to imagine yourself somewhere safe, Rat. The most magical place you can summon, like on the beach outside Tangier, you and Max and Vanessa and Morgan, with Morgan's mother, Souad, still alive. Back in a time when everything seemed simpler.

Or else picture this. You're in London with your granny. You're riding on the top of a bus—one of those red double-decker elephants that look like they belong in a circus. It's Christmastime. A wet winter's day that's sleeting into purple dusk, but inside, you're toasty warm. From the top story of the bus, you look down on the big boulevards festooned in Christmas lights. The bus is fuggy with warmth. And the traffic lights reflect off the melted snow in the street, making pools of shimmery red and green.

You are squeezed into a seat at the front of the bus, and beside you is your grandmother, Celia Kidd. Your grandmother's an old lady, but she's still whip-thin and her eyes are electric green, and she wears red lipstick and magenta leather gloves like the girl in the Hermès ad taped up on your wall. Even just thinking of those magenta gloves is a good way of banishing the image of snoring Thierry splayed wide across your mother's bed.

You and your granny have been Christmas shopping. You've been to all the fancy department stores, the shops that sell perfumed bath oil, the food shops that sell hams and caviar and chocolates and cheeses.

You've bought presents for your father and you've bought presents for your mother and you've bought presents for Morgan, and you've chosen something very beautiful for your grandmother.

Everybody in the shops recognizes Celia Kidd. And she tells them, This is my granddaughter, who is also named Celia. She looks just like you, the shop assistants say. It's nice to have a beautiful granddaughter named after you.

And now you are headed home to a white terraced London house, where Gillem is waiting for you in the midnight blue drawing room, in front of a roaring fire.

Celia will serve tea and cakes in front of the fire, the three of them will be snuggled tight on the pink velvet sofa, and Celia will tell you wild stories about London in the sixties.

"And tomorrow," she says, running her fingers lovingly through your hair, "I'll take you ice-skating in the park."

Two

CHAPTER

1

The radio alarm is jabbering again, cracking Rat out of sleep. Beady digitals say it's 6:58 a.m. The sky is silvery blue, the remaining streaks of snow on Mount Canigou are gleaming in the early morning light, the broad new leaves on the vines trellising their neighbors' terrace trembling pale green.

Rat can't deny it's day, even though it feels like somewhere between night and death. Radio's tuned to Radio Blue Roussillon, and the announcer's reporting on the third day of riots in Perpignan.

The radio announcer is summoning up last night's tally. This time, it's the downtown shopping streets that have been hit. A dozen buildings on the rue des Augustins firebombed, forty-some cars burned. Eleven people held for questioning in the Place Cassanyes murder.

It all started two weeks ago, in the middle of the Sunday market. An Algerian man caught a Gypsy boy trying to break into his car, and when he went after the kid with a knife, a bunch of Gypsies chased him and beat him to death. Broad daylight, dozens of people watching. Week later, a second Arab was shot dead in a drive-by shooting, and now the city's exploded into race riots.

Every night, kids are out with crowbars, baseball bats, jerry cans of gasoline, looking for Gypsies. But the Gypsies have all fled, so instead they're smashing up the city center, burning cars. And now everybody else is taking advantage of the mayhem— artful grannies rolling out of broken-glassed supermarkets, their shopping carts loaded with free heating oil. The extreme right planting their own bombs to make the Arabs look bad.

That's the idyllic South of France for you.

Rat doesn't want to get out of bed. It's May. Outside, in the noonday sun, it may feel hot as summer, but inside, early morning, it's arctic. She can hear the Tramontane whipping through the windows, sirening under the doors.

It's not easy wrenching herself out of bed and down the ladder into the cruel world. Tiled floors icy under her feet.

Roar of toilet flushing. In the living room, she almost bumps into Thierry, who is sleepwalking his way back to Vanessa's bed. They stare right through each other, Rat trying not to look at his skinny white legs covered in black hair, or the yellow flecks of piss he leaves on the toilet seat.

That's how she and her unofficial stepdad coexist these days. No more contact than two separate species inhabiting the same forest. Used to be, whenever Thierry shoved, Rat shoved back harder. But that's too much trouble. Life's too big to waste your time being petty as your adversary. If it weren't for Morgan, she'd have been out of the house long ago.

Her first job is to light the woodstove. She breaks up the side of a fruit crate and arranges its splintered slats in a little teepee surmounted by a flying buttress of grapevine. Takes a match to a crumple of newspaper inside. Crouching down, Rat puffs, making her breath into a bellows until the flame from the fruit-crate splinters has turned the gnarled gray whirl of grapevine reliably aglow.

She turns on the grill. Pours milk into a saucepan. Then she goes back into the bedroom to rouse Morgan. The sleeping child is curled up under his duvet. His body in its astronaut pajamas—pajamas she remembers back from when they were Jérôme's—is a small oven. She presses her face close to Morgan's, breathes in his toasty breath.

Rat can remember when Morgan's sleeping breath changed from being baby's breath, milky-sweet, to stale, like a grown-up's. She likes it even stale.

"Wake up, bedbug." She tickles him.

Morgan gives a great stretch that bops her on the nose and lunges back into sleep. She tickles him harder, and he grumbles, punching her again. Morgan sleeps the way he eats: hearty, even, indefatigable. Three square a day, ten hours a night. Unlike Rat, who's finicky, fretful, liable to upset stomachs and nightmares.

Rat opens Morgan's chest drawers—there's one that's splintered apart; in the old days when she and Thierry were still speaking, he would have fixed it for her—pulls out underpants, tracksuit bottoms, a T-shirt. Tries to find two socks whose toes and heels aren't completely bald. One sock Pokémon, one sock Bugs Bunny but at least they're roughly the same noncolor. Throws the bundle on his bed.

"C'mon. It's time for me to get going."

In the mornings, Jean-Luc drops off Rat at Victor Hugo on his way to work, while Morgan and Solenne, who aren't due at school till eight thirty, go with Marielle.

She gets out two bowls, scoops a tablespoon of Nesquik into each. Morgan is in charge of grilling the bread, because Rat always forgets and burns it. When she's grown up, she'll get a toaster like Marielle's.

Rat now attends to her own toilette: a perfunctory swab of deodorant under each armpit. Climbs back into the faded nest of last night's corduroys, grabs a 2 Many DJ's T-shirt that's somehow wound up in her drawer, slips into her flip-flops, considers running a brush through her matted hair and thinks better of it. She has a raw nerve in her broken tooth that she's been telling her mother about for months now.

And only then remembers, Today's my birthday.

When Rat gets into Jean-Luc's car, the radio is booming.

An agitated reporter describes last night's rioting. "As soon as darkness fell, they were out in the streets. Dozens of masked figures carrying tankards of gasoline, setting fire to cars, smashing store windows. I talked to the owner of a bakery on the boulevard Aristide Briand who'd had her shop windows broken."

The woman's voice, high-pitched, Catalan. In the background, sirens. "They had crowbars, I saw one man with a golf club. They were smashing every store along the boulevard—the pizzeria, the motorcycle showroom. When they reached my shop, I went out into the street, I begged them to stop. I said to them, What did I ever do to hurt you?"

"Did they listen?" the reporter asks.

"No, they didn't. One of them, he says to me, Madame, if you don't want to get hurt, you'd better go home. And they went right ahead"—she's crying now—"and smashed the windows of my bakery. Who's going to pay for it?"

Thick burry voice of a Gypsy pastor, saying Gypsies are peace-loving people. Voice of a young Arab man saying Gypsies break the law right, left, and center, and nobody does a thing. Voice of a sociology professor talking about the collapse of the Republican model of integration.

Bla-bla-bla. It's all a scam, a three-card monte game. They ask you to integrate, but they won't let you.

The radio announcer comes back on the air, saying that the Minister of the Interior has ordered fifteen hundred riot police to be bused into Perpignan from Montpellier and Bordeaux till order is restored.

Jean-Luc laughs. "That'll be the day. You know, I grew up on the rue des Remparts de St. Jacques, a block away from the place Cassanyes. When I was a kid, neighbors left their doors wide open. Didn't matter whether you were French, Gypsy, Spanish, Arab. Everybody looked out for everybody. There was an old Gypsy grandmother—if you didn't see her one day on her chair on the sidewalk, my mother'd be, like, Luc, go knock on Mamie Paulette's window, make sure she's all right. Nowadays, everybody in the neighborhood's got a dead bolt on their front door and a pistol in the bedside table. The little Arab who works for us, I was helping him load up his car, I see a golf club in the back, I say, I didn't know you were a golfer, Farid. He says, I have to protect my family, don't I?"

"*Putain*," yawns Rat, stretching. "What a mess."

"Fasten your seat belt; you got it all twisted up."

"Doesn't matter."

"It matters to me, if we get pulled over." Jean-Luc switches off the radio. "More and more, I think Marx had a point. Why are these kids smashing shop windows? Because consumer capitalism has sapped them of any political sense. Kids think what's wrong with their lives is they don't have enough money to buy the latest Adidas tracksuit, not that they have no access to power."

Rat yawns again, switches back on the radio, and tunes it to the hip-hop station. Fatal Bazooka boasting about how he's the big man in town.

Tuesday's Rat's easy day. All she's got is French and math in the morning, sports and civic education in the afternoon.

At lunchtime, she and Angélique go to their usual spot behind the skate park and sit, sharing a joint, each with one bud of Rat's MP3 in her ear. Angélique was the first kid Rat knew to get an MP3, but Angélique's is broken.

She finishes at four. When she gets through the metal detector, Jérôme's waiting for her on his motorbike. Two older girls in halter tops and cling-tight jeans are hanging around him, flirting.

Last year, when Jérôme was still at Victor Hugo, he was just this nerdy-looking white kid with an ass too skinny to hold up his jeans. No girl would give him the time of day. Then over the summer, Jérôme shot up three inches and started lifting weights. Now he's at Lycée Arago in Perpignan, and when he shows up at Victor Hugo on his motorbike, it's, Hey Jérôme, can you give me a ride to Moulin-à-Vent? Hey, Jérôme, would you like to come to a party Saturday night?

Rat suspects he's been going out with her friend Marie's older sister, but Jérôme would never tell.

"Did you bring my sleeping bag?" she asks.

He hands her the backpack with both their sleeping bags attached. She gets on the back of Jérôme's bike, and they take off, wobbly, engine sputtering.

To Vanessa, it's incomprehensible that Rat spends most of her waking and sleeping hours with a healthy adolescent male who nonetheless isn't her boyfriend.

Last summer, when the grown-ups finally agreed that Rat and Jérôme were old enough to go off camping alone, Vanessa's only question was, "Are you using protection?" Not, have you got ground cover, a lighter, a water bottle, but have you got a condom.

Rat was more nonplussed than angry. "Mama, I'm not sleeping with Jérôme! That would be, like, incest or something!"

Next time Vanessa tried to give Rat her little contraception speech (I don't care what you're doing as long as you're safe) Rat cut her short.

"Mama, I'm not sleeping with any boy. End of subject."

And Vanessa, offended, had inquired, "You aren't gay, are you? Because I think you should tell me. Not that I'd mind. I don't have any prejudices, as you know."

Rat burst out laughing, but Vanessa persisted. "*What?!* What's so funny? Well, I'm glad you think it's funny having a daughter like a clam. I mean, you'd tell me, right?"

"Tell you what? If I'm gay or if I need protection?"

"You think I'm funny?"

"Mama, leave me alone, I'm only fourteen."

"My pet, when I was fourteen, I wasn't sleeping on beaches with fifteen-year-old boys. Doesn't it drive *him* nuts?"

"Mama, would you feel better if I told you we were both gay?"

At that her mother finally gave up and started laughing, too. Vanessa must be the only mother in town actually trying to nag her teenage daughter into having sex. To Rat, boys are no different from girls—better, in certain respects. The last time someone tried to force a kiss—after she'd already explained she wasn't interested—she punched him. A question of basic respect.

Rat's just about sure Jérôme's sleeping with Marie's sister Céline.

Jérôme chooses the little back roads to get to Florian's place, chugging past miles of market gardens. The only traffic is tractors. It's the same route Vanessa used to take to get to the Perpignan hospital, and it gives Rat a mean flashback to Souad's dying.

She wonders whether Morgan remembers his mother. She wonders what her own life would have been like if Vanessa had died when Rat was Morgan's age. Who would have taken her— Mémé Catherine? The thought of being brought up by Mémé Catherine, Mass every week and Baby Jesus over her bed and "the Bon Dieu" this and the "Bon Dieu" that, makes Rat feel a little more forgiving of Vanessa. She may be a pervert, but she's not a fanatic.

They reach Bompas. Florian and his grandmother live on

the ground floor of a public-housing complex behind the municipal gym.

Jérôme raps on Florian's window. Florian opens the door.

He and Jérôme do their little pretend-gang-member ritual of touching knuckles to knuckles to heart, a language of the blind.

She and Florian exchange kisses. She's taller than he, so she has to stoop. She's taller than everybody (except Thierry, worst luck. She'd rather be littler than everybody else but bigger than Thierry). Vanessa's always telling her not to hunch to hide her height. You're a tall girl, enjoy it.

"How's tricks?"

"Not bad."

"What're you up to?"

"Chilling. Minding my own business."

Florian's business is dealing dope, and mostly business comes to him. Daytimes, his granny is out cleaning houses, which is her idea of business. In fact, his granny's business is every bit as illicit as Florian's, since she's supposed to be retired, living off her disability pension.

Apparently Florian's grandmother doesn't ask too many questions about the strange people coming in and out of her apartment. Once or twice, Florian says, she's asked him why he doesn't try to get a job with the electrician, which was what he trained for at school, but mostly she's pleased he's putting money on the table.

Florian struts into the kitchen, brings back three icy cold Kronenbourgs. "Man, these days you do not want to leave home unless it's *obligé*. This morning I had to go downtown, it was like World War Seven. Smoke, fire engines, police trucks."

"Fire engines?"

"Yeah, didn't you hear, they set some Arab cultural center on fire. Now that's really a case of pissing in your own bed. Place République was empty. Cafés boarded up, windows smashed. Not a mouse stirring, just all these riot police in their vans, barricading the streets. Spooky. I got back in my car, turned around, thought I was home free. Then up on Anatole France, just past Cassanyes, suddenly I hit this roadblock. Great big fucking cop makes me get out of the car. Registration papers, ID card, hands up in the air, and he searches me. First thing he finds is my knife. He's checking it out, making sure the blade's regulation length, no longer than my palm, and he's like, Where did you get this? And I'm, like, Well, actually my girlfriend won it at the amusement park, throwing hoops over plastic duckies."

They all laugh.

"Was it true?" asks Jérôme.

"Yeah, it's like this dinky little made-in-China piece of shit. And he's, like"—Florian narrows his eyes, grates his voice to steel—"Open the trunk of the car. *Now.*"

"What were they looking for?"

"Whatever."

"And were you clean?"

"Well, luckily he didn't think to look in the glove compartment. No, in fact, I was fine. But man, when I got back in the car and drove away, my heart was thumping so hard I thought I was going into cardiac arrest."

Rat and Jérôme have known Florian since elementary school. Back then, he was the kid grown-ups whispered about darkly and other boys sucked up to, because he didn't seem to have any brakes on him. Glamorous Trouble. Rat can remember hearing about the time they tried to send Florian home from school for throwing a chair at the teacher. Only there was nobody, it turned out, to send him home to. This was before his granny moved down south to look after him, when it was only his mom, who was always in and out of the mental hospital at Théza. He was living alone in the apartment like a wild animal, this ten-year-old kid. Empty cereal boxes all over the floor and mouse shit.

That was when Florian told everybody he wished he'd get put

in Care because that way at least he'd get a steady meal. Later on, when the Saint Féliu Youth Center got broken into—stereo equipment stolen, swastikas painted on the walls—he did get sent away. And when he came back, he wasn't glamorous anymore, he was just a loser.

That was the point where, to Rat's mind, a person gets interesting. A lot of the people she likes best in the world everyone else has given up on. So she wasn't surprised when Jérôme said he'd bumped into Florian, who was living over in Bompas with his granny, and said to stop by anytime. Or that Jérôme, who, like her, has a soft spot for so-called losers, chose to take it as an invitation not to come buy dope, but actually to chill with the guy, ask him if he wanted to go to the movies, get a kebab.

Rat takes a curious look around Florian's place. It's nice. There's a breakfront cabinet full of china collectibles. A clock on the wall with a picture of a waterfall, labeled "Souvenirs from the Cevennes." Crocheted doilies on the tabletop, potted plants in the kitchen window.

Florian is sitting in his tracksuit bottoms. On the table, a heap of plastic bags, a razor blade, a kitchen scale. He is weighing little lumps of hash, separating them and bagging them.

"I'll be finished in a minute. Check out my new Tony Hawk."

On a big-screen console is a skateboard game.

"Wanna play, Rat?"

Jérôme and Rat each choose a skater, name him, coiff him, outfit him. Jérôme propels his man into fantastical triple ollies up the walls of an empty shopping plaza. Rat, soon bored, allows her suicide skater to crash through the picture windows of the school cafeteria. She can't help it, she's really only interested in the part where you choose whether your hero has an Afro or dreads, camouflage cutoffs or baggies.

"I'm finished," says Florian. He disappears with the goods and returns. "Shall we bring some food?"

He opens the refrigerator, extracts a dish covered in plastic wrap.

"Take this," he orders Jérôme.

"What is it?"

"Swiss-chard-and-ham casserole."

Jérôme makes a face.

"It's delicious," Florian assures him. "First-rate."

"Are you sure it's okay to take it?"

"It's for me," he says. "My granny cooks me meals the night before, to heat up for lunch."

"It's not going to heat up so well over a campfire," warns Jérôme, but Rat can tell Florian's bent on bringing his granny's casserole.

"Did you tell her it was my birthday?" she teases, hopeful. "See, Flo, us poor suckers don't have grannies who bake."

"Get lost," says Florian. "You scum, you aren't worthy to eat the crumbs off her—"

He shoves Jérôme, who's sticking his nose back into the refrigerator hungrily.

"Here."

He throws a pack of cookies at him.

"Store-bought," Jérôme sniffs.

"I haven't brought anything," says Rat, guilty.

"Don't worry, we'll stop by Intermarché and fill in the gaps. Get some sausages, buy some more beer." Florian winks at Rat. "A bottle of champagne for the birthday girl."

They pack their stuff in the back of Florian's car, and leave Jérôme's motorbike behind.

The old dynamite factory sits on the shore just south of Port Vendres, along a craggy coastline of military watchtowers. It looks more like a nineteenth-century nobleman's estate than a factory.

There are tall chained gates and a ruined gatehouse whose windows are broken, and beyond them, thirty-two hectares of land overgrown into a dense dark Mediterranean jungle of umbrella pines and eucalyptus that runs down to the sea.

There are signs posted everywhere that say Danger: Explosives! but they haven't prevented the site from becoming a paradise for teenage raves and love-ins, a rendezvous for whatever monkey business gets smuggled back and forth across the Spanish border. There's room enough for a whole village of miscreants each to pursue undisturbed his contraband vocation.

Rat scales the gates quickly, and goes on ahead. It's a magical but slightly spooky place. There's a factory chimney, a watchtower, the remains of rail tracks. In one clearing, a spread-out sequence of long narrow buildings that could originally have served any function—laboratories, torture chambers, brothel. Prowling through the broken eviscerated rooms, she feels like the witness to a long-ago crime. Mattresses, old magazines strewn across the cement floor, plastic tubes. Pretty flowered wallpaper in what seems to be a bedroom, and a calendar on the floor. Did somebody leave in a hurry?

The main building is a huge cathedral-like structure. Now it's a half-roofless ruin. Fig trees have spread their lofty tentacles through corners of what once was ceiling. Rat, who hates warfare, appreciates that slow Bacchic metamorphosis from dynamite to figs. As she sweeps through its high crumbling spaces, she hears music coming from the main hall and then the noise of a dog barking. A shaggy sheepdog comes to greet her, wagging its tail and barking simultaneously.

"Hello, baby," Rat says softly. Kneels and buries her head in its golden fleece.

"Arnaque!" somebody calls. Has she heard right? Who would call their dog "Fraud"?

In the main hall, which still has its ceiling intact, there's a group of older kids camped out. No one she's ever seen before. One girl is lighting a stove. A boy seems to be folding laundry. The others are sitting around, reading. It looks oddly homey.

"Hi," says Rat.

Not much answer.

Now Jérôme and Florian appear.

At first sight, a flicker of tension between occupants and newcomers. A brief, territorial appraisal. The moment when hackles rise and fall, noses wrinkle, teeth are bared, covered, bared again, tail wags and then suddenly stills. Do you say hello, do you ignore each other, are they going to rob and kill you. But Rat's hugging their dog, so what can they do?

"Hey there," says Jérôme.

The others grunt.

"Nice dog," says Rat, and just to break the ice, "I forgot how much I love dogs. My stepdad has this really vicious Border collie that's totally made me forget how much I love dogs."

Tension is let out. The older kids aren't exactly friendly, but they're not outright hostile. There are maybe four or five of them, and they are a bit more hippyish looking than people from Rat's part of the world. One boy has dreadlocks, the other a big bushy blond beard. The girls are crew-cutted, pierced. They look as if they have been living in the dynamite factory for some time. They have installed a Primus stove, armchairs. A hammock is strung between two pillars. The ruin has become a cozy home for castaways.

Rat and her friends go find themselves a more distant building in which to set up camp. They unpack their knapsacks, lay out their sleeping bags, and then make their way through the underbrush down to the rocky cove.

It's a chilly afternoon. The sky is overcast, the sea gray and curdled. Rat and Jérôme scramble along the shaggy, barnacle-covered black rocks. But Florian begins to undress, tripping over his tracksuit bottoms and hopping on one foot.

"What are you up to, Flo? Getting in your pajamas already?" Rat teases.

"Isn't anybody else swimming?"

"You crazy, man?" Jérôme grumbles. "You're gonna freeze your fucking balls off."

Florian by now has stripped down to a pair of maroon Y-fronts, but has put back on his track shoes. His white body is runty, making his sneakered feet look disproportionately huge. His back is a wall of Chinese calligraphy, snakes, angels, mermaids.

He races down the beach, and plunges into the water, howling. Rises to the surface a moment later, seal-like. Drumming on his chest, he emits a long Tarzan yodel.

Rat laughs, just from the pleasure of seeing Florian so proud of himself. She always thought of him as being much older than her and Jérôme—when they were in kindergarten, he was—but he can't be more than nineteen. A kid, like them.

Back on shore, Florian gets dressed without first drying himself. Now his clothes are dripping wet, and his lips are blue, his teeth chattering.

Rat goes off in search of driftwood to make a fire, while Jérôme digs a little pit in the pebbles, sheltered from the wind. Soon, the fire is crackling, and Florian holds his wet sneakers on a driftwood skewer to dry them. The result is a stink of melting rubber, and shoes that are scorching hot but still wet.

"Shit." Florian gives up and lights a *pétard*. "Man, that really freaked me out, that riot policeman searching me," he says, suddenly. "Those guys are so jumpy, you twitch the wrong muscle and you're dead." He reflects. "These Gypsies got us all in the shit now. Beginning of the tourist season, just when everybody's ready to relax, party, have some fun."

Jérôme takes a drag, coughs. Passes it to Rat.

"You know, I actually knew that guy who got murdered," Florian continues.

"Which one?"

"The first guy. Dédé, they used to call him. His sister worked in a nail salon with my ex-girlfriend. Poor motherfucker. All he did was try to stop some punk from stealing his car radio, and he got beaten to death like an animal."

"What a way to die," Rat agrees.

"Can you believe it? Right in the middle of the place Cassanyes market? Hundreds of people looking, and nobody lifts a finger. No wonder the Arabs are going crazy."

"Yeah, I can see they're pissed off, but why burn people's cars?" Jérôme demands. "If you're angry, go burn Town Hall, don't burn some poor guy's car."

"That's too reasonable, Jérôme. Anger—you can't channel it like that. If you lose it, you lose it."

"Bullshit. Those guys who go to the service station, fill up jerry cans of gasoline—that's not losing it, that's premeditation."

"I don't blame them," says Rat, suddenly. "It stinks, being an Arab in France. My friend Angélique was out with some friends the other night, they go to Le Paradis, the bouncer lets them in no problem, there's a couple of North African girls right after them, he's like, Sorry, it's a private party tonight."

"They don't let me into Le Paradis, either," says Florian.

"Yeah, but that's just because you're such a supersize degenerate, Florian the flagrant," Rat teases.

Florian flicks a pebble at her, but he looks pleased.

"I wouldn't mind being Arab," he says, suddenly.

They both look at him, surprised. This, after all, is the boy who got sent to reform school for spray-painting swastikas on the wall.

"Like, if you're an Arab, you got this country of your own you go back to in the summers, all your aunts and uncles killing the fatted calf to celebrate your homecoming, you got this religion that scares the shit out of French people, everyone's looking at you like you're just about to explode a jumbo jet. You get a little respect because you're different. White French is, like, so nothing. You burn a car and you're Arab, everybody feels sorry for you 'cause of racism. You burn a car and you're white, you're just a nutcase."

"White is pretty nothing," Rat agrees. She thinks of Morgan, skin the color of honey. Will Morgan not be allowed into nightclubs when he's older? Will French ladies cross to the other side of the street when they see him coming?

Jérôme makes a screw gesture to his head. "You could always convert, Flo."

"If I were an Arab, I'd be married by now. My family would be picking me out some sweet little cousin"—Florian claps his hands over his head, wiggles his hips, mimicking Oriental dancing—"some superpure virgin who'd never been with a guy, who'd stay home cooking and cleaning, making a good home for our children, not like these French sluts. Excuse me, Rat."

"A virgin?" repeats Rat, incredulous. "And what about her? Isn't the girl entitled to a life of her own, aside from picking up your dirty socks?"

"It's different for women from traditional societies. They like to know who's boss."

"You are so full of it, Flo."

"I never knew you were such a reactionary," says Jérôme.

"A reactionary? I got values. Even 'degenerates' have values."

Later, Rat takes her cell phone and wanders off down the beach. "Mama?"

"My sweetheart. Where are you?"

"I'm down at Port Vendres with Jérôme." She doesn't say anything about Florian. Neither does she mention the dynamite factory. That's her and Jérôme's secret.

Her mother croons her "Happy Birthday." "What time will you be back?"

"We're going to sleep here on the beach, Mama. We got our sleeping bags; we've lit a fire. It's really beautiful, we watched the sun going down. Jérôme's gonna run me straight to school tomorrow morning."

Vanessa's voice goes suddenly frosty. "You're not coming home for your birthday?"

"I was home on my birthday, Mama. You just happened to be asleep."

There's a silence.

"What's wrong?"

More silence.

"Mama?"

"I made a cake for dinner."

"You did?" Stab of guilt through the heart. But how was she to know? Last year Vanessa wasn't even home for Rat's birthday; she and Thierry were up in the Aude, checking out some guy who had a set of bedroom furniture to unload. "Can we have it tomorrow night, Mama?"

"No, we can't. I've got other plans."

"What are you doing?"

"I'm going to Daniel and Zaza's for dinner. You sure are hard to figure, Rat. I mean, you're always complaining I'm not there for you, and then—"

"I know, I know. I'm sorry, Mama—it was just . . . Mama?"

"Yes, honey?"

"Can we have it another night? Day after tomorrow?"

"We'll see."

"Please?"

"I had everything fixed up for tonight."

"Fixed up" means made sure Thierry was going to be away. This is the big change in their lives: Thierry has a job now. He's looking after some vacation properties up in Brix. Easter to September's high season: often he sleeps there during the week.

"We'll find another time, okay?" says Rat. "Listen, Mama. I'm really really sorry I fucked up tonight. Give Morgan a big kiss from me. And a big kiss for you. I love you, Mama-do."

"Okay," says Vanessa, but she doesn't sound convinced.

Rat rejoins the others. Her stomach's all in knots, she feels like shit. But how was she to know Vanessa had gone and made her a cake? You can never tell when she's going to get it into her head suddenly to make a fuss over you.

"What's wrong?" asks Jérôme, at once.

"Vanessa'd gone and made me a birthday cake for tonight."

"That's what she said? You never know. She might just be saying it to make you feel bad. Vanessa's cakes . . ."

"Don't be rude; you're gonna have to eat it, too."

Jérôme groans. "Remember the time she burnt it so bad even Vesuvio wouldn't touch it?"

"Yeah, I remember—we had to throw out the pan. She did one for Morgan's birthday, though, that wasn't so bad."

"All this talk of food is making me hungry," complains Florian. "Shall we incinerate these sausages, or what?"

It's after midnight.

They've finished dinner, they've given Rat her presents—an Indian spirit-catcher from Jérôme, an old gray-green corduroy jacket from Florian that he says belonged to his granny's boyfriend, and which Rat instantly loves.

Now the three of them are lying on the beach, looking out to sea. Every once in a while, someone gets up to put some more driftwood on the fire.

In a couple of weeks, the nights will be thrumming with cicadas, but tonight it's still too cold. Silence, except for the low lapping of the waves on the shore.

It's a misty gray night. Stars faint; no moon. The only light in all this big gray-blackness is the lights of fishing boats at sea and the pulsing green Morse code of the lighthouse at Port-Vendres. All up and down the coast, lighthouses are talking to one another in their own secret language of beams and pulses.

Rat feels a wave of love for Jérôme, and for Florian, too.

"You know," she says, suddenly. "Next year's supposed to be the class trip to England."

"I know. My year, we didn't get to go because Madame Pujoulat was having a baby," says Jérôme.

"I don't think I wanna go, especially."

"Why not?" Jérôme demands.

"Angélique and Marina are being such jerks, they keep on telling everybody, Rat's English, she'll be able to show us around, or Rat's father lives in London, we can all go visit him. What am I supposed to say? 'Actually, we've never met. We could be sitting next to each other on a bus and not recognize each other.'"

"So they're jerks, but that's no reason not to go on the trip," says Jérôme, stoutly. "Everybody says it's great. No way you're chickening out, Rat."

Sometimes Jérôme gets like that, all bossy and parental.

"It's expensive. I don't know if Vanessa'll be able to come up with the scratch."

They subside into silence.

"Do you ever think of looking your dad up, trying to get in touch with him?" asks Jérôme.

Rat considers. How can she explain it to Jérôme, who's got both parents under one roof, an extended family still intact?

The honest answer would be that sometimes she doesn't think about her father for six months at a time, and then suddenly something goes wrong: a teacher makes fun of her in front of the whole class; Thierry comes home drunk and starts laying into her real petty and mean, and Vanessa just laughs. And Rat finds herself thinking, Actually, I don't belong here; I'd feel more at home in England.

These days it seems as if all the music she likes, all the video clips, the films, the fashions are British. She'll download a track from The Libertines or The Streets, and her friends will go, Yuck, but to her, it sounds really soulful and funny and true, even if she can't understand the words.

Lately, she's been obsessing about her unknown father. Wondering if they might not have something in common. Feeling fed up with her mother's side of the family. Thinking a change of genes might be oxygen. Gillem McKane as anti-Thierry.

"I don't know anything about him," she says, finally. "He might be dead for all I know."

"You could try Googling him," Jérôme suggests.

Rat reflects. "I never thought of that," she admits. "I'm not sure if I want to. I don't think I'm ready."

"You should go on that class trip for sure," Florian says, suddenly. "England's a really cool place. If your mom won't give you the money, I will."

She raises an eyebrow at him.

Florian looks injured. "I'm serious. How much is it—two, three hundred euros?"

"No way—it'll be, like, a hundred and twenty-five, max."

"A hundred and twenty-five? That's nothing. You know I'm loaded. If it wasn't that my granny gets seasick, I'd be living on a yacht in Monte Carlo."

"I'd be living in Corsica," says Jérôme. His aunt lives in Corsica.

"Well, I don't even know for sure the trip's gonna happen. They always find some excuse to cancel."

Later on, Rat and Florian and Jérôme make their way back through the jungle to the ruined factory and crawl into their sleeping bags for a few hours' sleep. But Rat's too excited to settle down.

Every now and then, she'll get up and go outside to look at the stars, and listen to the soft waves lapping at the rocks.

At dawn, just when she's finally drifted off, Jérôme awakens her. They climb down onto the rocks and watch the sun poke its rays above the sea's horizon. The fishing boats are heading back to Port-Vendres with their catch. And Rat will say, with some surprise, "It's not my birthday anymore. Now I'm going to be fifteen forever."

Jérôme turns to smile at her his fond shy smile, before ducking down out of the wind to light a last spliff.

You know those moments when you think this is the happiest time in my life, and just thinking it makes you sad?

Rat feels a pang she didn't bring along Morgan, and hopes Vanessa remembered to cook him something hot last night because he gets offended if you don't feed him a proper dinner, appetizer, main course, dessert.

It's still dark when they leave the dynamite factory. Jérôme, the lucky stiff, doesn't have school today, but Rat's first class begins at eight. The sun's high over the sea as they come around a bend of vineyard, Collioure lying below. She wonders whether Mémé Catherine still lives in the same house with the quince tree in the garden and the wisteria over the door. All these relatives that are strangers to her.

Florian drops her off at the school gates just before they close. Jérôme, head pillowed against his backpack, has already gone back to sleep.

2

"Sixty-eight entries," Jérôme says.

Rat's heart is pounding. "That's a lot!"

"No, it's not. And it's not necessarily him, either." He scrolls down the page. There are a bunch of Guillems and a bunch of McKanes, but none of them go together. They are all genealogical registers or runners in sports events.

"Nothing," he says.

Rat feels ridiculously deflated. It's like having your fortune told: you know you shouldn't, but once you've broken down and done it, you want to turn up trumps. "You sure there's really nothing?" she asks.

"Let's try something else," he says. "How about your grandmother? Wasn't she some famous actress or something? What was her name?"

"Celia Kidd. K-I-D-D," spells Rat.

Jérôme taps in Rat's grandmother's name, and they watch the machine hit jackpot. Hundreds of thousands of entries, all in English. Swingingsixtieschicks. Fan sites. Biography, awards, filmography.

She's even got her own entry in Wikipedia, on which Rat double-clicks. "Born in 1942 in Wiltshire . . . David Bailey picked her up on the street . . . Ken Russell gave Kidd a part in his . . ."

Jérôme switches seats with Rat, so she can flick through the material at her own speed. It's like sorting through boxes of used clothes in the market.

Then she catches the name she's looking for. "Son Gillem, by her first marriage to Canadian retail heir Malcolm McKane, started his artistic career working for . . ." Her heart's knocking hard, the blood's booming in her ears. She's scared to keep on reading, lest it say he died in a car crash or something.

"Hey," she says, "we were spelling it wrong. It isn't Guillem, it's Gillem. He's an artist."

"Oh, really? How do you spell that? *Putain,* what kind of name is that?" Jérôme taps the two names together.

One thousand eight hundred seventy-nine entries. This time the first name and last name are highlighted together. "Now we're onto something."

Rat scrolls.

Gillem McKane's name appears in a list of artists showing in a gallery, at an art fair in Switzerland and another in Belgium. Someone's offering a drawing of Gillem McKane's on eBay. She tries to scroll up a photograph of the drawing, but it's too small to see properly.

"I guess he must be a big deal," Rat says, wondering. She's never met a professional artist.

Jérôme's looking over her shoulder. "Has he got a Web site?"

"I don't think so."

He takes the mouse from her, scrolls down. "Yes, he does. Here's his Web site. gillemmckane.co.uk. That's got to be him." He clicks, clicks, double-clicks.

A pale green wave fills the screen. At the center of it is a little red hand, such as you see on Moroccan amulets, whose fingers waggle.

"Pretty," says Rat.

"Do you want to try to get in touch with him? Try zapping 'Contact.'"

"No. I'd just like to see what his work is like."

Friday night. Vanessa has invited Cristel and Laurent and the Cabreras over to celebrate Rat's birthday. Thierry, tragically, cannot make it: he's been spending the week up in Brix.

All day long, Vanessa's been decorating the room for the party. She has swathed the table in a leopard-skin silk coverlet, with fat pink candles studded in pearls. The plates are golden, and by everybody's place, there's a rose. Across the walls are draped Vanessa's feather boas, her sequined bolero, her painted Spanish fans. She's asked Jean-Luc to bring music.

They grill sausages on the barbecue. Everybody brings a dish: Marielle caramelized carrots with cumin, Cristel her famous rice salad, Laurent a platter of cheese. Vanessa's baked another chocolate cake, and this time she doesn't burn it.

Rat's wearing Cristel's birthday present—a T-shirt with a tattooed angel that's in a stretch material tighter than anything Rat usually wears. ("To show off your gorgeous figure," Cristel whispered in her ear, when Rat came to kiss her thank-you.)

Jean-Luc and Jérôme have mixed a CD that combines everybody's favorite music—Brazilian samba, Serge Gainsbourg for the older generation, hip-hop for the kids. Then Rat puts on this seventies disco tape that Vanessa found in the market, and everybody bops around the tiny apartment ecstatically, jumping and waving their arms and shrieking "I Will Survive!" Solenne goes whirling in circles until she falls over, giggling, and Laurent picks her up and dances with her in his arms.

Later, they go sit outside in the backyard to cool off. Vanessa serves the cake, with a bottle of champagne.

Rat blows out the lone candle quick, before the wind can, and the grown-ups drink a toast to Rat.

"Fifteen years old," sighs Vanessa. "Am I really old enough to have a fifteen-year-old daughter?"

"*Quinze ans et tous mes dents*," sings Rat.

"I remember the day you were born like it was yesterday."

"What was it like?" asks Rat, all attention. It's hard these days to get a story out of her mother: there's never a good moment.

"In brief? Hell," Vanessa replies. "Mémé Catherine, of course, had kicked me out of the house soon as I told her I was pregnant. I think what pissed her off most was my refusing to tell her who the dad was." Vanessa makes a shrugging face. "Anyway, I was living with a girlfriend, but neither of us had a car. She had to get a neighbor to drive us to the hospital. My water broke all over the passenger seat. I hardly knew the guy, it was so embarrassing."

"What water?" Morgan inquires.

"The little inland sea you baby-fish swim around in till you're born."

The new neighbors—a jolly-looking young couple with a two-year-old daughter—are sitting next door on their terrace. Rat brings them each a slice of cake and a glass of champagne.

"She's a classy girl, your daughter, Vanessa, you know that?" says Marielle. "A-one."

"I know. Just like me."

"And she's got character, too. Unlike her old trollop of a mother. Oh, Vanessa, I didn't see you there," jokes Jean-Luc.

Vanessa tweaks his ear affectionately. "You, I'll take care of you later."

It will be the last evening Rat sits down to a meal with her mother for a very long time. And somehow it's almost as if they both sense it, the way you savor what you know will be the last swim of the year, the last of the autumn figs. Neither of them puts a foot wrong. There are no explosive exchanges, no sarcastic rejoinders, bitter undertones, recriminations. None of that mother-daughter shit that can ruin a good time.

And then, one a.m. or so, when everybody's gone home except for Jérôme, there is the sound of a car turning into the drive.

The motorcyclish roar of the broken muffler is unmistakable. It's Thierry's Clio.

Vanessa glances at her watch, frowning.

Jérôme makes as if he's going to leave—Rat doesn't blame him, she would too if she had anywhere to go—then changes his mind.

Thierry takes a long time to get out of the car. When he comes into the house, followed by Vesuvio, he's moving slow. Eyes bloodshot. He casts a look around the room. "What's with the leopard skin? It looks like a bordello here."

"Where've you been?" Vanessa demands.

"Where do you think I've been? I've got a job, remember?"

That's the way the lovebirds talk these days. Snip, snip, snip. Voices tight and sour. Nastiness ricocheting back and forth like Ping-Pong.

"I got a call from Jens this morning, saying he needed to get hold of you urgent," Vanessa says. "I've been trying you all day."

"Yeah, my cell phone's out of juice. Anyway, Jens did get hold of me. I've just come from seeing him."

Vanessa does not seem satisfied. "He sounded pretty pissed," she persists. "He said there was some problem with a renter, and he couldn't find you anywhere. What was wrong?"

Jens is Thierry's boss. He and his wife are Danish; they have a restored farmhouse above Brix where they spend half the year. Jens is retired, but he's the kind of retired person who likes to keep busy. It just so happens that Jens's hobbies are more lucrative than most people's jobs. He can't help it, he has a golden thumb, as Vanessa puts it. Over the last decade, Jens has been buying up houses in the hill towns above Brix—little village houses, nothing fancy. Jens's wife, who is a decorator, then does them up very rustic in that style foreigners think of as French country, and they rent them out to vacationers.

For almost a year now, Thierry's been working for Jens as caretaker and general handyman. It's the perfect job for Thierry: he's handy; he can be charming, if he chooses; his English is good. There's even a little studio apartment over Jens's garage where Thierry can stay during the busy season, so he doesn't have to be constantly ferrying back and forth between Saint Féliu and Brix.

Sweet setup. All it requires is Thierry's being on call, in case a guest locks himself out of the house or the toilet backs up. Not much to ask, to Vanessa's way of thinking, especially when it's Vanessa who wangled him the job.

Vanessa is still looking at Thierry funny. "So what happened?" she inquires.

"What happened?" Thierry mimics. "What happened, apparently, is you decided to have a party without me. While the cat's away, huh?" He mock-bows to Jérôme, then sits down, heavily. "Aren't you going to offer me a piece of cake?" Leans over and harpoons himself a piece, scattering gobbets across the table.

"I thought you were staying at Brix tonight," says Vanessa.

"Would you rather I did? Sit, Vesuvio. Sit."

Vanessa gets up and pointedly shuts the front door he's left ajar.

"Do you mind?' he snarls. "I was just going to . . ."

He brings in a bag of groceries from the car. Unloads on the table a sack of dog food, a crumpled ketchup-smeared paper bag containing the remains of his dinner, a packet of cigarettes, a bag of peanuts.

Vanessa examines the cigarettes critically. "You got these from the gas station? Didn't I tell you Cristel was going to La Jonquera this weekend? You could have got a whole carton for the same price."

Thierry ignores her. "I didn't know you were having a party," he repeats, once again making a half-bow towards Jérôme. And then, "Hey, Momo, *mon brave*." He has this soft wheedling croon he assumes with Morgan, talking to the boy as if he were still a toddler. "You're very silent tonight. Don't you even come kiss me hello anymore? Come give Tonton Thierry a *bise*." Beckons, pointing to the spot on his cheek where he expects the kiss.

Morgan is a grown-up boy, too dignified to kiss men. His friends at school or at football, Jean-Luc, Laurent, he greets with a handshake. But Thierry uses this pseudokinship to force an intimacy that's more of an obeisance.

Once again he taps his own cheek, waiting for the kiss. Rat stiffens, ready to intervene. But Morgan rises to his feet, slowly, like a man after a hard day's work, and comes around the table. Places a cool, deliberate kiss a couple of inches offshore of Thierry's cheek.

"That's more like it." Thierry tears open the peanut packet clumsily, so that its contents spill onto the table. Scoops up a handful of nuts and offers them to Morgan. "Have a peanut."

Morgan jerks his head no.

"What, you can't speak? Can't say yes please, no thank you, Tonton Thierry? Or is it the barefoot contessa over there," nodding at Rat, "who won't let you take munchies from me? She's a tough one. Even tougher than her mother. Two she-wolves. Us men gotta stick together, huh, Momo? Huh, Jérôme? You heard of male solidarity? A circle of fire to keep the she-wolves at bay."

Thierry pours himself a glass of pastis. "Go get me some ice, Mo."

Morgan rises once again from his place beside Rat, slips a tray from the freezer, cracks the cubes into a bowl, and lays it before Thierry.

"That's my good boy."

Vanessa is pacing the room, chewing on a nail. She looks pretty wound up. "So what was the problem with Jens?"

"The problem?" Thierry repeats, laughing sourly. "The problem is the guy's a fucking cheapskate. He gets these builders off the bus from Ukraine to do the work for him half price, and then when something goes wrong, I'm the one who gets the blame."

"What happened?"

"Some Paris lawyer Jens wants to impress rented the house in Eus for the weekend, only it turns out the plumber installed the wrong kind of siphon in the shower. So suddenly the whole house is stinking like a cesspool, and it's all my fault."

Vanessa puts on her patient voice—a voice Rat doesn't get to hear too often. "I think the point is, you're supposed to be there, Thierry. On call. Available, in case there's a problem. Where were you all day, anyway?"

"Where were you?" mimicks Thierry in a shrill falsetto. "You should hear yourself, Vanessa. You're such a shrew."

Vanessa ignores this. "Did you straighten things out with Jens?" she persists. "He sounded pretty sore. He said it wasn't the first time you'd gone AWOL when a renter had a problem. I've never heard him that angry before."

Thierry smiles his thin-lipped ragged smile. "You don't know much about Jens, do you, sweetheart? You think he's this big cuddly teddy bear, just because he likes to grab your ass when his wife isn't looking. But you couldn't be more wrong. Jens is a real mean bastard, and crooked as hell."

"Did you manage to straighten things out?" Vanessa persists.

Thierry laughs. "Yeah, we straightened things out. I straightened *him* out. I'm, like, You try to fire me, I'm going straight to the Tax Office; I'm telling them who—"

"He's threatening to fire you?" Vanessa interrupts, her voice shooting up high.

"He's 'threatening,'" says Thierry, waggling his fingers in quotation marks. "But I told him where to get off. I know all the monkey business he gets up to, who he pays in cash, who pays him in cash. He won't think it's so funny when the tax man hauls him in."

Rat gets to her feet. "I'm putting Morgan to bed," she says. "Night, Jérôme. Thanks for my birthday, Ma."

She whisks Morgan through the door smartly, before there's any question of goodnight kisses.

Late into the night, Rat can hear her mother and Thierry fighting. She can't make out the words, but she can imagine the gist of it.

It's almost dawn when the noise awakens Rat, and she feels as if she's only just fallen asleep.

It's the sound of someone who's trying not to make a sound. A sound as small as a mouse eating away at something. A kind of rustle and squeak. She has startled awake with the idea that the squeak is Morgan crying, but it's not.

Rat makes herself motionless, holding her breath, so she can identify the sound. It's louder now, a rhythmic creaking of the bed. At first she wants to laugh, because it sounds like the noise of a couple having sex on a bed that squeaks. The creaking gets faster and she can hear somebody breathing hard, panting. Silence, and then the rustling and creaking begins again, and she hears Morgan grumble in sleepy protest.

Now she snaps fully awake.

She forces her eyes to adjust to the predawn grayness. Then she climbs down the ladder, trying not to make a sound. She trips over the duvet, which is on the floor.

There's someone bending over Morgan's bed. It's Thierry. He's kneeling, leaning over Morgan. He's murmuring words, he's breathing fast, she can't hear what he's saying, the sounds come out of him in little gasps and grunts. And the bed keeps rocking, squeaking.

Rat is looking for something heavy. Just as you might search for the right-size book with which to crush a mosquito.

The first weaponlike thing she sees is the standing lamp. She pulls its cord out of the wall just as she hears Thierry give a great groaning gasp, and she swings the lamp at him. She catches Thierry across the back with it, but it's too unwieldy, too floppy as a weapon. She tries to get hold of the lamp near its heavy metal base and club him with that, like a baseball bat, but it's falling apart in her hands.

Rat, dropping the lamp, starts kicking Thierry, who has now let go of Morgan and is doubled up, still trying to shield his face, groaning, but it's no good kicking with bare feet. She grabs the lamp again by its metal head.

I'm gonna kill him now, she thinks, and in that moment, it seems like a good idea. But Thierry lurches to his feet, he's stumbling out the door. A crash, a curse, and he's gone.

"You all right, Morgan?"

No answer.

"Did he hurt you?"

No answer.

She trips over the broken lamp, fumbles her way to the door. Switches on the overhead light.

Morgan's hands cover his eyes. He's still half-asleep. Rat makes him sit up and feels that both his pajamas and the duvet are wet. Not like pee, scattered gobs of slime. "Why are you all wet?" And then she realizes. "Let's get you cleaned up," she says.

"Who was that? Thierry?" Morgan asks.

"Yeah."

"Is he gone now?"

"Yeah. Don't worry, you're okay, I've got you. Are you all right?"

"Yeah."

She takes Morgan out into the bathroom, locks the door. Runs the shower till it's warm, but not hot. Then she finds him another pair of pajamas, strips the duvet, throws pajamas and duvet cover in the washing machine.

"Did he hurt you?"

"No . . ."

"Has he ever tried to do that to you before?"

"Do what?"

"Come into your bed like that, or . . ."

"No."

"Never? You sure?"

"Never."

Rat locks the bedroom door, and barricades it with a chair wedged under the knob, for good measure.

She takes Morgan up into her sleeping loft, along with his duvet. He can sleep on the single mattress; she will sleep on the duvet. It's baking-hot up in the loft, the two of them squeezed tight in the narrow space, but Rat's frozen. She lies awake till the blackness turns to ice-pale blue, listening to the low rumble of Morgan's breathing, and then she lets herself drift off into nightmares.

When Rat next awakens, it's broad daylight, and for a moment she can't remember why she feels that same sinking dread as if someone's died.

She can hear the buzz of Laurent sawing wood in his workshop and the bright chatter of the morning cartoons that Sabrina, their upstairs neighbor, puts on for her daughter while she does the housework. These cozy workaday sounds only make her feel the more estranged from what used to be her normal life.

Morgan is still sleeping. She climbs down the ladder, unfastens their bedroom door.

Both cars are gone. The house is empty.

When she climbs back up into her tent, Morgan is stretched out on his back, staring at the ceiling.

"You hungry, Mo?"

He glances at her expressionless, then looks away.

She feels oddly embarrassed in front of him. This isn't the world she'd meant to introduce him to.

"Is today Saturday?" he asks.

"Yeah."

"Is it time for football?"

She glances at the alarm radio. "In an hour. You all right?"

He nods.

After breakfast, she fetches her bicycle from the shed. Morgan, who's fastening his shin guards, bike already propped against the plane tree, looks up.

"Where are you going?"

"I thought I'd come along with you to football."

He looks at her. "I've been going by myself all year."

"Come on, Mo." She attempts a smile, but it must look pretty ghoulish. "I haven't seen you play in a long time."

"I'm not playing; I'm training."

"Indulge me."

He shrugs. "I think you need some air in that back tire" is all he says.

"What are you talking about, Rat? Thierry is not gay. You, maybe, he might try it on with, if he was drunk enough. But Morgan? A *little boy*? Are you out of your mind?"

"I'm telling you what I saw," Rat insists.

Vanessa reaches into the kitchen drawer, rummaging for matches. Lights her roll-up. Inhales hard. She's still in her shortie nightdress. Her smeared mascara is giving her raccoon eyes. Rat hasn't noticed how much her mother's aged in the last few years. There are gray roots to her red hair.

"*What* did you see?" Her tone is mocking, aggressive.

"Look, he scummed himself all over. Morgan's—the duvet cover was all . . ."

"Let me see."

"I put them in the machine."

Vanessa exhales smoke through her nose. Shakes her head. Paces, looks out the kitchen door. "I don't believe a word of it," she says. "I think you're outta your mind. What do you know about—suddenly you're the expert—"

"I caught him in Morgan's bed, he was groaning and panting and . . . and, like, trying to hump him, like Vesuvio when—"

"I don't believe you. You've always had it in for Thierry. I admit, there's plenty of bad stuff you can say about the guy: he drinks too much, he's a lazy bum, but he's not a pervert. He loves Morgan like a father, no way he's gonna . . ."

Rat's heart's beating so hard she can hardly breathe. All day she's been waiting for the moment her mother will get back from the market because then Rat will be rid of this thing, this burdensome secret, and painful as it will be for Vanessa, together they will figure out how to get Thierry out of their lives forever. But Vanessa is looking at her as if *she's* the enemy.

"You don't believe me?" Rat's voice has hiked up squeaky. "I've always told you he's had this weird thing about Morgan, the way he won't leave him alone, the way he's always trying to get him on his lap, calling him little love-names, and you've never believed me. And now he's gone and done it, he's tried to rape him. And you still don't believe me."

Vanessa's staring at her. "You're fucked up," she says, finally.

Rat is thinking about Morgan with a high-watt focus she hasn't had to devote to him in years. Wondering how he interprets last night's dreamlike violation. Wondering what it might do to him later on. No father, mother dead of AIDS, molested by your stepfather—the damage adds up.

Morgan is nine and a half years old. He is tall, like his mother was, with a lean muscular body, and long legs made for running. He is the captain of his football team, which means not just that he's the best player, but also that he knows how to organize the rest of the team to carry out a game plan.

He is a good-looking boy. He has eyes the changeable glint of chestnut honey, a fine hawk nose whose nostrils he flares to express comical surprise or disdain, a head of light brown curls that get tinged with gold in the summer. Solenne says that girls bring him presents, fight over who gets to sit next to him at lunch.

Rat realizes with surprise that Morgan is beautiful, and that this makes him prey, just as girls, once they start sprouting breasts, are prey.

But Rat is his protector. Has been from way back, almost from the time Vanessa and Souad used to drag him off to the Fandango at Barcarès, and Rat, who didn't even like him then, would catch herself worrying about what a toddler was gonna do all hours in that smoke-stenchy strobe-lighted hell.

Children like Morgan, poor, orphaned, go under every day, starve, die of diseases, get murdered. You see it every night on the news. But Morgan isn't one of those children. Morgan is Rat's brother.

"I feel like me and Mo, we got a secondhand life," Rat complains.

Jérôme says nothing.

"Do you know what I mean?"

"No." He's been pretty silent ever since Rat told him about Thierry. His first idea was to go over there with his mother's *croque-monsieur* griddle and castrate the guy. Once Rat made him promise not to tell anybody or do a thing, he's gone quiet. Quiet and green-faced, as if he's trying not to puke.

"Like, when I was little I used to read all these old comic books—same old comics Morgan's got now—and I'd go to Vanessa, all excited, saying, 'Mama, Mama, I'm gonna enter this Mickey Mouse contest: you can win a trip to Euro Disney!!' And Vanessa would take a look and she'd go, 'Sweetheart, this magazine's from 1992. The entry deadline expired four years ago!' Because all the comic books we ever had were old ones somebody threw away when their kids left home.

"Vanessa tries to dress it up like some political choice, like, Look at us, we're ecologically responsible, we don't even have a dishwasher, but basically, we're just feeding off other people's junk. Even Morgan, he's not even our own family, he's an orphan that nobody wanted. I can't look at a single thing and say honestly, That's mine."

"Is that bad?"

She shrugs.

"Or my dad. It wasn't like he and my mom were going out together, or even knew each other. It was just, like, Well, it's late and I don't have anybody else to fuck tonight, so I might as well go behind the bushes with this chick I just met."

Jérôme laughs quietly, a little shocked.

Solenne comes into the room, and stands looking over their shoulders at the computer screen. "What are you guys doing?"

"We're working. Beat it."

"I want to play Sims."

"Too bad."

"You guys've had the computer all afternoon. Me 'n' Morgan want to play Sims. Mama says—"

"Later. Get lost."

"But we don't have anything to do!"

"Where's Mama?"

"She's busy."

"Well, so are we. Get lost."

Surprisingly, she disappears.

"And close the door behind you!"

"Maybe it's not such a bad idea to try to get in touch with him," says Rat, thoughtfully.

Jérôme swivels around in his seat. "Who? Your dad?"

"Yeah. I always meant to, someday. I figured, if I ever got rich and famous, I'd knock on his door, say, Here I am, take a good long look. This is what you missed. Well, maybe now's the time to go find him."

Jérôme's eyes flick at her, surprised. "Now? In England?"

"That's where he lives, right?"

Jérôme considers. "What about Morgan?"

"I'd take him with me. That's the whole point."

"*Putain*," says Jérôme, wonderingly. "You're going to go to England? I've never been farther from home than Montpellier."

She smiles at him. "That's not true."

"Okay, Corsica. Big deal. It's still part of France."

There's something that's troubling her. "What should I do for Morgan?"

"What do you mean?"

"Shouldn't I be, like, taking him to a psychologist or something?"

Jérôme grimaces. "Thierry's the one who needs to go to a psychologist. A criminal psychologist, preferably."

"Yeah, but after something scary happens to you, after a plane crash or somebody dies, you're supposed to go for counseling, aren't you? Like, when those Russian terrorists break into a school and take all the kids hostage and kill everybody, you go to a counselor to talk about it."

"You sure you don't want to go to the police?"

"I can't. Vanessa and Thierry are gonna both say it didn't happen."

Jérôme is looking hard at her.

"I don't want to go to the police," she says, a bit defensively. "You promised you wouldn't tell anybody."

"I know. I won't. But I think you're making a mistake."

"Maybe. But I don't want people looking at Morgan funny, whispering. Even Florian, years later, people in Saint Féliu look at him and all they see is the kid who spray-painted swastikas all over the walls of the Youth Center."

"What if Thierry goes and does it to some other kid?"

Rat shrugs. "I don't feel responsible for some other kid; I feel responsible for people not telling nasty stories about Morgan."

Jérôme's still looking at her in a way that pisses her off. "Look, if I could kill the guy and make an end to it, I would, all right?" she says. "But that would just make things worse, and then we'd never be over it. Or if Vanessa believed me, and kicked him out of the house, like a normal person would. But she won't. So there's nothing left to do but for us to leave."

"Where are you going to get the money to get to England?"

Rat makes two cocked pistols of her hands and points them at him. "Bonnie and Clyde?"

"With a nine-year-old Clyde? Seriously, Rat . . ."

"I don't know. It's almost picking time, isn't it? How much does it cost to take a bus to London? I can work a season picking fruit, and we'll go. Work for one of those farmers who gives you a place to sleep. Like Angélique's sister did for the cherry season in Ceret—everybody slept in one big dormitory, it was really cool. Some people brought guitars, one guy had a conga drum, they sang songs every night."

"Cherries are almost over. You're too late for cherries, too early for everything else."

"I could go get signed up. They must be picking their work crews."

"You're too young still to work legally."

"Who said anything about legal? I'm sure I can find some farmer who'll pay me black."

"I bet Florian would give you the money."

"Oh that's right, I forgot about drug-running."

"Nah, he'd just give it to you. That's the kind of guy he is."

"Maybe."

Rat double-clicks, and once again the pale green wave washes over her. She clicks on the little hand with five waggling fingers. It opens up.

In one bubble it says Biography, and in another it says Exhibitions, and the third bubble says, Contact me, and that's where Rat clicks.

More words come wiggling across the page, red on pale green. The words say gillem@gillemmckane.co.uk.

"What do I do now?"

"You write him an e-mail and you send it."

"Oh." She ponders. "What do I say?"

"You say, hello, I'm your long-lost daughter, I'd like to come see you."

"You make it sound so easy!" she grumbles. "What if Vanessa was making the whole thing up, and he isn't my father at all?"

Funnily enough, this possibility has never occurred to her.

"Well, then he'll just tell you to buzz off."

"And then what?"

"We'll find somewhere else for you to go. You can always go live with my aunt."

Rat's met Jérôme's Corsican aunt, and she doesn't think so; she's never thought she was quite as cool as Jérôme and his family do, just because she lives with goats up a mountain. She rocks back and forth on Jérôme's stool, trying to formulate words so persuasive that this stranger who's never wanted to lay eyes on her will be irresistibly won over. She gets a sudden flashback to the last time she was agonizing over a letter to her unknown father. Remembering that long-ago birthday hoax makes her furious at her mother all over again, and she starts typing.

Under Subject, "I am your daughter Celia," because Jérôme has told her that people don't always open messages from an e-mail address they don't recognize.

"Hello, my name is Celia Bonnet. My mother is Vanessa from Collioure. I am fifteen years old now. I am coming to London, and I would like to meet you. Send me an e-mail to this address, or call me at. . . ." She starts to type the number, then remembers she's lost her cell phone.

When Rat presses the Send button and the message disappears, she feels as if she's walked off a cliff.

"Isn't there any kind of Help-I-really-didn't-mean-to-send-this button?"

Imagine being a spy on your own life.

That's how Rat feels, living at the Cabreras'. Morgan sleeps in the bottom bunk in Solenne's room; Rat has Emilie's old room to herself.

It's amazing how little difference it makes to their routine. In the mornings, Jean-Luc takes Rat to Victor Hugo, and Marielle takes Morgan and Solenne to school in Saint Féliu. In the afternoons, when they get back to Mas Cargol, instead of heading back to their own apartment, they go to Jérôme's.

The only difference is that all day, Rat finds herself almost subconsciously listening out for Thierry's car, glancing out the window every few minutes. And at night, she lies awake, imagining what she will say and do to him if he dares come back.

But evidently Vanessa's managed to persuade Jens to give Thierry one more chance, because all week he's gone.

Then one day, just when Rat might almost be beginning to relax, she awakens to find the Clio parked outside Vanessa's apartment, and her mother and Thierry smooching in the doorway, Thierry's hand grabbing her mother's ass.

How could Vanessa allow the man to touch her, knowing that what Rat said might be true, and that he'd actually rather be glad-assing her son? And somehow this sight, which makes her feel physically sick, simultaneously disarms her, taking away any capacity for confrontation.

All weekend, Thierry is back in evidence. Rat sees him bringing in groceries from her mother's van or carrying the garbage to the bins. On Sunday afternoon, she hears his high-pitched voice calling for Vesuvio. For a long time, he seems to be wandering around the *mas*, calling for his dog. Eventually he gives up.

When Rat gets home from school the next day, the Clio is gone.

That night, after dinner, Vanessa comes by the Cabreras. It's the first time she's been by since Rat moved out.

Rat stays holed up in Jérôme's room. She hasn't spoken to her mother, or even seen her face-to-face since the day she tried to tell Vanessa what Thierry did to Morgan, and she has no desire to. She doesn't ever want to see her mother again.

"What did she want?" she asks, when Jérôme comes upstairs to bed.

"She wanted to use the printer."

"What for?"

"Vesuvio's lost. They're putting up signs offering a reward."

"What—a reward for the person whose car finally flattened that nasty cur? So there is justice in the world, after all."

She's surprised, nonetheless—Vesuvio's not the kind of happy-go-lucky creature that goes bounding around the countryside in search of voles and rabbits—but she quickly forgets about it.

"Can we check your e-mails again, see if my dad's answered yet?"

"Sure, but take my advice. It could be weeks before he answers, or never. If you keep checking every five minutes, you'll drive us all nuts."

Rat is already nuts. Seeing Thierry again feels like a tarantula down her shirtfront. If her father doesn't answer soon, she's just going to have to show up on his doorstep in London.

"I need to talk to you, Mo."

Morgan is sitting at Marielle's kitchen table. The knife is balanced on the open jar of Nutella, and his *tartine* is half-eaten. He is buried deep in a comic book.

The Cabreras have an entire bookshelf devoted to comic books: *Astérix, Yakari, Arsène Lupin, Les Tuniques Bleues.* For hours every day, you can find Morgan and Solenne sitting cross-legged on the floor by the comic-book shelf. Silent, except for the occasional giggle.

There is a smear of Nutella around Morgan's mouth, and up by his ear. Rat reaches out with the dish towel to swab him clean.

Morgan jerks his head away and keeps reading.

"Mo? You listening to me?"

He grunts.

"We need to get out of here."

Morgan doesn't look up from his *Arsène Lupin*. She knows he doesn't want to talk about it. She doesn't much either.

"Morgan? You listening?"

"Yeah," he says, in exasperation. "You want to get us out of here."

"Put your book away and listen."

She takes his comic book and sits on it.

"Okay. I'm listening," he says.

"I want to take us to live somewhere else. I don't think we should be living anywhere Thierry has the right to show up."

"Where do you want to go?"

"I'm not sure yet. We might go down to my grandmother's in Collioure for a while."

"Is that a long way away?"

"Pretty long."

"How would I get to school?"

Rat reflects. "I don't think you'd be going to school for a bit."

Morgan looks at her. "I can't do that."

"There's only six weeks left in the year, it's not such a big deal. I don't know about you, I'm not learning shit at my school, I could really take it or leave it. How about you? You like Sandrine, don't you?"

"Mmmm," he says. It's true, it's been his best year yet, with a teacher who thinks he's smart and capable. "It *is* a big deal. I have all my football tournaments coming up. *And* exams."

"I know, I know. Me too. But we got to get out of here, Morgan. I don't get what's going on with Vanessa. It's like nobody's reactions are normal. Something like this happens, it kind of wakes you up. I don't think Vanessa can protect us anymore. I think she's losing it. She's more concerned about the dog than about her own children."

Morgan grunts. "Why can't we keep on staying with Jean-Luc and Marielle?"

"That'd be nice, wouldn't it, but—it's too close. I feel like I can't breathe, I'm always looking around, listening out for Thierry's car. I want to put a million miles between him and us."

"Collioure isn't a million miles."

"You know what I mean."

"Why don't we just kill him? Then we can keep on living here."

"Yeah, that's a good idea," says Rat, before realizing Morgan means it.

"He's big. But there are lots of ways to kill him."

She blows out her breath. "Nah, then we'd just go to jail forever. He's not worth it."

"To me, it is," says Morgan.

"Well, I'm not willing."

"I don't want to go into Care," says Morgan, suddenly, and Rat feels her breath disappear. Of course—that's what happens when people find out a kid's been abused at home; he goes into Care.

"You're not going into Care," she says, with as much authority as she can muster. "I'm old enough to take care of you."

Morgan looks at her, clearly unconvinced. "Okay," he says. "Now can I have my *Arsène Lupin* back?"

Sunday morning. Blazing blue of early summer. Just one or two white scars of snow left on the rock face of Mount Canigou.

The Cabreras have headed out for the day on Jean-Luc's boss's new boat. Rat and Morgan have opted to stay home.

No sign of Thierry.

When Vanessa comes back from the village with a loaf of bread, she finds her daughter packing. Both kids' sleeping bags are on the floor, along with a microtent Rat's borrowed from Laurent.

"Going somewhere?"

Vanessa looks over Rat's pile of provisions. She picks up an old horn penknife with a fork and spoon attached.

"That's not yours. Max brought that back to me from Switzerland."

Rat opens her mouth in protest, then shuts it. A change of underwear, socks, T-shirts, and a sweatshirt for each of them. Already she's searched the drawer in the kitchen dresser where Vanessa keeps official documents, retrieved her and Morgan's passports from the Morocco trip, blessedly still valid. Taken sixty euros from Vanessa's strongbox.

A windbreaker for Morgan, Florian's granny's boyfriend's corduroy jacket for her. A toothbrush to share. Jérôme's Indian spirit-catcher.

She's been waiting for Vanessa to relent, to introduce a note of doubt that possibly Rat could be telling the truth. Instead, she can hear from Vanessa's tone that her mother has, if anything, hardened.

"I can't believe you, Rat," Vanessa says. "You are turning into just the worst little lying fantasist. You have a sick mind, you know that? I asked Thierry about what you said happened. You know what he said, he said he heard Morgan crying in his sleep like he was having a nightmare, he came in to comfort him. Period."

"That's a total lie, just like everything else he says. Did he tell you how I whacked him with the bedside lamp, when I caught him trying to jump Morgan, and how he ran away, crying? I bet he didn't," says Rat. "I've been warning you he's a perverted sicko for years now. You didn't believe me then, you don't believe me now. When are you going to believe me? When he murders some little kid?"

"Morgan says it didn't happen, either—that Thierry never tried to touch him."

"That's not what Morgan says. Leave Morgan out of it."

"You are so damn jealous it's sick," says Vanessa.

"What?!" Rat stops, dumbfounded. "Jealous of what? That it wasn't me Thierry tried to rape?"

"You've always been jealous of me," Vanessa pronounces. "Everybody says so, everybody notices how jealous you are. Even Marielle and Jean-Luc. You've never wanted me to have anything of my own. Back when Souad was alive, you were jealous rotten of me being friends with her. You used to hate Morgan, remember? It really shocked me, how mean you used to be to that poor baby when his own mother was dying."

She's working herself up into it, getting more and more more sorry-for-herself self-righteous as she goes. Rat's done the same thing herself.

"All these years I've been so alone, struggling to keep a life together for me and my kids." Vanessa's voice is husky with tears. "Finally I've found someone who loves me and you just can't stand it, can you? You have to wreck every last little thing I've got. Maybe you're right, maybe it is time for us to separate, for you to get a life of your own. Then you'll see it's not so easy."

"Fine," says Rat. "That's what I'm doing."

"Where are you going?"

Rat doesn't answer.

"You're not taking Morgan with you."

Rat says nothing. She's trying to redistribute the weight, cram as much heavy stuff as she can into her knapsack, leaving Morgan's manageable.

"Look," says Vanessa. "You want to go sleep at a friend's house for a few days, that's fine. But you go on your own. Morgan stays with me. Don't drag him into this business. You have a problem with me or with Thierry, fine. You're a teenager, it's normal we have conflicts. But don't drag Morgan into it."

"I'm taking Morgan somewhere he'll be safe," says Rat.

"Where?"

"I'm going to take him to Collioure." She says it in order to hide the bigger fact of where she's ultimately aiming to go, but soon as she's said it, Rat sees she's hit a strategic nerve.

"To Mémé Catherine?" Vanessa's eyes swing round fast. "You've been in touch with her?" There's an edge almost of panic to her voice.

Rat doesn't answer. Fastens the sleeping bag to her knapsack, draws the cord tight. Vanessa lights a cigarette, paces.

"Okay, okay," she says, tone indulgent now. "You go visit your grandmother for a few days, that's fine. But Morgan stays here."

Rat shrugs.

"I don't think you understand how the Mémé Catherines of this world reason, Rat. You think everybody's like us, you know, antiracist, peace-and-love. Well, Mémé Catherine's from another planet. Mémé Catherine doesn't like Arabs. Period. No way she's going to let an Arab boy into her house. You tell Mémé Catherine that bullshit story about Thierry, you know what's gonna happen? She's gonna get straight on the phone to Child Welfare and get Morgan taken away that very same day. Perfect excuse. Is that what you want to happen, Morgan ending up in Care?"

Care again. Rat imagines Morgan in a strange town, in a strange house, in a strange family. Worse still, an orphanage. Not sharing a room with him. Not talking to him in the dark, not getting him up for school in the mornings. Seeing him maybe once a year. Or never.

But she doesn't believe it. Vanessa hates Mémé Catherine so much she'll tell any lie about her. Mémé Catherine's too Catholic, too duty-bound: like it or not, Morgan's her legally adopted grandson. In any case, they're not planning to live with her forever: it's just a road stop till Rat can figure out how to get them to England.

She hikes a knapsack onto each shoulder, and goes through the door. Out in the courtyard, Morgan and Cristel's godson are kicking around a football. Morgan drops it when he sees Rat emerge from the apartment, and comes running. Rat hands him his knapsack, with the sleeping bag attached.

Vanessa watches from the doorway.

"Come here, Morgan," she says. "Aren't you going to give your old Vanilla-do a kiss?"

Morgan goes and puts his arms around Vanessa. He is almost as tall as she is. She strokes his curls, kisses his face. Holds him at arm's length and looks at him. "So Rat's going to take you off for a few days' holiday, all right? Is that what you want to do?"

He nods.

"That's all right, then. You two go, enjoy yourselves. You need a bit of a break. You be good, my bedbug, you take care of Rat for me. She's a good girl, but she's stubborn as a mule."

She hugs him tight, then releases him.

"Rat?" she says. She holds out her arms to Rat, imploringly.

Rat doesn't move.

"Do you have your cell phone?"

Rat doesn't answer.

"Will you call me?" she asks, finally. A quaver in her voice. "Ratkin?"

No answer.

"Promise?"

Rat won't promise.

"Rat, you're a child still. And I'm your mother. I'm not giving you up that easy, Rat. I want to know where you are, and I want you to keep in touch. This is your home, here with me. You, me, Morgan. Us three forever. Okay?"

Rat moves her head in some equivocal way that could just mean a fly has alighted on her ear. And turns to go.

They trudge down the drive, Morgan bearing the knapsack

with his sleeping bag, Rat hauling a larger backpack with the tent and both their sleeping mats attached.

When they are almost out of sight, Morgan turns to wave good-bye, but Vanessa's gone back into the apartment.

When they reach the road to Saint Féliu, Morgan remembers he's forgotten his water bottle.

"It don't matter, Morgan. That metal one weighs a ton. We'll pick up a plastic bottle somewhere."

CHAPTER

3

If you were around in the seventies and eighties, long after Celia Kidd had quit modeling, you might have seen her traipsing about Europe with her son.

She, an impossibly leggy woman with milk-white skin and a merry mocking laugh. The boy, black hair down to his shoulders, a kind of negative Lord Fauntleroy, radiating unease, yet unable to think of a better game than tagging after his mother and trying to keep her suitors at bay.

They were at fashion shows in Paris. They were at outdoor cafés in the Piazza Navona. They were on the beach in Majorca, she sitting under a parasol in a droopy straw hat and a ruched bathing costume, he, diving off high rocks. They worked the fancy flea markets, the auction houses, they went to film festivals and art openings.

Celia Kidd had two husbands and a great many lovers. She sent her son to school when she thought of it. There was a progressive English boarding school from which the boy was expelled for smoking pot, a Swiss one from which he was expelled for taking heroin. He signed up for art school in Paris and then dropped out. Got a job stretching canvases for an important British painter who was a friend of his mother's.

Celia Kidd occasionally reappeared in the gossip columns, once for getting arrested for driving drunk after her license had already been revoked, another time when her secretary stole several hundred thousand pounds of art from her.

And Gillem dallied, unable to break loose. Until there came a day when Celia Kidd's son decided it was time to draw up accounts. He thought about what he loved: painting, the English countryside, a woman he'd met at a dinner party who looked absurdly voluptuous but acted strict as a schoolmarm. And what he hated: waking at noon with a head like a rotten melon. Fooling himself that his real life had not yet begun.

His mother, meanwhile, was beginning to forget things she'd always known. And Gillem, censorious, blamed it on the booze and pills.

He and the voluptuous schoolmarm (in fact, she worked for a film producer) married and bought a house in West London, with a shed at the bottom of the garden where he could paint. Eventually, they had a son.

Gillem would never have a big career, but he had a kind of mental, not to mention financial, freedom which meant that he didn't need much recognition in order to keep doing what he pleased. God knows, it had taken him long enough to find it.

Gillem is sitting in the darkness, staring at his computer.

On the screen is a fifteenth-century altarpiece by Jan van Eyck from a cathedral in Ghent. Its name is *The Adoration of the Mystic Lamb*. Twice—in winter when there are no tourists—he's been to see it. It is probably his favorite picture in the world.

Gillem is examining van Eyck's full-length portraits of Adam and Eve. They stand on the outer edges of the altarpiece, Adam on the far right, Eve on the far left, in a kind of banishment, a state of extreme privation. The painting's palette—the emerald greens and flame oranges that bedeck its angels and prophets and emperors—is brilliant, new-washed as countryside after a hard rain. Only Adam and Eve are condemned to puritanical gray, brown, black. Each stands, naked, alone, in the mental purgatory of his shadow-world.

Each is electrifying in the fullness of his interiority, his self-awareness, which is why to Gillem these two portraits symbolize the very essence of what it means to be human in a fallen world.

Eve is holding an ugly wrinkled little citrus fruit. She is holding it aloft, as the priest holds up the sacrament, her expression, to Gillem's mind, defiant, mildly challenging. She will outcountenance God or anybody else, too, so poised is she, so whole. You feel if she had the choice again, knowing the sequence of expulsion, pain, mortality entailed, she would still eat the fruit. Because she's ready to grow up, move into a world where people fend for themselves.

Adam is less stable, more deranged, a brown-bearded naked man, wild, primitive, sinewy, with a weather-beaten face and springy shoulder-length hair. If you saw him on Kensington High Street, he'd be a mad homeless person.

Adam is in motion. His right foot is raised; he is stepping forward out of the picture frame, into the future, into our world. And yet his left arm crosses his chest as if to shelter a private heartache. His dark brown eyes express a kind of beaten, harrowed acceptance of sin, a dogged cognizance of all the world's suffering that he's unleashed and all that lies in store.

Gillem has tried hard to purge his youthful sins and make himself into a decent reliable man. But those sins, it turns out, won't stay purged. They have come creeping out of the past in search of him. And now his family, too, will have to suffer for them.

He feels as if the home life he and his wife have so painstakingly constructed for themselves and their son is a fraud. The only thing that seems real right now—real as the ugly wrinkled yellow fruit seems real, compared to the unreality of the angels' psychedelic wings—is the rocky cove in Collioure, where one night he had sex with a local girl he'd picked up in a nightclub.

He clicks a series of keys on his computer, and the altarpiece vanishes. What scrolls up in its place is the e-mail message he was sent a week ago, and which he's been unable to answer.

He rereads it, taps "Reply." Considers a long while, types a few words, then once again presses "Cancel."

"Have you any idea where we're headed?" asks Morgan, in his sweet trusting way. Just because Rat's saving his life and honor doesn't mean he's going to give her a break.

No Sunday bus to Collioure till 4:45 that afternoon, they've discovered, so Rat has decided to hoof it to Canet to see if there's an earlier bus from there. Cutting across the fields to stay off the big roads. When they get tired of walking, they can hitch.

"Short-term or eventually?" asks Rat. "Short-term, we're going to stay with my granny. Long-term, we're going to go meet my father."

Morgan looks puzzled. "You have a father?"

He's got a point, that kid. What father? The only father in anybody's life is Jean-Luc, poor guy, stuck serving as communal surrogate to all Mas Cargol's single-mothered mites.

"Remember, I got this father who's English, who lives in London? I thought maybe it was time to go look him up, say here I am, your wonderful daughter you've been longing to meet all these years."

Doesn't sound very convincing, does it? Especially since the supposed father still hasn't bothered to answer her damn e-mail.

If anybody ever sent Rat an e-mail, she would answer straightaway now that she knows what torment it is sitting around waiting.

Vanessa used to tell her Gillem McKane had become a sort of hermit. That was why he never answered her letters, or why Rat couldn't go meet him. But that was probably just Vanessa-mush because the guy didn't want to see her. Hermits don't publish their address in cyberspace.

Sliding under the electric fence dividing one field from the next, Morgan snarls his leg on a thistle. Hops, rubs it.

"Lemme see. I got a Band-Aid somewhere in this pack. Shall we put a Band-Aid on it?"

"No."

"You wanna change into long trousers?"

"Nope."

"That way you won't get cut so bad."

"I don't care."

Something isn't right with Morgan; he won't look at her.

"What's the matter?"

Long silence. Then, "I didn't say good-bye to Solenne."

"That's all right; I told Jérôme we were going."

Rat doesn't tell Morgan that in fact she's waited on purpose till the Cabreras were out for the day. Marielle and Jean-Luc aren't as easygoing as Vanessa: she can just imagine their faces if she tried to tell them, Me and Morgan have decided to begin our summer vacation a month early. Don't worry; we'll send you a postcard soon as we get where we're going.

They walk for a while in silence. The midday sun is beating down hard on their heads. Rat realizes she forgot to pack Morgan's hat.

The rough sandy land they're traversing is desolate. A hundred years ago, it would have been wheat fields, rice paddies. Fifty years ago, orchards. Now it's a parched moonscape of hummocks, thistles, barbed wire, garbage. In one field, a white horse, curious, starts following them.

Morgan is getting a funny look on his face, there's a little smile twitching at the corners of his mouth, an expression of bottled-up joy Rat recognizes.

"Tell me the truth, Rat. No messing around. We're going to Collioure, or we're going to England?"

"Eventually? England. That's my intention, at least."

"To London?"

"Yup."

"You're not fooling?"

She smiles at him. "We're going to London."

"*Putain!*" he says, softly. "And are we ever going home again?"

"Oh sure," she replies. "Soon as Vanessa dumps Thierry, we'll be back."

"What if she never does?"

"Never's a long time. Let's just think as far as Collioure."

In a stand of poplars by an irrigation canal that runs into the sea, where they stop to eat their sandwiches, they find someone's old campground: the rotten foam-and-ripped-plastic seat from an old car, charred remnants of wood, cans of beer, a rain-soaked magazine. Plastic sheet as roofing. Somewhere they too could sleep, if they had to.

Occasionally they pass allotments of lettuces, peas, beans, flowers. Corrugated tin sheds. A scarecrow, dressed in blue over-alls faded almost pink by the sun. What looks, from a car window, like wasteland turns out, on closer examination, to be land minutely used, semiclandestinely inhabited.

When they reach the river Têt, they are obliged to wind their way back onto the highway bridge. Ahead, you see the beachside apartment blocks of Canet Plage. And beyond those, the high dark green wall of the Pyrénées.

On the far side of the bridge, Rat takes them down a fisher-man's path that leads through an Indochinese jungle of bulrushes to the riverbank. There they rest for a while gazing out into the wide rushing swell of cement-gray waters, the swirling eddies, the camel-humped mud bars where plastic bottles and tankards of detergent get marooned.

Farther downstream, the multibranched saltwater-freshwater deltaland of river merging into Mediterranean.

To Rat, it feels like the first time she's breathed free since the night of her birthday party.

"Rat?"

"Mmmmm?"

"Which direction are we going?"

"You see the mountains?" She points south.

"Yeah."

"That's where we're headed."

"And on the other side of those mountains is—Spain?"

A mischievous smile is once again frisking around the corners of Morgan's mouth. "You're sure we're headed the right way for England?"

Rat grins back. "This don't look like the way to England? You accusing me of getting us lost?"

Morgan laughs.

"Let's get lost," sings Rat. "Remember that song, Morgan?" She tries to imitate Chet Baker's soft wispy voice, but she can no longer remember the words.

Vanessa's old boyfriend Max had a Chet Baker tape he used to play over and over when they were on the road. Vanessa loved it, too. She and Max used to sing along to the tape, Max making fun of Vanessa's lousy English. Max's English was almost as good as his French, and he knew the lyrics to all the songs. *"Let's get lost,"* sings Rat, but these are the only words she remembers.

"Remember when we used to drive around in the van, looking for yard sales, and we'd beg Vanessa to get us lost on purpose?" she asks.

"Yeah. That was fun."

"We'd, like, wind up in some farmer's artichoke field. Remember the time the back wheels got stuck in the sand, and we had to go ask those surfers to dig us out?"

"Yeah."

"Well, listen, boy, I guarantee you I can get us a damn sight more lost than that."

Morgan laughs. "England?" he says, after a moment, wonderingly.

"England," replies Rat.

They grin at each other, immensely excited.

"Hey, Rat?"

"Yeah?"

"No offense, but—can you actually speak English?"

"Me? It's the only class I've ever gotten decent grades in."

"I know, but can you speak it?"

"Sure," Rat laughs. "I speak it great. So long as nobody tries to speak it back to me! Look, once we get to England, soon as there's anybody we need to speak to, I know just what to do, I go up to him, I say, *Mister, let's get lost!* We go into the bakery, I point at a loaf of bread, I say to the lady, *Missus, let's get lost!*"

Both now are rolling around, helpless with giggles. Doesn't matter they're hot and footsore, that Morgan has a nasty red scrape down his leg, that Collioure is still miles to go, and they have no idea where they are going to sleep that night. They're happy to be together, out in the open countryside, free of Thierry.

It is late afternoon before they reach the causeway that runs between the sea and the lagoon of Saint-Cyprien. It's a good place to hitch a lift, because there's parking on either side of the road, where people stop to look at the flamingos, or to walk on the beach.

Rat and Morgan get a ride from a vanload of windsurfers from Banyuls, who deposit them at the turnoff for Collioure.

.   .   .

The road down to Collioure is steep, and there's no room for pedestrians. On the far side of the crash barrier is a gulley too slant-sided to walk in. Rat decides they are better off taking a shortcut down through the terraced vineyards. But as soon as they get off the asphalt road, they find themselves sliding down the scree of a hillside steep as cliff. Rat had imagined there must be some kind of path, but although it is possible to proceed horizontally across each terrace of vines, there appears to be no vertical descent except an irrigation drain.

In the end, she takes Morgan's knapsack as well as her own, and they slide down, half on their heels, half on their bottoms, from terrace to terrace.

Collioure is still miles below.

In the end, Rat gives up, and they scramble back up to the road.

Rat was a little girl last time her mother took her to see Mémé Catherine. Back then, she had no need to pay attention to directions. She can remember the name of the condo complex in which her granny lived, and that it was somewhere in the upper town, but once they get to what seems like the right elevation, she can't find it. All the turnings they take lead to dead ends backing onto ravines, so that they are continually obliged to retrace their steps.

Morgan says nothing, but his face is drained of color.

It's Sunday evening, and darkness is falling.

A town can be unfriendlier at night than the countryside. Every human enclosure seems to exclude the wayfarers. There isn't a single bar or café open, and all the shutters of people's houses are closed so tight you can't tell if there's a light on inside.

Rat is chilled to the bone, and infinitely weary, which means Morgan must be feeling even worse. She tries not to let herself think of the Cabreras' house, where at this moment, Marielle will be cooking supper, Solenne probably playing with her Barbies in the bath. A hot bath. And Jérôme? Knowing Jérôme, he's probably worrying about them.

"How's your scrape, Morgan?"

"It's okay."

"Are you cold? It gets cold once the sun goes behind the cliffs. Let's change you into your long trousers."

"Here? In public?"

"Well, there aren't exactly a lot of people around, are there?"

Circling and circling in the deepening dusk around the area that seems right, Rat finally strikes lucky. A sign to Les Glycines.

"Are we there?"

"Yeah, we're there."

Eureka.

But no, not quite. Les Glycines, it turns out, is a maze of half-moon streets, where all the streets have flower names and all the houses are identical. Rat remembers that Mémé Catherine lives on rue de Jasmin, but she has no idea where that is. And there isn't a living soul on the streets, not even a cat, and not a light visible in anybody's house. Lost in a labyrinth of shuttered flowers, where Honeysuckle Row and Morning Glory Drive monotonously recur. Finally, they hit Jasmine, and she has a faint recollection of its being a house on the corner, but which corner? From which end have they arrived? How did she used to recognize Mémé Catherine's house when she was a child?

"We're on the right street, but I'm not sure about the house. Why don't you stay here with the bags while I go look?"

Morgan clearly doesn't want to be left behind, but he sits. Ten minutes later, Rat's back.

"I found the house," she says.

"Is she home?"

"I don't think so. But come."

Rat takes the knapsacks and helps Morgan to his feet. Her grandmother's house is a hundred meters down the road. And yes, it's on a corner. But there are no lights on inside, and the white metal shutters that open and close with an electric button look definitively shut.

"Are you sure it's her house?"

"Yeah," says Rat. "You can't see it over the wall, but that's her quince tree."

She rings the bell several times at long intervals, but there is no answer.

"What do we do now?" asks Morgan.

"Let's go get something to eat, and we'll come back later."

"Can we leave our stuff?"

She considers. They could climb over the gate and pitch their tent in Mémé Catherine's garden, camp there till she came back. But Rat's getting a bad feeling about this town, and the last thing she wants is one of Mémé Catherine's invisible neighbors to go reporting to the police that some dangerous drifters have broken into Madame Bonnet's property.

Instead, they shoulder their bags and hike back down to the bottom of the town. "There'll be a café or something open on the seafront," Rat promises. "Even if we can't get a full meal, we'll be able to have a *croque-monsieur* to warm us up."

No such luck. It's Sunday night. Every damn bar and pizzeria on the corniche is shuttered tight, lights out. And it's cold.

They sit down on a bench overlooking the sea, picking through the bread and cheese and ham and cucumber left over from lunch. Morgan, Rat can tell, is still ravenous. Hunger makes him colder, the cold makes him hungrier. Isn't there some story about the three wolves of hunger, cold, fatigue? She wonders what she was thinking of, prying him away from the Cabreras' cozy home, before she had a sure place to take him to.

After hiking back up to Mémé Catherine's once more to make sure she hasn't come home, they return to the small playground that Rat's reconnoitered as the safest, driest place for them to spend the night, and lay out their ground rolls and sleeping bags in a small plywood hut that has an extremely cold metal pole running vertically through it.

It's early still, but there's nothing for it but to try to sleep.

Climbing into their sleeping bags, each tries to wriggle himself into a tolerable position, in Rat's case, with knees drawn to her chin.

For years Morgan's been asking her to take him camping, just the two of them. Somehow she'd imagined their first night alone under the stars a bit more festive.

"Rat?"

"Mmm?"

"I'm still hungry." Morgan voices this observation as neutrally as if they are conducting a scientific experiment in how much it takes to fill a person's stomach.

"I know, Mo. We'll get you a big breakfast tomorrow, I promise. Hot chocolate, pastries, the works." Pretty soon she'll have to start husbanding their sixty euros, especially if there's no Mémé Catherine to take them in, but not yet.

"Rat?"

"Mmmmmm."

"You know how you see pictures of children, posted up on walls?"

"Mmmmmm."

"Who are those children?"

"They're missing children," says Rat, puzzled. "Kids who've been kidnapped, or who've run away from home."

"Are we missing children?"

"No, not a bit. We told Vanessa we were leaving. She waved us good-bye, remember?"

"You don't think Thierry's going to come after us, do you?"

"That coward? No way."

"He was putting up posters for Vesuvio. You don't think he'll put up posters for us?"

"Are you kidding? I think he'll be dead-relieved we're gone."

Morgan subsides, apparently satisfied.

The next morning, Rat awakens at dawn. She routs them from

their playground hut—sore, frozen—as soon as the sun's risen above the sea, and packs up. Even if they have Vanessa's say-so, last thing she wants is to attract the attention of anybody official.

On the corniche, a lone bakery is open. Rat picks up *L'Indépendant* from the stack of newspapers by the door.

"*Putain,*" she says, glancing at the front-page photograph. "There's cars getting burned all over the place now—two cars in Canet last night!"

The blonde woman behind the counter is looking at them as if they aren't children but something alien, potentially threatening. "Anything else?" she asks, pointedly.

They eat their *pains au raisins* sitting on the seawall, looking over the beach, but it's too cold to linger. They climb back uphill, and make their way once more to Les Glycines, where they sit themselves down on Mémé Catherine's doorstep.

Not long before a woman next door is parting her kitchen curtains to peer out at them. A man comes to join her. Together, they look at the children. Rat jumps to her feet and rings their bell. For the longest time, she thinks no one will answer. Finally, the woman opens the front door a crack.

"Yes? What do you want?" she calls.

"I'm looking for Madame Bonnet," Rat shouts back.

The woman examines Rat from the safety of her doorstep. She's clearly not going to budge. "Are you the same people who came by last night? She's not here."

"Has she gone away? I'm her granddaughter."

A long pause. "She's at the clinic."

"Is she sick?"

The woman looks over Rat, probably wondering why this so-called granddaughter isn't better clued in about her grandmother's health. Rat wishes she'd packed a hairbrush.

"Madame Bonnet is doing rehab for her hip replacement," the woman says, finally. "She won't be back for a good month. What

did she say, Gérard? End of June, I think. Are you the granddaughter who lives outside Lille?"

Lille? This must be Aunt Marie-Christine and her children.

"Yes," lies Rat.

It takes them longer than Rat expected to reach the dynamite factory. This time, she opts to go along the main road. Below is
sharp black cliff, paler sea. The distance from Collioure to the
bay of Paulilles, a few minutes in Florian's car, proves interminable on foot. It's scary to make one's way through the miles
and miles of dark tunnels, with only a few inches of pedestrian
curb clearly intended only for emergency use. When cars and
trucks hurtle past, she and Morgan press themselves tight against
the cavey walls.

When they finally reach the factory, Rat first throws their
backpacks over the gates, then helps Morgan to scale them.

But once they are safely inside the park enclosure, she feels
oddly at peace. It's as if everything ugly and menacing—
Thierry, the lady in the bakery, Mémé Catherine's neighbors, the
loud angry cars that seemed to be trying deliberately to crush the
two children against the tunnel walls—remains on the far side of
the chained gates of the dynamite factory.

No one can find us here, she thinks. Only Jérôme and Florian
know about it, and they will never tell.

Together, she and Morgan explore what was once a formal
park. There are parasol pines and cedars, palm trees and eucalyptus trees and oleander. Hibiscus and snakey wisteria are draped
across a tumbledown wall. The undergrowth is a solid mat of
brambles.

Unhurried, they make their way towards the ruined outbuildings.

Morgan, dancing on his toes like a boxer, is caught between

delight and trepidation. "Can we really stay here? It's like—it's like a fairy tale."

They reach the cathedral-like building where she and Jérôme and Florian camped the night of Rat's birthday. There's no one home, but she can see that the older kids are clearly still in residence.

Rat takes advantage of their absence to take a good look around their living space. It's been ingeniously equipped. The cement floor is carpeted in old rugs, empty sacks of grain. A couple of the smaller rooms have been converted into sleeping quarters: yellow crushed-velvet cushions from an old sofa, mattresses, sleeping bags unzipped and hung up on a laundry line to air.

Another area is kitchen, with the Primus stove and a box where onions, poatoes, rice are stored, a metal trolley with wire-mesh shelves containing plates, kitchen utensils. A plastic barrel full of water. Somebody's accordion. Candles. A lantern. Several crates of books and papers. Homemade-looking pamphlets, printed in block letters, crude black-and-white drawings.

Rat picks up a flyer from the top of a pile.

"Don't Let Machines Play with Your Children," she reads aloud.

"What's that?"

She reads on. "Something about the government using biometrics in schools."

"What's biometrics?"

"Don't you remember, Jean-Luc was talking about it the other night. This new supersonic way they have of taking your photograph, so they know you're not illegal."

Morgan's lost interest. "People actually live in this place?"

"Yeah, a bunch of them. Kids—older kids. They're okay. Me and Jérôme met them the other night."

"Are they coming back?"

"Looks like. Let's go decide where we're going to sleep. Dry ground, preferably."

"Will they mind us staying here?"

"Well, it's public property, isn't it?" says Rat. "We'll try not to get in their way."

Together, they pick a space at the far end of the building, a room whose ceiling is still intact, its floor relatively dry. Rat lays out their mats and sleeping bags, unpacks their knapsacks. Their settlement looks sparse compared to the well-embedded hominess, the good husbandry of their absent neighbors.

She checks their water bottle. "We'll fill up in the morning," she says. "There's got to be a spring somewhere near; otherwise, those guys wouldn't be living here. It'll be fun camping here awhile, don't you think?"

"Mmmm. Are there wolves?"

"Morgan, there are only about three wolves left in the whole of France and they're way up in the mountains."

Easy to believe in the daylight, but come nightfall?

Just to be safe, Rat hangs Jérôme's spirit-catcher over Morgan's sleeping bag.

It's turned into a glorious afternoon. Late in the day, when the sun's going down, Rat goes swimming.

The water is so salty it stings your skin. She swims out far enough to see around the curve of the cove, up the coast to the high-rise hotels of Saint-Cyprien and Canet. Above her, dark blue sky, steep red-gray hills terraced in vines, the leaves palest newborn green, and beyond, the high wall of the Albères. On one peak, she can see the gray hulk of a pilgrimage site where she and Mémé Catherine picnicked one Palm Sunday.

Morgan waits on the beach, convinced that Rat is going to get eaten by a sea serpent. Only when she comes up on shore and threatens to throw him in the water will he venture in, and then no farther than his waist. He stands in the sea, clinging tight to Rat's hands as she holds him from behind. His shoulders are hunched up high, and he squeals in terrified glee, like a toddler about to be tickled. Every time Rat tries to loosen one hand, he clings tighter.

They are whooping in the water, when Rat notices a group of people coming down the overgrown path to the beach. A girl and two boys, preceded by the sheepdog. They are carrying crates.

Rat extracts herself from the sea as inconspicuously as she can, grabs their one towel, and dresses behind it. She emerges, and helps Morgan dry himself and put his clothes on. Her skin feels uncomfortably prickly, her clothes are drenched. Then she goes forth to meet their fellow campers, Morgan shadowing her to keep out of the dog's reach.

"Hi again," she says.

"Hey."

"I'm back. This time I brought my brother."

The older girl has a crew cut and very bright blue eyes. She's wearing black punk combat trousers with the legs tied together and a heavy black sweater and a pair of Doc Martens high-tops that look too hot and clunky for the weather. When she strips off her sweater, she's wearing a white tank top underneath, and she's flat-chested as a boy. She's tall and slender. Tall as Rat. She is one of the prettiest girls Rat has ever seen. The bright blue of her eyes make her look as if she's smiling, even though she isn't.

Morgan is still hiding behind Rat.

"He's not sure about your dog," Rat explains.

"She's gentle," says the girl.

"Is her name really Arnaque?"

"Why not?"

The older kids set about making a fire. They have brought down to the beach crates of vegetables, fruit. Potatoes.

The girl offers them each a nectarine, and bites into one herself. Hunkers down on her heels, haunches long and sinewy. Wiping her dripping cheeks with the back of one hand, she gazes at them.

Morgan wolfs the nectarine down in an instant. Sits, staring fixedly at the remaining food.

The girl reaches into a crate, and tears off a great hunk of bread. Hands it to him.

Rat feels embarrassed. She's been trying to provide Morgan with regular meals, but Morgan isn't a boy with a regular stomach. Morgan's got a stomach like a dump truck. "We had lunch, but . . ."

"These potatoes will take a long time to roast. It's not exactly fast food. Have some more bread."

The older girl's manner is reserved, but she nonetheless makes it clear that she considers these child-invaders their guests.

"Do you live here?" Rat asks.

The others exchange glances.

"We're in transit," one of the boys says.

"Long-term transit," adds the other.

"Terminal transit!"

Everybody laughs.

"Do you mind if we camp here a while?" Rat asks. "We stashed our stuff in one of the rooms . . ."

"We saw," says the girl in Doc Martens. "It isn't ours; it's a Free Zone. For the time being, at least. I guess you know the government's planning to turn it into a marine research center."

"That'd be a shame," says Rat. "I've been coming here since I was a kid, but I never thought of staying here long-term. What do you do for fresh water? Is there a spring?"

"Yeah, in the woods. We've tested it; it's fairly pure."

"Cool," says Rat, appreciatively. These guys are organized.

That evening, over dinner, Rat learns more. There are five of them, three girls and two boys, camping at the dynamite factory. Until recently, they were squatting with a bunch of other friends in a very beautiful medieval building in the center of Lyon. But the government finally succeeded in getting them expelled, and its occupants have been obliged to find other accommodations. They have been staying at the factory a few weeks.

"Are you students?" asks Rat.

"We're gleaners," says the girl in Doc Martens, whose name is Pauline.

"Parasites," says the blond-bearded boy called Dany.

Pauline explains. They have worked out a fairly simple and portable way of living virtually without money. They go around the markets, after they are over and the sellers have packed up, gathering the leftover fruit and vegetables that have been thrown away. When they lived in Lyon, they baked their own bread, but now they retrieve the day-old bread that bakeries give away. It's not just that they are cheapskates, like Vanessa, or can't be bothered to get jobs or sign up for welfare, Rat gathers: it's more a matter of principle. A demonstration that society is so wasteful you can live pretty decently off its leftovers.

"How do you get around?" Rat asks.

They have a van which they run off used oil from deep fryers, Pauline says. "You go round to a kebab shop, most people are pretty happy to unload their dirty oil on you, saves them hauling it to the dump themselves."

For the first time Morgan speaks up. "You can run a car off cooking oil?"

Pauline is more than willing to describe the exact chemical process by which a car's engine converts vegetable oil to carburant— of course, you have to mix it with a little diesel—but this part's too much like school for Rat.

"So you guys live pretty much without money?" she interrupts.

"Pretty much. We do a lot by barter."

"You can't live a hundred percent moneyless, though, can you? I mean, what happens when you get your period, you go round to somebody and say, can I please borrow your used Tampax?"

Pauline laughs. "We have some money. Sometimes we work a season here and there, picking fruit, or painting someone's house."

"Or somebody's great-aunt dies."

"Even better if you have a technical skill—Dany's an electrician."

"I'm on unemployment. That takes skill!" jokes Julie.

"It all goes in the kitty."

"My mom would love you guys," Rat says. "She tries to live like that too, but she's not so scientific about it."

"You're lucky," says Dany. "Most of our parents are pretty pissed we're using our graduate degrees *not* to earn money."

"You guys have graduate degrees?"

"Oh, we have dozens. They're totally addictive. It's only after you have a degree in philosophy and a degree in sociology and a degree in economics that you realize all you really need to know in this world is electricity and plumbing."

These kids are a lot friendlier than most twenty-something-year-olds Rat's encountered. If you ask them questions, they answer readily. But they themselves ask no questions, exhibit no traces of an encumbering curiosity. And under the circumstances, Rat finds their discretion an exquisite form of courtesy.

After dinner, Rat fishes for advice.

"You guys move around a lot. Maybe you can tell me the cheapest way for me and my brother to get to England. How much do you think bus fare would be?"

Yannick considers. "Bus fare's the least of your problems. Do you have papers?"

"Yeah, we both have passports."

"That's a good start. Mind if I ask how old you are?"

"Fifteen."

"That's not old enough."

"For what?"

"To take a child out of France. Legally. That makes you both unaccompanied minors. That's your problem."

Rat's heart has sunk. It's never occurred to her that she and Morgan might not be allowed to leave France. For her, it was just a question of do we hitchhike to London, or do we take a bus.

"Bad timing," says Pauline, finally. "Pre–September eleventh, pre-Schengen, you could talk your way through most borders, more or less. After the Soviet Union collapsed, there was this little pocket of freedom. Nowadays it's Paranoiaville—they're looking for terrorists, they're looking for illegal aliens, they're looking for pedophiles. It's a minefield. Even trying to get onto a train these days is, like, a major production. Sometimes you get lucky."

"Maybe they should try a ferry," Dany suggests.

"What ferries?" asks Rat.

"Up north, across the Channel."

"Where do they leave from?"

"There are ferries from Calais. Where else? Le Havre, Dieppe."

"Where's that?"

"Normandy."

"They're not cheap. But you could try."

"That would be fun," says Rat, brightening. "You want to take a boat to England, Mo?"

Morgan grunts.

"You can just walk onto a ferry?"

"Walk on, yes. Or drive on."

"Yeah, me and Morgan did that when we went to Morocco. Remember, Morgan, when we went across the Strait? That was back when Morgan was a toddler."

They smile at her. "Sure. Find some family to adopt you for the crossing."

Rat makes a face. "It's family we're getting away from."

That night, lying in her sleeping bag on the hard cement floor, Rat twists and wriggles in search of an endurable position, a more padded corner of hip or bottom to rest on.

Morgan's breathing tells her he's awake, too.

"Morgan?"

"Yeah."

"Do you like this place?"

"Yeah."

"This is where Jérôme and Florian and I came for my birthday."

"It's nice."

"And those kids are nice, too, aren't they?"

"Yeah." A pause. "Why's he called Pauline?"

"Who?"

"The one with the metal in his mouth. I thought Pauline was a chick's name."

Silence. Rat reflects on Morgan's misunderstanding—goes down the checklist of all the things that might constitute womanliness in Morgan's book—breasts, hair, makeup, jewelry, a fundamental indifference to a car's inner workings.

"She *is* a chick, she just doesn't have tits, that's all. There are lots of different ways of being a chick. Do you think you can go to sleep now, Mo?"

She reaches over and takes hold of his hand. Morgan eventually falls asleep, still clutching Rat's hand. When she's sure he's sleeping soundly, she frees it.

For what seems like hours, she lies awake, listening to the sound of Morgan's sleeping breath, her mind racing.

They can stay at the dynamite factory as long as they choose, she figures. The days will be getting longer and warmer, more conducive to camping out, closer to the time she'll be able to find work picking fruit. If Pauline and her friends are going to sign up for the season, then Rat will be able to join their work crew inconspicuously, without too much fuss about her being underage, and Morgan will have a safe place to hole up while she's off picking.

But the longer they stay in the Pyrénées-Orientales, the greater the danger that one day they will be spotted by someone they know. For all Rat knows, Vanessa's already called Mémé Catherine to check up on them. And if she finds out they're just plain missing, who knows what she might not do to find them?

You need to call Vanessa to let her know you're both okay, Rat tells herself, but she's still too angry to call. What they really need to do is get to England. She wonders whether her father has finally answered. It feels like months since she e-mailed him. Out of the sixty euros they started with, they have a little less than thirty-eight left. Not much. Better get going, and skip the harvest. Better try to hitch to London.

But Thierry's scumminess has shaken Rat. A few weeks ago, she would simply have headed for the nearest highway, stuck out her thumb and hopped into any car that stopped. Now she finds herself wondering, What if we get picked up by another child molester? How will I be able to protect Morgan this time? She loathes Thierry even worse for making her think about these things, for having undermined her blithe assumption that other people were basically well-intentioned.

The world looks uglier, more menacing than it did when she was younger. You can't just assume your innocence will keep you safe.

Morgan's known this all his life. Now she too is having to catch on.

CHAPTER

4

"You are such a prat," says Kate.

Her face has gone bright red, and she's trying to laugh, but Gillem can see she's fighting back tears. "Why did you never tell me? *That's* what I can't understand."

"I never think about it," he admits. "It was such an abysmal period in my life, I did so many shameful things. I find it very hard to think about."

"This daughter of yours exists, she's been growing up, she's—she's a teenager. You've never thought about her? That's pathological. Not even at the back of your—you are so closed, you don't even know what you're thinking. That's serial-killer mentality."

"Why serial killer? Women give babies up for adoption all the time." Not very long ago, the home secretary's wife had been confronted with the son whom she had given up for adoption forty years ago. "Do you think Pauline Prescott allowed herself to—"

"When I miscarried all those times, when Artemio was finally born, didn't you think—"

"No." Gillem's lying. In fact, he'd thought Kate's miscarriages were divine punishment for the child he'd abandoned, but that's just the kind of sick bastard he is.

"You didn't think of how it might have been for this woman, going through pregnancy, giving birth all by herself, with no husband? She must have been *young*."

"Look, do you want to know the truth? I felt taken advantage of. If a girl wants a baby and doesn't tell you that's what she's after—There's—there's an unspoken agreement nowadays— there's the pill, there's birth control, it's meant, you know, AIDS aside, we can sleep around all we like, that women can be as carefree, as it were, as men. It's true I didn't ask, Are you protected, because we weren't teenagers, I assumed she—"

"Because it would have been inconvenient for you to stop halfway and put on a condom."

Gillem looks down at his hands. He is miserable. Kate is miserable. And because he's the one who's made them both miserable, he's being obliged to talk about things he doesn't know how to talk about. He clears his throat.

"She didn't tell me she was operating by other rules. She had this sort of groupie thing going, she wanted *my* child," he explains, wearily. "I don't mean that in a big-headed way, but here we were, rich foreigners renting a holiday house in this tiny village, Mummy was still getting her picture in the papers, not always for the most salubrious reasons. This girl and her friends had been following my mother around all summer; she knew all sorts of things about her. If she had this hidden agenda, if she'd decided she wanted to get pregnant by an utter stranger, well then, it was her look-out."

"Well, she certainly miscalculated, didn't she, poor girl? I do find everything you are saying utterly baffling, Gill. Cold, paranoid, self-pitying. Very well, forget the mother—gold-digging star-fucking stalker. What about the child?"

"If *she* didn't want to give her child a father—"

"What about the child?" Kate repeats.

"I pay child support. That's what I owe the child. If you choose to make procreation something utterly unilateral, non-consensual, that's what you're left with—a biological father whose connection to his offspring is about as profound as a snake's or a—"

"And you're willing to be the snake."

"No. I wasn't willing. I was furious, I was sick about it."

Kate shakes her head. "I feel as if I don't recognize you anymore."

"You've been pregnant before, but you had abortions. If it had been up to me, this woman would have, too."

He makes an impatient gesture. Kate is demanding from him what seem to him unreasonable reparations—more, in fact, than the child's mother has ever asked. Kate, in her woolly high-mindedness, is insisting that he admit this daughter into his life, after all these years, because she belongs there. Because she's been wrongly excluded. She is the ghost of his old lostness, his former debauches, his miserable shy drugged efforts at promiscuity.

But Kate's back where she started. *"But why didn't you tell me you had a child?* I've told you about every boy I ever kissed, every time I ever fell off my *bicycle*. How could you hide something that huge? Didn't you know I'd want to see a child of yours, that I *hate* it that I wasn't able to have dozens of children with you?"

"I didn't like the mother," Gillem says finally. "I wouldn't much want to know what came out of her. I wouldn't feel especially connected to it. You know, genetics doesn't feel very real to me, compared to what one puts into a child emotionally, culturally."

"Well, that's either ignorance or denial," she snaps. "If you really believed that, we would have adopted. Hasn't she tried to get in touch with you—the mother, I mean?"

"Not directly."

"What, all that goes through Dickie?"

"It's not something we talk about, especially. I see the transfers on my bank statements, that's all. A few years ago, she asked for a hike in payments, I told Dickie fine. That's it."

"Has she ever married?"

"I gather not."

Kate throws up her hands. "Look. The truth is—we both know it—this is something completely banal, run-of-the-mill. We both know loads of people this has happened to—suddenly these illegitimate children show up, or your mother tells you on her deathbed that actually your biological father is Winston Churchill, or whatever. It's no big deal. This is not—er, *The Scarlet Letter*. But what you do have to face—"

"Easy, Kate. Why are you being so aggressive?"

"All right. But it happened. This poor child. And now, quite understandably, she wants to get to know you. It's not her fault you decided her mother was trying to take advantage of you. Why should she be made some sort of nonbeing? It's just—well, sex is wonderful and mysterious, and there are sometimes utterly unintended consequences that one has to accept. So now this child—*your* child—has come into our lives, and it's up to us to welcome her."

"Watch what you're doing, Kate. I don't want her in my life."

"Too fucking bad—she's here!" Kate's laugh is loud and bitter.

"Why are you being so aggressive? What do you want me to do about it?"

His tone is so defeated that she softens.

"Well, invite her over, of course. We must invite her to the house. What's she doing, is she studying here?"

"I don't think she's arrived in London yet. She said she was coming soon."

"Does she have somewhere to stay? What's her name?"

He's reluctant to answer. "Celia," he says, finally. "Celia Bonnet."

"*Celia!*" Kate explodes again into laughter. "That does take some nerve. What a shame your mother's non compos mentis. If the girl's pretty, she'd have loved her. And French, too! Well, I suppose we'd better tell Artemio he has a sister."

"Do you really think that's a good idea?"

"It's the truth."

He grimaces.

"It's the truth," Kate insists. "He has a half sister. People need to know the truth in a family—I don't want to be part of a cover-up that he'll find out in some way that will hurt worse, and make him feel as if *he* never knew you, either."

Gillem pauses, as if waiting for her to relent, then rises to his feet.

"Are you going out?" Kate asks. Her tone is frosty.

"I was going to visit my mother," he says. "Would you rather I went tomorrow, instead? It's just that I've been putting it off all week . . ."

"No, of course you should go." She's going to be like this—chilly, polite—until he can't take it any longer and they both break down and admit that they love each other so much it hurts. "You don't suppose you could pick up Artemio from his piano lesson on your way home?"

"What time does he finish?"

"Half past six."

Gillem glances at the kitchen clock. It will make it an even thinner wafer of time with his mother than he might have liked, but he daren't say no. "What number is it, again?"

"Thirty-seven Cleveland Square."

Thirty-seven, thinks Gillem to himself as he closes the front door. Thirty-seven is the age van Gogh was when he shot himself. Sometimes numbers comfort Gillem with their stolid incontrovertibility. But these days there is no comfort in this number, or in anything else . . .

When they get back from the market, Rat can tell at once that someone has visited their camp. Her and Morgan's sleeping area smells of dope, and there's an imprint of somebody's body on Morgan's sleeping bag. A pot-smoking Goldilocks.

She goes through to the Great Hall. The Paulines are unloading their booty: salads, fruit, bread. They've bought some cheeses and a long string of Catalan sausages to grill for dinner tonight. Some friends from another squat are arriving tonight on their way to an antinuclear demonstration in Marseille.

Dany has picked up his accordion. Morgan has already settled himself in the hammock with a *Titeuf* comic book he got from a secondhand bookseller.

"Hey Mo," says Rat. "Looks like Jérôme and Florian have come to find us."

"Oh yeah?" Morgan doesn't look up from his comic book.

These days Rat hardly sees Morgan, except at bedtime or in the middle of the night, when he occasionally wakes up from a bad dream. He has attached himself to Yannick and Dany, joining in their chores, gathering firewood, fetching water, watching them dive for mussels and sea urchins. The other day they went into the woods and came back with a basket of wild strawberries. Morgan had on his face what is almost Rat's favorite of his expressions: lips compressed in a look of utter solemnity, supreme satisfaction at a job well done.

Rat's happy enough, too, in the day-to-day, but at night she worries. The Paulines aren't going to stay at the dynamite factory much longer. From what she can make out, none of their living arrangements are intended to last long, and the groups in which they live are constantly mutating, splitting into smaller cells or going off to join larger collectives. When they leave the dynamite factory, Yannick and Dany are planning to help set up another squat in Toulouse. Pauline and Sara are going to join some friends who live on a sheep farm up in the Ariège, and Julie, who is Belgian, is going back to Anvers to get her midwife's training.

Rat likes Pauline a lot. At first, when Pauline would start talking about how prison was this laboratory where the state tests everything later to be diffused throughout society, or why it's wrong to recycle your garbage, Rat tended to daydream. Now she's getting a bit more interested. It's even occurred to Rat that if London doesn't work out, she wouldn't mind living on a sheep farm in the Ariège, although Pauline has made it clear it's an all-female collective, where even a nine-year-old male might not be welcome.

Rat makes her way down to the beach, followed by Arnaque.

Two figures are standing by the shore. One of them is skipping stones into the water. She breaks into a run, throwing her arms around both boys at the same time, enveloping them in a joint hug.

"You found us!"

Jérôme is looking sour. She can also tell from just one look at him both that her father hasn't answered her e-mail and that Thierry's still around. "Yeah, nice of you to keep in touch. Of course, I didn't worry a bit."

"Oh. I didn't have my cell phone."

"Yeah, well, cell phones have existed for about five minutes. What do you think people did before? There's an excellent system of public pay phones in this country, you know. You put in your money, and you . . ."

"I'm sorry. I guess I thought it was safer for you not to know where we were. I didn't think you'd—well, it sure was smart of you to find us here."

"Process of elimination. I saw your grandmother's house was all closed up, so . . ."

"How did you know where my granny lived?"

"Ever heard of a phone book? You really are clued in to all amenities of civic life, girl."

He gets like that, Jérôme. Usually Rat gives him time to cool off, but today she's too happy to see him. She sits down on the rock beside him, snuggling up till she feels his body relax, his shoulders unhunch. She didn't realize how much she'd missed him. Now that she's broken with Vanessa, Jérôme and his parents feel like the only family she and Morgan have got.

News from Mas Cargol. Thierry is still vaguely in the picture, although everybody seems to be telling Vanessa she should get rid of the guy. Vanessa is saying that she and Rat had a spat—you know, adolescent hormones, mother-daughter conflicts—and that she's sent Rat and Morgan to live with Mémé Catherine for a few weeks.

"Morgan and Solenne's teacher took my mom aside to ask her what was really going on with Morgan. She said he was doing really well, and she didn't want him to fall too far behind. Apparently, she'd tried to talk to your mom, and your mom just blew her off."

"I bet."

"Your mom's really a number, Rat."

"Why, what's she up to?"

"Aw, suddenly she wants to be my best friend. Cozying up to me, asking me questions, trying to figure out where you are. Watching me like a hawk. You should call her, Rat. She's your mother; she needs to know you and Morgan're safe. Like, if I've figured out you're not staying with your granny, she must know it, too."

Rat reflects. "Look, you can tell her you've heard from us, if you like. Tell her I called you to say we're safe, we're living with friends, and that we're keep in touch. But that I refused to say where we're staying. Okay?"

Jérôme looks uncomfortable; he's not a good liar.

"Just give me time to get out of here, Jérôme. I mean, this place is paradise, we've been having a fine time, hanging out with the Paulines—these guys are superintellectuals, they've got some ideas that would blow your mind. But, like, today was the first time me 'n' Morgan have been beyond the gates since we got here. We went to the market at Banyuls and the whole time, I'm nervous as a cat someone we know's gonna spot us. Any day now someone's going to notice our campfires, and the police will come. I'm getting real itchy to get out of the Pyrénées-Orientales, head up to England. No news from my father?" She knows the answer already.

"None."

"He still hasn't answered my e-mail?"

"No."

"Fuck," she says, and ponders. "What should I do, should I send another one?"

"Yeah, maybe you'd better."

"I'll tell you what to write, and you can send it. Maybe the address wasn't any good. Maybe we should send one to that gallery place that sells his stuff, too."

Jérôme is still looking worried. "And if you don't hear back, what are you going to do?"

"I'm going to go to London anyway. Go to his gallery and find him."

"You can't go to England if you have no money and nowhere to stay. You want to end up sleeping in the street, Rat? London's the most expensive city in the world."

That's Jérôme for you, cautious. Small wonder he's planning to be an accountant when he grows up.

"We'll be fine. It's just a question of how we get there."

Over lunch, they discuss strategies with the Paulines.

Florian thinks the ferry idea is bogus.

"Why complicate things? Why don't we just put 'em on a plane?"

He pulls out his cell phone, wanders down to the beach where the reception's clearest, comes back a few minutes later, looking triumphant. "There's a Ryanair flight from Perpignan at eight tonight, with plenty of seats available."

"Did you book them? Did they ask you who was traveling?" asks Dany.

"Nah. I don't think it'll be a problem. These airlines are so busy running each other outta business, they don't care if you're Osama bin Laden. You want to go for it, Rat?"

"I don't think we can afford a plane, just now. I think we're better off hitching. Did you ask how much it costs?"

Florian winks at her. "I already promised you a trip to England, didn't I? You can pay me back once you're reunited with your millionaire daddy."

Rat's not proud. In her view, money is—or should be—a collective amenity. Whoever's got it, pays. She reaches over and squeezes Florian's hand. "Thanks."

"You want to go for it, Rat?"

"Sure. Why not?"

"I'm not going to be able to take you tonight. I have my aikido qualification." Jérôme glances at his watch. "I've got to be at Moulin-à-Vent by seven. Will you be taking them, Flo?"

"I'm taking them," says Florian. "It's okay. We got plenty of time. We'll drop you off on the way."

Rat catches Pauline's gaze and suddenly her throat dries up and she doesn't want to leave. Pauline glances away, then looks back at Rat again with her bright blue eyes that are always smiling, even when she's not. Frowns, embarrassed.

Jérôme's staring at Rat's bare feet. "You did bring a pair of shoes?"

It's been ages since she's had to think about shoes. "I'm sure I have that pair of flip-flops somewhere. Will they do?"

"Barely."

Rat clears her throat. "You willing to try it, Morgan? You ready to go to London this evening?"

Morgan shrugs. Morgan's ready.

The ticket lady is a plump young North African woman with acned cheeks.

When they get to the head of the line, Florian does the talking. He sounds pretty businesslike, although he does stink of dope. He's already got his credit card out of his wallet, their passports laid on the counter.

"I'd like to buy two tickets for the eight p.m. flight to London."

"Who are the passengers traveling?" she asks, smoothly.

Florian indicates Rat and Morgan.

"How old is the little boy?"

"Nine years old."

"And the young lady?"

"I'm fifteen," says Rat.

"Is anybody traveling with them?"

"No, it's just them."

Rat's heart starts beating faster.

"I'm sorry, Ryanair doesn't allow unaccompanied minors on its flights."

"That's bullshit," says Florian, his voice shooting high. "This girl's fifteen. That's hardly a minor. I mean, girls get married and have babies at fifteen, but they're not allowed to get on a plane?"

The woman is unmoved. "Children have to be accompanied by a passenger who is sixteen or over."

"What, so we have to, like, camp out in your offices till this girl turns sixteen?"

"I don't make the rules."

"And what about if I go along with them?"

Rat, startled, stares at Florian.

"What's your date of birth, sir?"

"I'm nineteen. Born February 24, 1986."

"Are you these children's legal guardian?"

He hesitates. "No, I'm not."

"In that case, they'll still need authorization from their parents to travel."

"Are those the same stupid rules for every airline, or is this just a Ryanair special? If we go to Air France, will they take us?"

"I don't know, sir."

"Well, could you please find out? Let me speak to your supervisor."

Rat tugs at Florian's sleeve, says softly, "Let's go."

There are people who know how to lose their temper strategically, but Florian isn't one of them. Browbeating this poor girl isn't going to get them anywhere.

Outside, Rat and Florian take a seat under a palm tree, near a group of Scandinavian backpackers who are sprawled in the grass, drinking beer. The sun is still high in the sky. The young men are shirtless; their fleshy shoulders and hairless chests are already sunburnt scarlet. Come Easter, the whole of northern Europe comes swarming as if by biological compulsion down to the Mediterranean. Only countercyclical Rat is fighting her way up to the cold foggy north.

Florian is still fuming. "What a swindle," he complains. "Fucking France, fucking bureaucracy. I bet in other countries a kid's got a right to take a vacation."

"We're not taking a vacation; we're running away," Rat points out.

Florian looks at her, annoyed. "Running away, vacation, what's the difference? It's a question of individual freedom."

"You sound like Pauline."

"Who's Pauline?"

"The girl at the dynamite factory. That's what they believe in, freedom."

"Don't you?"

Rat looks around. "Where's Morgan gone?"

They go back into the airport, where they find Morgan trying, with a plastic dummy, to coax a Twix from the candy machine. Morgan's generally pretty law-abiding, but he's missed his afternoon snack and it's almost dinnertime. Not so long ago, he would have come told Rat he was hungry: his sojourn at the dynamite factory has made him more autonomous.

"Here, kid," says Florian, handing him a handful of coins. "Buy yourself a drink, too. Want something, Rat?"

"What are we going to do now?" Morgan asks Rat.

Florian sighs. "So those guys say the Channel ferry's a better bet?"

"That's one idea." Rat's optimism has taken a beating. She too had been sure all they needed was Florian's credit card and they would be up and away. Thirty thousand feet above the Massif Central by now. "It's all a gamble, I guess."

"Well, I tell you what. Why don't you guys stay at my place tonight, and we'll figure out what to do from here." He looks at the airport clock. "Shit. I have to drop something off at Bas Vernet. You can wait in the car; I won't be long."

He takes out his phone. "Granny? How's it going? I'm bringing two friends home for the night. Do we need anything for dinner? Sure? *Gros bises.*" He makes a kissing noise into the phone, and Rat and Morgan avoid each other's eyes so as not to laugh.

Superhighway, three lanes in each direction.

Mountainous pine forest on either side.

On the sound system, "Clandestino."

Florian's got a really sad collection of music. If you'd asked Rat what kind of music Florian was into, she'd have said heavy metal, maybe electro-groove. No, turns out he's into music-hall variety, octogenarian crooners his granny must love. The only decent CD he has is Manu Chao.

"Clandestino" is old now, but Rat still loves it.

All the songs interconnect, there's this same weird Spanish-language radio broadcast running through it, the same late-night Arabic lullabies for some baby that never seems to go to sleep. And this loneliness that's not just personal but elemental, worldwide. It's the loneliness of migrants to the big city, people who work night shifts and sleep in illegal dormitories, twelve to a room, who on Sundays crowd into long-distance-phone shops hoping to hear for just one moment the voices of their loved ones back in Macedonia or Senegal. The loneliness of people who, unlike Rat thus far, have actually managed to smuggle themselves across a border into the land of the lucky and can't stop longing for what they left behind.

"*Mano Negra clandestina / peruano clandestino / africano clandestino / marijuana ilegal!*" she and Morgan chant. Florian starts howling like a wolf. He's really crazy, that boy. Last time they stopped for gas and a pee, he asked Rat if she wanted to drive.

"I'd love to, but I can't."

"You know how to, right? A fifteen-year-old who doesn't know how to drive is unnatural."

"I know how, but"—she pointed out the obvious—"I don't want to get us arrested."

"What about Morgan, can he drive?"

Morgan split his sides, giggling.

"What's the matter, Morgan, you can't drive? Don't feel bad about it, there's lots of nine-year-olds can't drive. I can teach you in a jiffy."

"Yeah, it don't look so hard," Morgan sassed. "Judging from you, all you have to do is put your foot down hard on the pedal and curse at all the other drivers."

"Have a toke, Morgan: it might make you less saucy."

Morgan clicks his tongue in a "no." "I'm an athlete," he says. "I don't put anything in my lungs but oxygen."

Morgan has been full of surprises. Last night, staying with Florian's granny, Rat had taken advantage of their first plumbing in weeks to do laundry. Emptying out the pockets of Morgan's shorts—bubblegum wrappers, football cards, the one-euro dummy—suddenly she'd come upon two little medals, one brass, one stainless steel. Magpie Morgan's voodoo charms, she'd figured. Except engraved on one medal was "Indexel Electronic Identification" and on the other Thierry's name and cell phone number.

She was curious. "What're these?"

Morgan shrugged.

She was genuinely baffled, then it clicked. "Aren't these Vesuvio's?"

No answer.

"Did you find these somewhere?"

No answer.

"Why'd you take his ID medals?"

Slow to draw conclusions, since Morgan was so damn phobic about dogs.

"Well," he said, finally. "We got rid of him."

"Who's *we?*"

"Me 'n' Jérôme."

"What d'you mean?"

"We fed him rat poison."

"Vesuvio? Are you kidding me? You and Jérôme killed Thierry's dog?"

Morgan said nothing. Rat chewed over this revelation, genuinely shocked. Sure, Vesuvio was a horrible beast. But how could you kill a poor animal for what was Thierry's fault?

"When was this?"

"Last time Thierry came back."

"Where'd you get rat poison?"

"Jean-Luc has some in the garage."

"And Jérôme helped you?"

"Yeah."

Cross-questioned, Morgan divulged that Jérôme had brought him a hamburger patty into which they'd stuck pellets of rat poison. Sunday morning, when Thierry let the dog out of the house for its morning pee before heading back to bed himself, they'd lured Vesuvio into the garage and locked the door. Came back later to make sure he was dead, loaded him into a garbage bag, and hauled the body off to the communal bins. Easy-peasy. Took off his tags so nobody could identify him.

Rat feels as if her world's gone mad.

"Why didn't you guys tell me?"

"I knew you wouldn't like the idea, 'cause you love animals. I know you'd say it wasn't Vesuvio's fault. But that's only because you haven't been bitten by him as often as I have."

"And Jérôme went along with it—with this *dog* murder? It sounds so cold-blooded, so planned out." She's nonplussed as much as anything. She always thought Jérôme was such a peaceable guy, far less of a hoodlum than she.

"Yeah, Jérôme said he'd rather kill Thierry, but if I was happy with taking out the dog, fine."

Rat is silent for a moment. Much as she loathed that dog, she is totally creeped out. "You know, you can't just keep on killing everything you're scared of. Otherwise, you'll never stop being scared."

Morgan shrugged. "I didn't kill him because I was scared; I killed him to get even."

That was Morgan for you. Liked his revenge the way other boys liked candy bars or video games. What do you want for your birthday, Morgan? See that kid over there, the forward from Barcarès, who tripped me up when the referee wasn't looking? Break his leg.

All the same, it gave Rat the creeps to think of that speckled piebald body going bloated, putrid, the blue eye maggot-ridden, in some municipal dump, while Thierry and Vanessa rode around town, putting up posters.

It was at a picnic area just north of Clermont-Ferrand that Florian tried to make the moves on Rat.

Morgan had settled down to sleep in the tent. Rat and Florian were sharing a companionable joint before bed. When suddenly Florian inhaled, leaned over, and blew a big puff of hash fume into Rat's open mouth.

"Did you like that?" he asked.

Rat was doing her best not to choke or pass out, but Florian, taking her silence as assent, followed it up with a kiss. Stuck his tongue in her mouth, before she knew what he was doing.

Rat was so surprised she bit him.

"That was supposed to feel nice!" the boy complained, laughing and cursing at the same time.

"Sorry, I just don't . . ."

"Don't what?"

"I don't do that stuff."

"Have you tried?"

She shrugged. "A bit."

"Maybe it was the wrong guy."

He approached her again, gently, stroking her hair, kissing her lightly on the lips, but she pushed him off.

Afterwards, she felt bad, hoping he didn't think it was because he was such an ugly little squirt, or because she believed the stories about his being HIV.

Maybe Vanessa was right. Maybe she was gay. Maybe she was waiting to sleep with Pauline.

Next day, they're following signs to Orléans, when Florian's cell phone rings.

Florian checks the number. Florian's way too paranoid to take a call from an unidentified number.

"Jérôme," he says, and passes it to Rat.

Rat takes the phone. "Hey, dog-killer, how's it going?"

"So Morgan told you, huh?"

"I have to say, I don't approve."

"I didn't think you would. Where are you?"

"We're—I don't know. Somewhere south of Paris. Where are we, Florian?"

"There's an e-mail from your father," says Jérôme's voice.

Rat feels the prickles spread all over her body. She can hardly breathe, let alone speak.

"When'd it come?"

"Late last night. I just picked it up now."

"What's it say?"

"Do you want me to open it?"

"Yes. The reception's not very good."

"Can you hear me better now?"

"Wait . . ." Her chest feels like lead. "Tell me first. Is it good news or bad?"

A pause. Then, "Good. Definitely good." Jérôme clears his throat. "Ready?"

"Ready."

"Okay. Here goes. Can you hear me?"

"Yeah. Read it."

" 'Hello Celia,' " Jérôme reads. " 'I would be pleased to meet you whenever you come to England. My telephone number is such-and-such. Looking forward to meeting you. Cordially, Gillem.' "

When he's finished, she asks him to read it again. She scrambles for the Magic Marker that came with the Mickey Mouse comic she bought Morgan at the last service station, and scribbles the number on her hand.

"Do you want to answer?"

"Yeah, tell him thanks and that I'm on my way—should be in London in the next few days."

The connections's cutting them off, so she tells Jérôme they'll call him when they stop for the night.

Florian's eyes are on the road, but he's smiling. "So what'd he say?"

Rat snuffles, wiping her nose on the back of her hand. "My dad? He gave me his telephone number, and said to call him when we get to London. I can't believe I'm saying that as if it's something completely normal!" The tears are running hard now, dripping from her nose.

She feels small warm hands on her shoulder. Morgan is leaning forward from the backseat and is trying to hug her from behind. "Congratulations, Rat," he says.

She swivels round to stroke his cheek. Wipes her nose and eyes on the back of her hand. "I don't know why we're all acting as if I just won the lottery. He should have got in touch with me fifteen years ago!" Now laughter mixes with tears.

"Yeah, but you wouldn't have had much to say, would you, aside from 'goo-goo ga-ga,' " Morgan points out.

"What can I tell you," says Florian. "Guys are shits. I have a two-year-old daughter, I try to make sure I see her every month or so, she's the cutest, but I don't always make it."

"I didn't know you had a kid, Florian."

"Yeah, she's a total cutie-pie. Megane, she's called."

"Nice."

Florian takes her left hand, examines the back of it where she's scribbled the number in blue ink. "I guess you're not going to wash for a few days, huh?"

"My father," she says to herself, wonderingly. "First word I've heard from him in my whole life! So he really does exist, that father of mine. Vanessa didn't just cook me up in a home science kit. I got a real live father of my own, and he'd be happy to see me. He fucking better be happy to see me, after all these years!"

They reach Dieppe at nightfall, check out the ferry terminal, and then go in search of the closest campsite. The next morning, they're awakened again by Florian's cell phone. He takes a look at the incoming number, jumps out of the car in his underpants, wanders off to where he can't be overheard.

It's a good twenty minutes before he's back, not looking happy.

"What's the matter, Florian?"

"The police have arrested a supplier of mine coming across the Spanish border."

"Shit."

"Shit is right. He had, like, eighty kilos of hash on him."

"What's it mean for you?"

"Well, the stupid fuck's probably got my number on his cell phone. It's not good." He glances at his watch. "Let's go, let's get this over with."

On their way out, Florian buries his cell-phone chip in the remains of last night's kebab, and dumps the paper bag in a campground bin. Then they drive down to the ferry terminal. It's a massive zone like a military camp, acres of barbed wire, surveillance cameras, floodlighting. Customs and immigration officers. Florian is looking more and more unhappy. The guy really has no luck.

Rat goes into the ladies' room to wash and brush her teeth, change her clothes. When she comes out, Florian is on a pay phone.

"What's happening?" she asks.

"I don't know. I can't seem to find out."

"Why don't you head on back to Perpignan? Unless it's a good time for you to get out of the country."

"No way," says Florian, casting a nervous look at the over-muscled border police posted at the corner. "I'm not walking right into their jaws now. You gotta be in the right frame of mind, real Zen, real relaxed, otherwise, they smell the fear. Besides, I got all my shit stuffed in a shoe at the bottom of my closet. I gotta hide it somewhere more devious."

"Well, go on back now. Hide your goods. We'll be fine."

"Are you sure? I brought you all this way, might as well finish up the job right, get you safe on the boat."

"It's been great," says Rat. "Best trip of my life. You really saved our hides. But you get going now, we'll be fine."

"You want to see if you can get on the noon ferry?"

"No, it'll be fine."

"Listen, I'll wait for you outside till eleven. If it's no go, come tell me and I'll bring you back to my granny's, we'll find another way."

"Okay."

He makes to kiss her. "No biting, all right?"

Awkward kisses. Florian musses up Morgan's hair. "Let me give you my granny's number. Call her and tell her what's happening. And here," Florian reaches into his tracksuit pocket, pulls out his wallet, peels off three yellow fifties. "That's for your trip."

"Thanks, Daddy."

"Don't mention it, sugar-pie. Anything for my little girl." He winks at Morgan. "You, too, buster. Stay cool."

He starts walking towards the automatic sliding doors. "I'll wait here till eleven. After that, you can call my granny, if you need me to come back and get you."

"Good luck."

Rat watches the scrawny little bantam rooster strut out the door, watches him turn once and wave. Then she and Morgan shoulder their backpacks and head over to the ticket office.

A youngish man in uniform, brush-cut hair, but nice-looking.

"Two tickets on the twelve o'clock, please."

"Foot passengers?"

"Yeah."

"Round-trip?"

"One way."

"Do you have any special discounts?"

"I'm a student, my brother's nine," she says.

"Let me just check on the fares." He taps on his computer.

Rat deposits their passports on the countertop. Unable to breathe from the tension. Checks the back of her hand to make sure her father's telephone number is still legible. She should memorize it, really, before it disappears. Repeats in her head his e-mail message. Maybe she will like this man. Maybe he will like her. Maybe he's shy, as Vanessa always said, and he's just been waiting all these years for her to make the first move.

She wonders whether he will kiss her or whether they will shake hands. English people are formal. They don't kiss strangers, even if the stranger is their daughter. Probably they will shake hands.

Later on, when they get to know each other better, then it will be different. She wonders if he will ask her about Vanessa, and what Rat will say. She won't mention Thierry, that's for sure: she wants her mother to look *good* in this man's eyes.

The young man in uniform has called over an older woman. "I'm not coming up with any fares," he says.

The older woman stands beside him, looking over his shoulder. She takes a look at Rat and peers over the counter to catch a glimpse of Morgan. She looks again at Morgan. It's a look certain kinds of French people get when they see an Arab, even if that Arab is a small boy. She says something to the young man, and he too glances at Rat and Morgan, but Rat can't hear what they're saying.

The woman now addresses Rat. "Is there an accompanying adult?"

"No, just me," says Rat. "Our dad is waiting for us at the other end."

"Is he your legal guardian?"

"No, my mom is."

"And where does your mother live?"

"Here in France."

"You need an authorized parental consent form for this child to leave French territory without an adult. Your mother should know that. In any case, we don't accept unaccompanied minors."

The woman is wearing brown foundation. Her fingernails are unnaturally thick and square ended, more like tools than nails, and they are lacquered chocolate brown. She has a short, layered haircut with purplish highlights. Rat hates this woman, but the hate isn't going to do them any good.

"He isn't unaccompanied: I'm taking him. We're going to stay with our dad."

"Yes, but you're a minor, too. You need to be over the age of eighteen."

"You mean we need a letter from our mom?" Rat is considering rapidly whether she could possibly bring herself to call up Vanessa and ask her for this favor. No. But maybe they can forge a letter themselves.

The official snorts. "No, I don't mean a letter from your mother. It's a stamped and notarized form your mother needs to get from the *préfecture.*"

"But our dad's waiting for us at the other end. What if he calls you and says it's okay?"

The woman is getting annoyed. There are people waiting behind Rat. She says, in a tone of mounting irritation, "I've already told you. You need authorization from the *préfecture.* Next, please."

Rat and Morgan walk away. The sun is beating down on the asphalt. Florian's car is gone. Rat can see from the gingerly pigeon-toed way Morgan's stepping that he's sprouted another blister. Somewhere at the bottom of her pack is squirreled their last Band-Aid.

She looks at the cars lining up in their allotted lanes to board the noonday ferry to Newhaven. The cars are all British, with yellow license plates, steering wheels on the wrong side. It's June still, too early for school holidays. Many of them are SUVs, loaded up with cases of alcohol in the back. And if two of those cases weren't filled with wine and spirits, but with children? Rat is too big to pass for a bottle of Beaujolais, but what about Morgan?

She'd better get something over Morgan's head or he's going to catch sunstroke.

"What are we going to do now?"

"We're going to buy you a hat."

"Yippee," says Morgan sarcastically. "I'd been hoping we were going shopping. And after that?"

"Lunch?"

"Are we going to ask Vanessa to get us that form?"

"No," says Rat. "Not if we can find another way. I don't want to talk to her just yet. You know what I mean? I don't want to ask her for any favors. I'm not even sure she'd do it if we asked."

She can't quite imagine how Vanessa would feel about Rat's going to England to meet Gillem McKane, all on her own. If something that exciting were happening to Rat, she suspects, her mother would want a piece of the action herself.

"Are you still mad at her?"

Rat reflects. "Yeah, I'm mad at her. She should have believed us. She should have protected you. She should have put us first. That's what a mother's supposed to do. I'll get over it someday, but not yet."

Morgan doesn't say anything.

"But you love her, don't you, Morgan? I mean, she's a great person. We both know that. Heart of gold."

"She's supernice, Vanessa."

"Yeah, well. Thierry won't be around forever. Let's keep our fingers crossed that he finds a new girlfriend. Maybe he'll run off with Jens's wife, just to teach Jens a lesson."

They laugh, uncertainly.

"Anyway, my dad wants to meet us, and that's something."

"Why don't we call him?"

"Well, he said he'd be happy to see me if I came to London, he didn't say he'd be happy to come to France to pick me up. Besides, same problem. We don't have the same name, he's not our guardian."

In her head, Rat's running through the possibilities of how to smuggle Morgan onto that ferry.

She thinks of Manu Chao. She realizes this is something clandestines do every day—secretly infiltrate this salty border, span the sleeve of water beween continental Europe and the British

Isles. You see it on the news, ever since they closed the refugee center at Sangatte. Grown men and boys, women and girls now too. They hide in trucks, they stow away in freight trains crossing the tunnel. Every day, a thousand Kurds, Iraqis, sub-Saharan Africans broach that border. Some of them are found asphyxiated in the backs of trucks, many more are turned back, but maybe a couple dozen get across every day. It can't be that hard. Some crossings are more porous than others. And after all, it's not as if she and Morgan are illegals, they're European nationals with proper passports, all they're missing is some piddling little stamp from the *préfecture*.

"Let's go get you a hat," she says, finally.

Half a kilometer from the ferry terminal, but still within the Zone, there's a mall. A duty-free mall intended for travelers. There's a mammoth food court, with a McDonald's, a string of fake-French croissant shops, and a megasupermarket selling duty-free alcohol.

Rat is ostensibly looking for a sun hat for Morgan, but actually what she's doing is checking out the prospective passengers, seeing if there is any kindly family she can imagine approaching to ask if they'd be willing to sneak two French children across the border.

It's mostly middle-aged to elderly British couples, loud and bleached blond and wearing spandex. They are pushing shopping carts full of liquor and cigarettes. Everyone looks bent on his own consumer pastimes. The longer Rat watches, the less she can imagine approaching any of these loudly impervious bargain hunters. For one thing, her English isn't good enough, and judging from most of these shoppers' transactions with salespeople and cashiers, they are strictly monolingual.

She finds Morgan a turquoise blue cap for twelve euros that says in English "Enjoy the Spirit of Summer Fun" on its peak.

"It's completely lame," protests Morgan.

"So's sunstroke."

"I'm not going to wear it."

A moment later Morgan's pestering her to buy him a Happy Meal, and Rat begins to say no and then relents. She buys herself a burger and fries, too. Wolfs the food down too fast and feels like throwing up. On Morgan's face, by contrast, is an expression of divine contentment. He's extracted from its plastic packaging the miniature skateboard that came with his Happy Meal, and he's spinning it across the floor of the food court. A little English boy comes to watch. Rat checks out his parents as potential smugglers. More fat hot blond red-faced people in spandex. Not likely.

After lunch, Rat puts a new Band-Aid on Morgan's heel and they hike back to the ferry. For a long time, they sit on a manicured grassy bank and watch the cars going through Immigration. Watch the uniformed man in the pill-box checking people's passports, waving them through. Nobody gets stopped, nobody gets searched. It's a cinch. If only Rat can find some suitable adults willing to smuggle them onto the ferry, they'll be home free.

"Where are we going to sleep tonight?" Morgan asks. He's lost his burst of fast-food energy, and his nose is running. His eyes look gluey, as if he's coming down with a cold.

She considers. "I guess we'd better go back to the campsite, figure out what we're going to do in the morning."

But the thought of hauling their packs and sleeping bags all the way back up that hill is more than she can face. Normandy's colder and wetter than the Pyrénées-Orientales . Last thing Morgan needs is another night sleeping in the damp. No wonder he's getting sick.

Rat can smell her own sweat. It's hot in the sun, and she's been wearing the same clothes for three days, but it's a sweat that reeks of fear, not heat. That damn lady with the chocolate nails has really psyched her out.

"Let's go back to the mall. We'll get some food for tonight, and we can have a wash."

The food in the supermarket is crappy and overpriced and not really intended to provide anybody with a square meal, but they end up with salami baguettes, a bag of potato chips, a jumbo pack of Twix, and a liter of Orangina. Salt and sugar. Grease. Chemicals.

"Come on." Rat jerks her head towards the ladies' room.

"What?" Morgan stands stock-still.

"We both need a wash. You're filthy."

"I'm not coming into the girls' bathroom with you."

"Yes, you are."

"You've got to be kidding." His mouth is set. He has gone stubborn, immovable on her. He's gone into Mediterranean macho mode, a position against which Rat has little leverage.

And Rat all of a sudden feels unable to cope. Too many officials, too many border controls, too many security cameras, none of which are able to prevent any of the world's everyday atrocities from happening.

"You have to, Morgan." Her voice is high, shaky.

"Into the girls' bathroom? No way. I am not going into the girls' bathroom." Morgan lowers his head like a bull, folds his arms across his chest.

And Rat, to her own surprise, finds herself totally losing it. Why now, just when she's finally heard back from her father, don't ask. But it's as if all the month's strain is suddenly pitching into an inconsolable panic and rage, and it's all Morgan's fault.

"You are such a fucking pain in the ass, Morgan. Don't you understand a thing by now?" she shouts at the startled boy. "Places like this are, like, the most unsafe places in the world. We are in this place where I don't dare let you out of my sight for a second. I can't let you go in the men's room by yourself. You want to know about those Missing Children posters? Well, this is where all those kids get lost. Someone grabs you in the men's room and you end up dead in a ditch."

He looks at his feet. "I don't need a wash that bad."

"Yes, you do. You are fucking filthy. And if we want to have any decent chance of getting out of here and into England, we both have to look squeaky-clean. Understand? Now you come into the ladies' room with me now, right now, or else I'm gonna . . ."

For a moment, they face each other, grim. Then Morgan snuffles, hikes up his shoulders, and follows her into the bathroom. Too tired and sick to fight.

Their hike back up to the campground is an almost silent ordeal. It takes far longer than Rat anticipated to get free of the ferry area, with its wasteland of grills, parking lots, and feeder roads. The sun is still hot, but Morgan is sneezing, snuffling. Walking hop-legged from his blistered ankle. Rat shoulders his knapsack as well as hers.

She takes off her flip-flops and stuffs them into an outer pocket. The asphalt is burning, there's broken glass everywhere, but she still feels freer barefoot. They trudge up the road that rises in steep loops straight from the sea onto cliffs overlooking the Atlantic. It's a landscape that must once have been beautiful Normandy coast, a countryside of little fishing villages, and that now has been transformed into a Zone, reconfigured as a commercial transit point for cars and trucks pouring back and forth between other Zones within the European Economic Area.

From time to time, they try thumbing for a lift, but the cars are all British, and nobody stops.

It's seven by the time Rat and Morgan reach the campground where they spent the previous night. The sun is still high above the horizon, but Rat feels all her accumulated exhaustion, her guilt at having yelled at Morgan, flooding her. She's suddenly so tired she wants to cry. It's as much as she can do to find a patch of grass on which to unload their knapsacks. She flops to the ground, stretches out on her back. Later on, after she's had a rest, she can begin to think about the driest spot to pitch their tent.

Morgan seats himself at a distance from her.

"Don't wipe your nose on your shirt."

"I don't have anything else." He's still being a bit formal with her.

She reaches over to feel his burning forehead. "Damn, I meant to buy you some Doliprane." She searches in her pockets for a tissue, finally extracts a T-shirt from her knapsack. "Here, wipe your nose on that. I'm going to have a sleep; I'm zonked."

"Yeah, you have a sleep."

"Don't go anywhere; don't talk to anybody, okay?"

She curls up on her side, with her sleeping bag as pillow. When she awakens, the evening sun has vanished behind clouds, and it's chilly. Morgan is sitting a few yards away, still playing with his Happy Meals mini-skateboard, and humming through his head cold. She sits up and surveys her surroundings. She feels better.

The campground is not crowded; there are maybe half a dozen trailers and a few cars, all with English plates. There is one couple, however, sitting beside a very beat-up station wagon, who inspire her with a flicker of hope. It all depends on which direction they're headed, whether they've just arrived in France or if they're going home. "Wait here a moment, Mo."

When she comes back, she says, "Let's move our stuff."

"How come? Isn't this a good spot?"

"I have a plan."

"What?" Morgan's tone is skeptical.

"I'm not going to tell you, except that it involves your being very sweet and charming to whoever I happen to start talking to. Think you can handle that?"

Morgan attempts a dimpled simper.

"Yuck. Better not smile. Just stick to your usual glowering self. Please."

They set down their knapsacks a couple of yards away from the English couple. The woman smiles at them.

She isn't young, but she looks funky. She has dyed black hair and a knob-nosed face like a wooden doll's. She is wearing a red-and-white crocheted wool skirt that looks as if she might have made it herself. Her companion is tall and pudgy, with a shock of gingery hair and a dirty pink jacket. They have a brocade quilt spread out as a picnic blanket, and a two-liter carton of rosé. On the picnic blanket is laid out an array of pâtés, pizzas, quiches in French butcher paper. They are clearly at the end of their holiday, as Rat's already confirmed from the arsenal of wine stocked in the back of their station wagon.

Rat and Morgan pitch their tent, unpack their knapsacks.

The woman looks over, and Rat smiles at her.

"Bon appétit," she says.

"Bon appétit," the woman replies, smiling back.

"I like your picnic rug," says Rat.

"Thanks," says the woman. "It's our—what do you call it, the thing you put on the bed?"

"Bedspread. Have you had a nice time in France?" Rat inquires, politely.

"No," says the man in the pink jacket. "In fact, we've had an absolutely godawful time in France."

They all laugh loudly. The man has a gulping laugh, as if laughter were a form of oxygen he was short of.

"That's not so strange," Rat replies. "France is an absolutely godawful country." In fact, she's never once in her life considered "France" as if it were an entity separable from herself that she could compare to other countries, as you compare teachers or other people's parents.

"It is fairly godawful," the man agrees. "Except compared to every other country in the world. Anyway, it wasn't France's fault. We came to buy a house, but it fell through."

The woman catches Morgan gazing hungrily at the spread of pizzas and quiches and *pâtés en croûte*. "Would you like one?" she gestures at the selection. "We bought loads too much."

"No, thank you," says Rat, on Morgan's behalf. "We have our own food. It just doesn't look quite as good as yours."

"Go on, have some," urges the woman, and this time Rat allows Morgan to accept a slice of pizza.

"One," Rat says, sternly. She herself takes some quiche. They try not to gobble their food too fast, but still Rat catches the couple exchanging a glance.

"You want to buy a house?" Rat repeats, her mouth full. "In France?"

"Well, we're fed up with England."

"What do you do?"

"We're French teachers," says the man. "Can't you tell?"

They all laugh again.

"In fact, I teach French, and Jane teaches special ed. My name's Charlie, by the way."

Rat and Morgan introduce themselves.

"I'd offer you some wine, but I don't suppose you're old enough to drink."

"On the contrary," Morgan pipes up. "I adore a good red."

This time, they all laugh.

"So you want to live in France?" says Rat.

"We'd heard that for the price of a bedsit in Exeter, you can buy a sheep farm in the Pyrénées."

"You're going to raise sheep?" Rat looks at Charlie's pink jacket, Jane's crocheted miniskirt. Funny how everybody she meets these days seems to be bent on raising sheep.

"Well, no, I thought we could get rid of the sheep and teach English. But it wasn't any good."

"Why not?"

"Because the man was insane. Turned out, he didn't want to sell at all. Or rather, he wanted the money, but he didn't want to move out of the house. He said, Where am I going to live?"

"And you didn't want to live with him?" asks Rat, politely.

"No, because he was completely mad."

"Well, a different sort of mad from us," says Jane, laughing.

"So you're going back to Exeter?"

Charlie heaves a theatrically deep sigh. "Yes, I suppose. Till we find the next dream house somewhere cheap and remote. Someone told us to try the Spanish side of the border, but I don't speak Spanish. Or Basque, or whatever they speak there, and the thought of learning a new language at my age is rather dispiriting. What's your story?"

Rat is feeling emboldened. She has a hope that this couple's semisloshed jokiness might make it possible for more serious business to slip through almost unnoticed. She has been trying inconspicuously to check out the inside of their station wagon, see where there's enough space.

"We're trying to get to England."

"How do you mean, trying? Are you Serbian war criminals or Liberian child-soldiers, or do you just not have enough money for the ferry?"

"No, we're French. And we've got the money, but it turns out we don't have the right papers. The woman at the ferry says my brother's too young to be traveling without an adult, unless we have a special paper saying it's all right. I mean, we have passports, but we don't have this paper that's got to be signed by our parents and stamped by the prefect."

"How very unreasonable. Aren't bureaucracies mad?"

"They are."

"So you're going to have to get your parents to—to—"

She looks him over. "I can't. It's a signed paper."

"And?"

"My parents—well, my parents aren't exactly paper sort of people. They can't read, can't write. Didn't even want us kids going to school. Well, just me, because that way I can fill out the benefit forms for them."

"Are you having me on?"

Jane has been sneaking a glance at Rat's bare feet. "You wouldn't happen to be Roma, would you?" she asks, very tentatively, as if she were afraid of offending them.

"What's that?"

"Gypsies," translates Charlie.

"Of course we're Gypsies," Rat replies. "What did you think we were?"

Jane beams. "I thought you might be, but I didn't want to . . . I've had a number of Traveler students in my courses—English Roma. They are always very surprising and very . . . rewarding."

"Downright pains in the ass is what she means," Charlie says.

"Is your family nomadic?" Jane asks Rat.

"What's nomadic mean?"

"Always traveling."

"Nah—well, part-time. We live in Perpignan. We spend the winters in Perpignan, and then come spring, we hit the road."

"Don't Roma usually travel in a big gang?"

Rat's enjoying this. It's like opening up your voice and suddenly remembering you can sing. "We got left behind. My older brother Florian, he's been detained by the police because he'd been a witness to one of the killings. You heard about the anti-Gypsy riots in Perpignan? Well, everybody scattered. Some families went to Montpellier, some went to Paris. Well, us, we were supposed to travel with my brother Florian, but . . . by the time Morgan and I made it to Paris, our cousins said, Hey didn't you know, your dad and your mom and everybody went on to England. You see, there's going to be this humongous Gypsy gathering outside London. We're trying to meet up with the rest of our family. If only we can get across the Channel, we'll be fine."

"Hmmm. So what are you going to do now?"

"I thought maybe you could adopt us for the day," says Rat, cheerfully. "That way—if we were in a car with grown-ups—we'd just slip right through customs unnoticed. Me, I'm fine, I'm fifteen, and we both have valid passports and everything, but Morgan's still too little to get across without a parent's say-so. So him, we could hide under your picnic spread or something. Looks like there's plenty of space in your car. He's little, but he can stay very quiet. And me, if they ask any questions, you can just pretend I'm your niece or something. Me, I'm perfectly legal."

The woman obviously hasn't followed a word, so Charlie translates. His tone is deliberately neutral; Rat can't tell whether he thinks the request is preposterous or worth considering. Then he turns back to Rat and his manner is once more facetious.

"You want us to smuggle you into England in our car? You're asking us to traffic in human bodies?"

"Well, yeah, just until the boat lands and we get out the other side. We were supposed to be traveling with our big brother, but he's still . . . A station wagon like yours, it would be easy to hide Morgan under a blanket, bedspread, whatever."

"What if we got caught? Won't they put us in jail as child-slavers?"

"We won't get caught. Morgan's very good at keeping still. Houdini. I've been watching the other cars go through. They don't search them or ask questions or anything, you just show your tickets and passports and they wave you along. Because otherwise, what with nobody in my family knowing how to read or write, and us all being scattered, there's no way we can get across to our parents. I mean, we can't exactly swim, can we?"

"What are you going to do once you get to Newhaven? You know, it's still quite a long way to London."

"Aw, that doesn't matter. Once we're across, we'll hitch. Or we'll take a bus. We've got money. Florian gave us plenty of money. All we have to do is get across that"—she nods towards the sea—"and we're fine."

"Hmmmm," the man considers. "Well, it's a tempting idea, to be honest—staging our own little act of civil disobedience against border controls, but I'm not convinced. With our roll of luck, we could all end up in the clink."

"We've got EU passports," repeats Rat, desperately. "We're French."

"Let Jane and me talk it over between ourselves, all right?" He looks at her quizzically. "You're not wanted by the law, are you?"

"No."

"Promise?"

"I promise."

"We're not going to get arrested for assisting fugitives, are we? Juvenile narco-terrorists?"

"No. It's just some stupid rule that kids can't cross borders by themselves, that's all. I'm fine, I'm fifteen. Ten months later, and I'll be able to take him myself. We haven't done anything wrong, I promise."

"Mind if I just take a look at your passports?"

He leafs through them. "Celia Bonnet, eh? My God, is it possible that anybody could be born as late as 1990 and already be sentient? You have different last names."

"Yeah, Morgan's got our dad's name, I've got our mom's."

"Is Perpignan nice? Any cheap farms to be had?"

She smiles. "If you get us into England, I'm sure somebody we know could find you something. Us Gypsies have plots of land all over the place, even up in the mountains."

"Is that so? Well, why don't you and your young friend go off and sit under that tree while Jane and I talk it over? I'll give you a wave when we've made up our minds. No, I tell you what. If we decide yes, I'll give you thumbs-up. If it's no, thumbs-down. And no means no, no begging or pleading, you just go away and you're not to bother us again, because I hate being made to feel guilty. Is that understood? Because what you're asking us to do could get us all in a great deal of trouble."

"It won't get you in any trouble. I was watching for hours. They just waved through every single car really fast. But yes, it's a deal."

Rat takes Morgan off, and they sit and wait while the couple talk it over. Rat tries not to look back at them. She is tired of this sickening suspense, this holding her breath while strangers decide her fate. Not much difference between Charlie and Jane and the lady with brown fingernails. Everybody just wants to obey rules they know are inhuman.

Rat's considering what they should do next if this way doesn't work. Try another crossing? Stow aboard a Eurostar? They have what's left of Florian's 150 euros; it's nerve and stamina she's running short of.

And if they really can't leave France?

Encouraging as her father's e-mail was, she can't quite see herself on the strength of it ringing him up to say, Glad you're happy to meet me; how about coming over to France to get me and my brother and bringing us back to London with you?

"Do you think they'll take us?" asks Morgan.

"I think they're both pretty soused. If they say yes, I hope they don't think better of it in the morning."

"Why did you have to say we were Gypsies?"

"Didn't you see the look on her face when she asked us if we were Gypsies—all hopeful and excited? She wanted us to be. They're arty types. Arty types think Gypsies are exotic."

"Do you think they'll say yes?"

"I'm pretty sure."

"What makes you so sure?"

"They're bored," she says. "It's an adventure, and it makes a good story. They came to France to buy a farm, turns out the crazy man doesn't want to leave the farm, and then they meet these Gypsy children and smuggle them into England, and the Gypsies promise to find them some land. They're looking for adventure. And it makes a good story to tell their friends. That's what I'm hoping, anyway."

"Are there more checkpoints on the other side?"

"Good question. Hope not."

Morgan starts coughing an ominously deep croaky cough. Rat's first shameful reaction is to hope Jane and Charlie don't hear it. Gypsies is one thing, tubercular Gypsies another.

After what seems like a very long time, the man gestures to get their attention. It's thumbs-up. The children come over. Jane and Charlie are both smiling. Even Morgan starts beaming.

"Look, we're on," Charlie says. "But this is the deal. I don't fancy getting caught with a seven-year-old in my duty-free bags—"

Morgan's smile vanishes.

"He's nine," says Rat.

"So sorry, Morgan. A nine-year-old. So this is what we'll do. It's much better to be straightforward. We'll just bung you two in the backseat and try to look as if we're an ordinary family returning from holiday. Just a family who happen to have two British parents and two French children, with three different last names. You said you had enough money, right? I don't even have a clue what the fare is for children."

Rat pulls the wad from her pocket. "I'll give you the money right now. In fact, I'll treat you two to the boat fare."

"Later, my dear." He examines her, mock-suspiciously. "Are you sure you're really Gypsies? I've never heard of Gypsies lavishing money on non-Gypsies, one gets the impression that usually traffic flows the other way."

Rat grins. "Well, if you'd said no, you would have found out fast whether we were Gypsies or not."

Charlie screws up his eyes at her. "You'd have put a well-known Gypsy curse on us?"

"Well, Morgan's pretty good at letting the air out of people's tires."

"Charming. And one more thing," he concludes. "I don't want to sound inhospitable, but when we get to the other side, you're on your own. Our ways part there. I have no wish to meet the rest of your doubtless delightful family or be involved in your affairs ever again. Is that understood?"

Rat nods. She doesn't much want to see them again, either.

The next morning, the cars line up for the noonday ferry, and Charlie spends a long time discussing with the man in the booth what kind of tickets he should buy, and whether they are likely to be coming back to France in the next six months. In the end, he buys a one-way pass.

"Funny," Jane says, sadly. "When we came over, we were so sure it was for good."

Charlie grimaces. "I could strangle that nice Monsieur Vollin. Voleur, more like. Now, Celia," he catches the girl's eye in the rearview mirror.

"Yes, Charlie."

"I would suggest when we reach passport control, you children start squabbling in the back. You know, pull each other's hair, poke each other's eyes out. We must act like a real family, you know."

"Have you got children?" asks Rat, curious.

"I have a daughter, but she's grown. She lives with her mother."

Rat fishes her MP3 out of her knapsack and hands it to Morgan. "Put it on," she says. "And don't give it back to me, no matter what." He looks puzzled, because the battery's dead, but complies.

As they pull up to the immigration booth and Charlie rolls down his window, Rat complains, loudly, "Daddy, Morgan won't give me back my MP3! He's had it all morning!"

She tries to grab it, but Morgan ducks down, hands hugged tight to his ears to keep the buds secure.

"Children, will you please—Quiet, you abominable brats," says Charlie, with almost frightening sincerity. "Jane, do you have the passports?"

The woman takes their four maroon EU passports out of her fake-crocodile handbag, and the official hands them back with barely a glance.

The station wagon moves through, and trundles onto the ramp of the ferry. Rat can hear Morgan beside her letting out his breath. She squeezes his hand.

"That was easy," he says, happily.

"Easy?" says Charlie. "Easy for you, perhaps. I nearly had a heart attack. I've never been so nervous in my life."

"You didn't act it. You two were valiant," says Rat. "You've really saved our lives."

"Never mind that," he replies. "Do you suppose the bar is open yet?"

They have left the car, and are standing in a great throng of passengers waiting to climb the metal stairs to the upper deck.

Rat offers Charlie what's left of Florian's money—120 plus. It's more than the total car fare, but he slips it into his wallet without demurral, and Rat doesn't think it would be diplomatic to ask for change. They are now officially broke, except for a handful of coins.

"Do they have a McDonald's on this boat?" Morgan inquires.

He has a thick cough by now, his forehead is worryingly hot, but nonetheless he is in good spirits.

"Can't remember offhand," says Charlie. "But they've certainly got some serious amusement arcades."

Rat feels as if it's been years that she and Morgan have been subsisting in this antiseptic fluorescent-lit no-man's-land of fast food, computer-game arcades, and soda-pop dispensers. She can't even remember what it feels like to sleep in your own bed or pee in your own bathroom and not behind a bush or in a roadside service station. No wonder Morgan's come down sick.

Never mind. Four-and-a-half-hour crossing and they'll be free. She looks at the back of her hand once more. Don't get your hopes too high, you'll probably hate each other. What kind of father would never have wanted to lay eyes on his own child all these years?

"Let's get out on the deck," she says to Morgan. "We need some air. Good sea air to clear your lungs."

"I'm hungry."

"Tough. We don't have any money left. We're going to look at the sea."

Last time they were on a boat was with Max, Vanessa, Souad, crossing the Strait of Gibraltar. Back when Morgan had a mother, and Vanessa had a decent boyfriend. Back before everything in their world got broken.

BOOK

Three

Do you ever feel as if you're living a life that's not yours?

This is the question that's been pounding through Gillem's head since Celia Bonnet first contacted him.

He drifts downstairs at three, four a.m.—sleep now seems a fad he outgrew years ago—and looks around his own kitchen with the eyes of an intruder. At the refrigerator, whose front is tacked with brightly colored alphabet magnets displaying emergency contact numbers (Kate's mobile, Gillem's mobile, Kate's office, pediatrician, Kate's sister, police, fire, hospital), notices from Artemio's school, drawings of robots and war machines that Artemio made years ago.

He sits down on a stool at the kitchen counter, and wonders, Why do we have those age-yellowed drawings and preschool alphabets tacked to our refrigerator? Why do we sit on high stools, like dunces?

And he knows the answer. Because everybody does. If you have stools in a kitchen around a countertop, then your children will perch on them, chattering to you while you cook, and then you will be a happy family.

Because if you don't have emergency medical numbers and the dates of your child's school play tacked to the refrigerator, then it means you don't care whether or not he chokes to death from a bee sting, or if nobody shows up to his *Peter Pan*, and if you don't mount his drawings in that actually quite derogatory space—how would he, Gillem, feel if his own artwork were affixed to the refrigerator?—then he will think you don't value him.

They do these things to be like everybody else. They do it as more traditional peoples hang amulets of upraised palms and blue glass eyes over the baby's cradle, to avert destruction. In next-generational overcompensation, because in neither his nor Kate's childhood was there ever a mother in the kitchen cooking supper, or a father who knew whether or not you'd learned to read.

They do it in a show of legitimacy. This is how we enshrine our modern trinity: wage-earning Mummy, chores-performing Daddy, high-achieving Child. If you don't do this, it's helter-skelter. The floods will engulf you, and everybody will revert to savagery. You will father strange children off strange women, bastards who grow up and who eventually come to find you in order to—to what? To cut your throat? Or simply to confront you with the howling futility of your life, the utter fraudulence of everything you've made and said you stood for.

Why has she come?

Gillem tries to imagine the home in which his daughter grew up. Alone with a single mother? With grandparents, as the French still sometimes do? Or was she the eldest child in one of your more up-to-date reconstituted families with mother, stepfather and a slew of younger half siblings and steps? And Vanessa Bonnet's refrigerator door? At least she, he can be quite sure, is not so much of a flaming hypocrite as he.

He comes in from his studio for a midday break. It's Friday, when Kate works at home, which actually means talking on the phone to her sisters, picking up Artemio from school, cooking something wonderful for dinner. She's a homemaker, Kate: she only pretends to work. All her real creative energy goes into soups and stews and Gillem sympathizes, because he's just the same, except he cooks on paper, and for nobody's sustenance but his own. At this moment, she and their housekeeper, Mirjana, are talking shop, while the radio blares the hip-hop station Mirjana favors.

"We'd better make up the spare room," says Kate. "She *is* going to be staying with us, isn't she, Gillem?"

"Yes, when is she arriving, your daughter?" inquires Mirjana. Faintly sulky, because the spare room is her room when she sleeps over: her clothes, her music, even a teddy bear from a boyfriend she's since chucked are stowed there, to Kate's annoyance.

"It wasn't very clear. Sometime in the next couple of days?" Gillem forces out the words over the knots in his stomach.

"I put in the spare-room sheets with the last load of washing: they just need an iron," says Mirjana. Terrifying, the efficiency of the bourgeois domestic machine, whose digestive juices have already broken down Gillem's agonizing secret into a question of sheets to be ironed. *Why didn't you tell me, Gillem?* Because I thought it had gone away. Because I'd come to believe it—she— was nothing more than a sum that got automatically debited from my bank account each month.

Kate is busy making a shopping list: "Loo paper, dishwasher liquid, cereal, milk, yogurt, juice. Balsamic vinegar. Oh yes, and tea. Anything I've forgotten, Mirjana?"

She is still unable to look Gillem in the eye, although he can see she is trying to get over it. He wonders if she has stopped loving him. I don't know you anymore, is what she'd said. She'd thought he was someone upright. Not an unfeeling coward, a sneak.

"Cif. *Lemon* Cif. None of your generic brands," pronounces Mirjana, with a mock-stern glare at Kate.

"Mirjana, you are such a snob," says Kate fondly. And, glancing at the kitchen clock, "Goodness, I'm late." In answer to Gillem's inquiring glance, "I'm having lunch with Constance."

"If you get a chance this weekend, you might get Artie a new pair of trainers," Mirjana puts in. "The whole front of the shoe is coming off . . ."

"Already?" groans Kate. "Those Nikes bloody well cost a fortune. Forty-eight quid. I only bought them a month ago."

Gillem remembers first going to bed with Kate—remembers her ripe woman's body, already heavy in its curves, the deep animal cries that were ripped from deep inside her. He had felt by contrast timid and constrained in his approach to her, as if he were trying to play lawn tennis with a lioness. And hoped with a kind of dread that she would free him.

Am I the one who's done this to us, Kate? Am I the one who's retooled you into this bustling, bargain-hunting mum? Or are you, too, seeking refuge in the banal, using bathroom bleach and new trainers as amulets to fend off the demons of doubt?

He comes in from his studio late that same afternoon, when Artemio is home from school, sitting on a high stool, reading *Beano*, while Kate makes shepherd's pie for his tea. Peeled potatoes boiling. The mince from Tuesday's leg of lamb sizzling in the pan.

"Are those white specks onions, Mumma?"

Kate rolls her eyes at her son. "No, my darling, they are *great big* globules of fat!"

"Mumma, you are so revolting. You did remember to order the *Pink Panther* collection, didn't you?"

And Kate says, triumphantly, yes, she did, because she knows that had she forgot, Artemio, who's a volatile child and under a great deal of pressure at school, might well fling himself on the floor, wailing that nobody cared what he wanted or needed. And meanwhile all Gillem can see is the back of Artemio's neck, a slender white knotted rope that seems far too reedy to bear the weight of his disproportionately big head. What were we thinking of, bringing such a preposterously frail and needy creature into the world?

Some impermissible inner self of Gillem's remembers a drawing by Géricault of a man having his head chopped off. Imagining Artemio's white neck upon a guillotine, the blood spurting, the inner tubes of vocal cords, esophagus cross-sectioned. Imagines the head dropping. Thinks, This isn't my life. I meant to be lighter on the earth, not to leave such a trail.

"You should have had it sent by overnight delivery," Artemio is grumbling. "It's going to take *weeks* by ordinary post."

You have an older sister, Artemio. You have never heard of her and she has never heard of you, you don't even speak the same language, but she is coming towards us, your paths are about to converge, and what will be left of us after this convergence?

"Artemio," he says. "I've got to go down to the art-supply shop. Would you like to come?"

"Where?"

"Kensington High Street."

"All right," Artemio shrugs.

Kate, whose cherry-red mouth has quite unconsciously pursed as soon as Gillem mentioned slipping off on some private errand when his son's only just arrived home from school, now looks almost stricken when she guesses what he's up to.

"Have a good time, boys," she says. "Don't be too long."

On their way home, Gillem takes Artemio for hot chocolate at one of those Italian-style chain cafés next to the tube station. They sit down at high stools in the window—stools again!—looking out at people hurrying home from work. June, but a raw gray day that could easily pass for late autumn. Artemio is chattering about a Blake Edwards film he has just seen for the twentieth time, in which Peter Sellers, playing a comically clumsy and obtuse Indian actor, is accidentally invited to a Hollywood mogul's party.

"Darling," Gillem interjects gently, taking his son by the hand.

But Artemio continues, undeterred. "So then he starts talking to the parrot, because none of these, like, celebrities want to talk to him," he pursues, "and he's like, Pretty Polly, Pretty Polly, and the parrot has this food called birdie num num, so Peter Sellers is, like, going around to all the guests, saying—" Here Artemio tries to assume an Indian accent, mid hysterical giggles, " 'Nice parrot eat birdie num num!' and the Hollywood producer's, like—"

Gillem looks at his watch. "My darling, hold on a moment," he persists. "I need to talk to you."

Artemio halts, annoyed.

"There's a girl who's coming to stay with us from France," Gillem says. "A big girl—sort of, well, Tarquin's age. She's your half sister."

Artemio's glance swings up at his father, panicked, then veers away, unreadable. "My *what?* What's a half sister? Which half?" he inquires, facetiously.

"You know, like Rufus and Camilla. They have the same father, but not the same mother. I had a child before I married Mumma."

"You—were—married—to—someone—else?" Artemio screws up his face in comic disbelief—a gesture he's copied from somewhere—perhaps an actor in a television series, or another child at school.

"We weren't married. It was a . . . it was a sort of summer romance. Years before I'd ever met your mother. In France. Where Granny used to rent a house. This woman and I went out together. And she had a baby." He's not quite sure how much Artemio knows about sex. "The girl grew up with her mother. She's fifteen now. I've never met her. Her name is Celia. And she's coming to see us here in London."

"What for?"

"Because she'd like to meet us all. And I'd like to meet her. I've invited her."

Artemio is momentarily silent. "She's French?"

"Yes."

"So what's she to you?"

Gillem hesitates. Even saying it seems like a betrayal. "She's my daughter."

"Your half daughter?"

"No, my daughter."

"And you've never met her before?" Artemio considers a moment, then screws up his face again in this expression that Gillem, in the midst of his own very real distress, finds disproportionately irritating. "Do you think *I've* got children I've never met?"

Gillem laughs.

Artemio looks very serious. "Daddy?"

"Yes, my darling?"

"I don't much like my flapjack. It has, like, cherries or something really random in it. Can I get something else instead? That brownie thingy with Smarties?"

"No, my darling. It's late. It's almost six. Mumma has a shepherd's pie waiting for you at home." He makes another stab at it. "Celia—your half sister—she's coming to London, and I imagine she'll be staying with us."

"Where's she going to sleep?" Good God, just like Kate. This primal sin, the spurned child coming to claim her rightful mite, is once again getting reduced to a question of housekeeping.

"In the spare room."

"Where Mirjana sleeps when you and Mum are out late?"

"Exactly."

"Daddy?"

"Yes, my love."

"Can't I please, please have a brownie? I promise I'll eat my tea."

"All right, my darling. If you promise to eat your tea."

"Daddy?"

"Yes, my darling?"

"Where was I? Did I tell you about dinner yet? So then they all sit down to dinner, except Peter Sellers has this chair that's much too short for him, and every time . . ."

"Hello?" The man's voice is cautious, as if he's not used to answering the phone.

Before Rat can speak, the operator breaks in, asking him, presumably, if he will accept a reverse-charge call from Celia.

A moment's terrifying silence. Then, "Yes, yes I will," says the man's voice. Him. Gillem. Her father.

The operator says something else.

Then, "Celia?" He pronounces the name English-fashion. SEEL-ya. He's talking to her. He's saying her name.

"*Oui, bonjour.*" Her voice comes out croaky.

"*Vous êtes où, maintenant?*" His, by contrast, is pleasant, low, with a strong British accent. An old-fashioned accent, like when the Queen of England came to France and spoke on the radio. Rat's not used to being called "vous."

"I'm in Newhaven."

"Newhaven? In Sussex? Can you speak up? I can't hear you very well."

"Yes."

"Are you coming to London?"

"Yes," she says, trying to bring out the words from a throat that's closed tight with nerves. Coughs to clear it, and chokes on her cough. "Maybe this evening," she ventures. "It depends how quickly I get a ride. Is it far?"

Pause. "You have friends who are going to drive you?"

"No, I'm hitchhiking." She needs to tell him now that's she's not alone. She stammers a bit, then dives in. "I'm traveling with my little brother."

There's an unnerving silence, as if he might have hung up on her. Then the voice says, "I don't think it's a very good idea to hitchhike. Why don't you take a train? I'll come meet you at the station. Or do you not have money for train fare?"

"We don't have any more money. But hitching is fine; I always hitchhike."

"Do you have a place to stay in London?"

She hesitates. "No, not yet, but I'm sure we'll . . ."

"I can't hear you very well—the connection's not very good. Would you like to stay with us?"

"Yes. Thank you."

"Look. What shall we do about getting you here?" the voice ponders. "Hold on a moment." There's a clatter of the telephone receiver and of departing footsteps and voices in English. A moment later, the voice is back.

"I tell you what to do. Find a taxi driver who will drive you to London—if you have any problem, call me up again and let me talk to the driver. You can come straight here, and I'll pay at this end."

"That would cost a fortune!"

"Don't worry, it's simpler. Have you got our address?"

"No."

"Have you got something to write with?"

"Yes."

"Do you know London at all? We live in West London."

Hawkridge Road is a street of rather grim brick-fronted Edwardian houses, in a neighborhood wedged between a highway overpass and the train tracks.

Number 39 is the house at the corner. It has ugly bars over the windows and a big medallion advertising its security system.

The door is opened by a woman.

"Hel-lo," the woman says, in a loud, ringing voice. "You must be Celia. I'm Kate, Gillem's wife."

Rat blinks. In all her years' speculations about her father, it has never occurred to her that he might be married. She has taken too literally Vanessa's description of Gillem as a hermit. She has pictured her and Morgan sleeping on the floor of an artist's studio, with him on a single bed at the other end. Even his reiteration over the telephone of "we"s and "our"s had not prepared her. She had assumed, with solemn satisfaction, that he meant him and Celia Kidd.

Isn't that what she's so long dreamed of, being ensconced with her father and her grandmother in the midnight blue sitting room? Imagined, in this afternoon's variant, as the minicab roared up the highway, her and Morgan cuddled on the sofa with Celia Kidd, making the grand old lady laugh, making her huge eyes pop, with stories of their misadventures—the dynamite factory where lost boys and lost girls lived off garbage and plotted their own parallel economy, Florian and his intercepted dealer (this, after all, is a granny with a wicked tolerance for drugs), the English schoolteachers to whom they pretended to be Gypsies, who were scared Rat and Morgan's Gypsy clan would descend on their Exeter bedsit. All those harrowing scrapes and tender friendships transmuted into a fireside story, a story that would show Celia Kidd that Rat was plucky and resourceful, just like her. That would make Gillem realize, You are one of us. We were wrong to exclude you. Now you are ours and we will never let you go.

She has been so busy trying to decide what to tell Gillem about why she and Morgan have suddenly appeared on his doorstep— what cocktail of truth and evasion and pure wishful thinking to toast him with—that she's utterly forgotten that he might have a story of his own.

There is no room for a wife in her conception of Gillem. There is barely room for Rat herself. If there is a wife, there may be children, and if Gillem has children—real planned wanted children, not just accidents—then Rat will have no reason to exist, nothing to offer this man in exchange for her huge frightening need.

The woman facing Rat looks indisputably wifely, even motherly. She has red cheeks and a cherry-red mouth and masses of curly brown hair, kept back, rather ineffectually, by a tortoiseshell clasp. She is plump, with an exaggeratedly curvy bosom and hips and, as much as Rat can see, bottom, too. She is wearing a flowery skirt and a lacy top. Her enormous round brown eyes, which have a lot of white around them, give her an air of astonishment.

She doesn't ask the children in; she just stands there, goggling.

Rat doesn't blame her. She and Morgan are both very bedraggled. Rat feels about as ugly and embarrassing as she ever has in her life. She had another go at getting them both washed in the bathroom of the ferry terminal in Newhaven, but it wasn't a great success. There wasn't enough water to rinse the soap from her hair, and she feels sticky all over.

There was a set of cleanish clothes she'd been saving for this meeting—cutoff army fatigues and an antinuclear T-shirt inherited from Pauline, shorts and a Pokémon T-shirt for Morgan—but their knapsacks have been full of dirty clothes so long that their clean clothes smell equally rank. And she hasn't shaved her legs in so long that they look downright wolfish.

To make matters worse, Rat's period's come on when she wasn't expecting it, and since she didn't have any English change for the Tampax machine, she's had to make do with stuffing her underpants full of stiff paper towels.

Nonetheless, Rat does as you do in her part of the world, she makes to kiss the woman on both cheeks. The woman looks startled, then laughs, as if she's never been kissed before, and then she hugs Rat to her big bosom, and laughs again.

"*Est-ce que tu as payé le taxi?* No?" She disappears down the path and is back in a moment. "Let me see you," she says.

She puts her hand on the girl's shoulders.

"My God," she says. "*Tu es très, très grande.* What are you, five eleven, six feet?"

Rat feels as if the woman is pushing her down, trying to make her smaller. "I dunno."

And then the woman spots Morgan. "Hello there, who are you?" Now her voice is bright and cheery, the same lilt with which she greeted Rat.

"His name is Morgan."

"Morgan?" repeats the woman. She laughs. "That's a very odd name for a French boy."

"Not really. It's pretty popular. There are a couple of other Morgans in your school, aren't there, Mo?"

Morgan nods noncommittally.

"Well, pleased to meet you, Morgan, *je suis Kate, la femme de Gillem.* And Morgan is—how old? *Quel age as tu, Morgan?*"

"Nine."

"Shouldn't he be in school? *Ecole? Tu ne vas pas à l'école?*"

"He's on holiday."

"So your sister's taking you on holiday? Aren't you a lucky boy. Come in. You two must be exhausted. Dinner won't be a moment; we'll eat as soon as Gillem . . ."

Rat follows Kate inside.

They have come into a large living room. The walls are painted a saffron yellow. There is an enormous canvas on one wall, clotted with gashes and splotches of violent blacks, dark reds, purple. At the far end of the room is a red lacquer table, set for dinner, and beyond it, French doors leading out into what looks like a garden.

A man comes through the garden door into the room. He's talking on a cell phone, as he walks. Rat can see that he's tall and gaunt, and that he's wearing baggy corduroys that hang off his scarecrow body. He is wearing a button-down shirt, but the collar is ragged. His long narrow feet are bare. He looks almost as disheveled as she and Morgan do. Rat can't make out his face yet, because he's against the light, and she hopes he can't see hers, because she's fighting back tears, she's not sure why, probably just nerves or fatigue, because it's been such a bitch to get them here.

Rat wipes her eyes with one hand. With the other, she's holding on to Morgan's hand, even though they never hold hands anymore, especially not in public, she's squeezing his hand so hard it must hurt, but he doesn't complain or try to wriggle free, and for that she's grateful. After all, it's because of Morgan that they're here.

The man's making good-bye noises to whomever he's talking to. He is looking at Rat as he speaks, in a sidelong sort of way. Then he puts the phone back in his pocket, and ambles across the room to meet her.

"Sorry," he says in French.

He doesn't kiss her or shake her hand. This time Rat knows enough not to make the first move.

He has a large head. He has freckly skin with a faint flush to it, narrow green eyes, a wide thin mouth. There are a thousand tiny wrinkles around his eyes that suggest that sometime he must smile, but he isn't smiling now.

Somehow she'd thought he would still be a boy her age, all beautiful, the curly black-haired boy on the drawing-room floor. She's come too late.

He's a middle-aged man. He's the same age as Vanessa, but he looks older, as if he's lived through wars and sickness. His hair is gray and close-cropped. There are broken vessels around his nose, pouches under his eyes. He isn't even an especially handsome man.

Then Rat looks down at his bare feet. They are horned and calloused, the way feet get if you rarely wear shoes. The toenails on one foot are blue. It's an unappetizing sight, and yet it's the first thing that arouses a sense of kinship in her.

He, too, has been looking her over obliquely, and she hopes he can't see that she's trembling so hard she can hardly stand.

"How was the taxi ride?"

"Fine, thanks. Thanks a lot. It was quicker than hitching."

"I didn't think anybody dared hitch nowadays, especially not young girls."

They look at each other in silence.

"What did you do to your foot?" she ventures, finally.

He looks down, as if trying to remember. "I seem to recall it was a packing case that savaged it. I was trying to clean up my studio."

"The place is a tip," adds his wife.

"*Un bordel,*" translates the man. Rat and Morgan exchange glances at this faintly racy word.

Gillem looks at Morgan, as if for the first time. "Hel-lo," he says, with the same upward lilt as his wife. "Who's this?"

"This is my brother, Morgan."

He pats Morgan on the shoulder. "*Salut,* Morgan."

At the end of dinner, a boy in striped flannel pajamas, squinting against the light, appears on the stairs. He's clutching a large plush pig. He is rail-thin, high-shouldered, with his mother's cherubic red lips and curly brown hair. He looks very young.

"Artemio," his mother says, in exaggerated reproach. "What are you doing out of bed? Did you have a bad dream?"

"I can't get to sleep," the boy complains, although he's clearly been asleep.

"But darling, you must. It's a school night. It's almost eleven."

He hovers, staring at the newcomers. Then he catches sight of the bottle of medicine on the dining room table that Kate has produced for Morgan.

"Is that for me?"

"No, darling, it's for Morgan. He's ill. Come say hello. This is Celia and this is Morgan. Morgan is nine." She holds out a hand.

Artemio hangs back, still staring at the guests. "I'm ill, too. My throat hurts," he quavers. "I think I've got a temperature. I need some Calpol. Now."

Kate rises.

"Shall I do it?" asks Gillem, also getting to his feet.

"I'll do it." Kate leads her son back upstairs, leaving Gillem for the first time alone with Rat and Morgan.

"Where did you say you were living now?" Gillem asks. They have cleared the table and are loading the dishes into the dishwasher.

"Saint Féliu," says Rat.

"I'm afraid I don't know it. Is it nice?"

Rat's never thought about whether or not it's nice. It's her home.

"It's on the beach," she volunteers, finally.

"That sounds lovely. Do you like to swim, Morgan?"

"No," says Morgan, snuffling.

"He's scared of sharks," Rat explains.

"Quite right, too," says Gillem. "Nasty creatures."

There's an awkward pause. Then, "Are you anywhere near Collioure?"

"A bit farther north."

"Ah. I used to love that coast. One of the most enchanted places in Europe. I suppose it's probably spoiled by now?"

Rat doesn't know what he's talking about.

"Lots of new development? Hotels?"

"No, not too bad."

"My mother used to rent a house outside Collioure, right over the cliffs. It was absolutely stunning."

"I know," says Rat. "The house is still there."

He laughs awkwardly, as if made uneasy by her knowing more about him than he does about her.

"You never went back?" she asks.

"No—I think the man who owned it died. I seem to remember we talked to his heirs about buying it, but they hadn't made up their minds yet what they wanted to do. After that, we used to go to the Atlantic coast of Spain, near San Sebastián. Do you know that part of Spain?"

"No." She wonders if he has children there, too, whom he's never met. She wonders if he's thought about her even once in all these years. Did he know if she were a boy or a girl, did he know Vanessa had named her after his mother? She wonders what he thinks of her now, and why he won't look at her head-on, whether it's because he's angry that she came.

She's a bit angry, herself. In all the years she's fantasized about coming to meet him, it was always in a more triumphal manner, look at how brilliantly your daughter's turned out. Now because of sleazebag Thierry she's shown up like a beggar.

"Oh, it's a magnificent coast—wild. Huge waves. Those Spanish villages have a bit more life to them, too, than French ones. You know, you go into a bar and at midnight, it's still jammed with little children running around. Festive. You ought to go one day, if you haven't been."

Rat ignores this. It's not really for him to tell her where she should go. "So you've never been back to the Pyrénées-Orientales?"

"No. To other parts of France, yes. I go to Paris from time to time. Normandy. Kate has a sister who lives near Caen. But Collioure, never."

She figures it must be her fault, and feels defiantly pleased even to have had this negative effect on his life: spoiling his taste for a place he once loved.

She studies the picture on the wall. At first glance, it looked like meaningless gobbets of rucked-up paint, but now she thinks she can make out shapes in it, scratched in and then smeared over. "Is that one of your pictures?"

He smiles. "I wish it were. It's by a very great British artist whom I worked for when I was young. How are you feeling, Morgan?"

Morgan wipes his nose on a soggy scrap of toilet paper. "Fine, thank you, mister."

Gillem looks at the kitchen clock. "You two must be exhausted. Has Kate shown you where you're sleeping? I hope you don't mind sharing a room?"

"Me and Morgan always sleep in the same room," says Rat, stoutly.

The bedroom is on the ground floor, just beyond the kitchen.

There are signs of someone's part-time presence: a pile of pop music magazines, an arsenal of candy-flavored toners and gels in the adjoining bathroom.

There have been efforts, too, to prepare the room for its current inmates. There are two fresh towels folded on the sofa bed. A bottle of mineral water, with two glasses, on the bedside table. Somebody has made up a child-size mattress on the floor, with a flannel duvet cover depicting teddy bears in space rockets.

There is one window rather high up, with bars across it. The high barred window makes Rat feel like a prisoner, but she knows that Morgan will find it reassuring. She climbs up on the ledge to look out the window. It looks straight into someone else's pantry.

Kate, turning off the downstairs lights, sticks her head round the door to say goodnight. She is looking harried. "Have you got everything you need?" she asks. "Sleep as late as you like tomorrow. I take Artie to school at about half past seven, so you'll have the house to yourselves. Help yourselves to breakfast, lunch, whatever. Gillem's studio is at the end of the garden. I've told him to keep an ear out for you. If you need something, you can knock on his door. I've left my office number on the dining room table. And then Mirjana will be in in the afternoon. Has Gillem explained to you about the burglar alarm? Oh, never mind—I'll explain to you how it works tomorrow. I should be back about six." She lingers in the doorway, looking around the room. "Goodness, it is a bit cramped in here. Are you sure you'll be all right? I left the Calpol on the kitchen counter, along with the thermometer. If Morgan isn't any better tomorrow, I think we ought to take him round to our pediatrician, don't you, Celia?"

Rat and Morgan breathe easier when she leaves. They aren't used to such strenuous hospitality.

Morgan has taken possession of the sofa bed—ever since Thierry, he's gotten a bit fussy about where he sleeps. So Rat winds up on the child's mattress on the floor. This way, if an intruder comes through the door, it's Rat who's on the front line.

Rat reaches a hand up to Morgan's forehead. It's sweaty, which she figures is a good sign. The medicine must be bringing down his fever.

"So that's your brother." Morgan's knitting his brow in an expression of comic puzzlement.

"*Putain*—so it is."

"How old did they say he was, again?"

"Eight?"

"And he still sucks his thumb and goes around with a stuffed toy?"

Rat laughs. She tries to get into her head that this child glimpsed on the stairs is indeed her brother, one of the very few relatives she's ever met, that he is her biological kin and Morgan isn't, but it doesn't make sense to her.

"Why'd you have to tell the man I was scared of sharks?"

"I have no idea. It just kinda slipped out, I was so desperate for something to say."

"You could have said *you* were scared of sharks."

"I'm sorry, Mo."

Rat gets up on her knees, and rubs Morgan's back. Pats him on the bottom. "Time for sleep, okay? Tomorrow we can relax, concentrate on getting you well again. No more border crossings. No more sleeping in the rain. No more pissing in the bushes, burying our shit in a hole. No more eating out of the garbage. We're safe."

They are both silent.

"You know what?" Morgan says, finally.

"What?"

"I kinda liked our life on the road. I'm gonna miss it."

"Me too." She gives his shoulder a last squeeze, before climbing back into her own bed. "Well, you know, we can always try asking Kate, Mind if we go out in the garden? No, we don't want to look at the lovely flowers, we want to take a shit. And by the way, no bacon and eggs, or whatever you English people eat for breakfast, please can we just pick around in your garbage instead, because you see that's what we're used to."

Morgan explodes into little squeals of laughter.

"I'll be, like, 'Watch it, Artemio, better hold on tight to that stuffed pig, else Morgan here's likely to wolf it down, too.'"

Morgan starts rooting around, squealing like a little piglet himself, pretending to be gobbling up Artemio's toys, until he laughs so hard he falls off his bed and onto Rat's mattress on the floor.

Rat grabs him tight and hugs him. "Got you, piggy!" she says.

That first day, they don't get up till two in the afternoon.

Every time Rat awakens, it's so dark outside she thinks it's not yet dawn. Until finally she realizes it's not going to get any lighter.

It's raining. The floor is icy, and her bare legs, emerging from beneath the child-size coverlet, are freezing. Last night she'd tried to block the draft that was coming through the window with a couple of T-shirts, and now they're soaking. She hasn't packed the right clothes for England. She at least has Florian's corduroy jacket, but Morgan has nothing warmer than a light windbreaker. No wonder he's sick.

She climbs into Morgan's bed to get warm, and for a moment it's as if they're back at Mas Cargol, and soon Jean-Luc's going to be driving her to school. Except outside you hear the oily rumble of buses, cars honking, people talking on the street. Amid her homesickness, a curiosity to get a gawk at this great city of London, which during last night's taxi ride seemed not one unified metropolis, but a stream of small towns, each with its own post office, Laundromat, hairdresser.

Rat takes a leisurely shower, basking in the luxuriance of limitless hot water, of a showerhead the size of a satellite dish, whose spray you can adjust from mere fog to bouncing hailstones big enough to make you duck and wince.

"Morgan, you want to try this supercool shower or are you too sick?"

"Too sick," says Morgan, snuffling.

Dressing, Rat remembers one of her going-back-to-sleep dreams, which was a variant on a nightmare she used to have of losing Morgan. In this particular version, she and Morgan were in England, but he was younger, no more than a toddler. They're in a crowded mall and suddenly Morgan's gone. In a horrible flash, Rat realizes he's been nabbed by those same English boys who years ago had murdered a two-year-old they picked up in a shopping mall. And hadn't she seen on the news that those boys'd just been released from prison? She is pushing past shoppers, howling, wailing, knowing that he is dead or about to die, and mid her bottomless grief, the thought, How am I going to tell Souad?

Until now, Rat realizes, what she and Morgan had in common was that they were each the product of a one-night stand. There were plenty of other kids in Saint Féliu being raised by single mothers. But nobody, besides her and Morgan, whose fathers had never even laid eyes on them once. Now Rat has changed this equation, managed to track down and claim hers, thanks to the hazard of Vanessa's having ducked into the bushes with a fancy Englishman, and not a truck driver on the A7. But what are the chances of Morgan's ever finding his dad? None. Unless Pauline's right, and one day soon, everyone's DNA will be on an easily readable chip.

The house appears to be empty. In the sink, breakfast plates, a saucepan gummed in yellowed milk. Rat's first quest is for a washing machine. Opening various doors, she comes upon an entire laundry room.

"Wow—wouldn't Vanessa flip? They got a whole machine just for drying clothes!"

The sum total of her and Morgan's dirty wash adds up to a paltry little bundle, not enough even to make an appetizer for the washing machine's steely maw. She adjusts the setting to Eco, pushes a button, red lights blink, and it starts to roar.

"Are you hungry, Morgan? I'm ravenous. Hey"—catching sight of the kitchen clock—"you know what time it is? It's ten past three! That makes four p.m., French time!"

Rat picks around in the refrigerator and the kitchen cabinets. There's plenty of food, including some leftovers worthy of Florian's granny, but she's trying to avoid anything that looks as if Kate might be intending it for dinner. Eventually settles on half a dozen eggs, a lettuce, olive oil, mustard. No vinegar visible. The only salt, unsettlingly enough, is pink and claims to come from a Jurassic salt pan.

"What's Jurassic? I thought it was some kinda dinosaur. Want to try some dinosaur salt, Mo? Think they've got dinosaur eggs to go with it?"

No bread. After a vigorous hunt, unearths something labelled "Irish soda bread" that's vaguely cakey. It's underbaked, which makes it more filling. She cuts Morgan a thick slice while he's waiting.

"Shall we put on some music?"

She rummages through the McKanes' CD collection, looking in vain for something she's ever heard of.

When Gillem comes in from his studio later that afternoon to check on his guests, he finds the two children seated at a laid table like an old married couple, Bach's *The Art of Fugue* playing in the background.

There's a smell of melted butter, an order, a ceremoniousness to the scene that's touching in this pair of waifs. On the table, an omelette and a green salad. The girl, a ferocious-looking penknife in hand, is hacking off a slice of soda bread. A beggar's banquet.

She is saying something to her brother in her rapid southern street-French, gesticulating with the knife in her hand, and the boy gives a dark rich little chuckle. When he looks at his sister, his face is completely different—not wall-like impassive, but vivid, shining.

The girl now catches sight of Gillem and rises to her feet, wiping the knife clean on her corduroys before folding the blade and slipping it back into her pocket.

She's cleaner than she was last night, black hair slicked back wet. She's not so ghastly white-faced, either, though she still looks wary, feral.

How was it Kate described her looking? "Like an alley-cat version of your mum."

Because what is shocking is how much this child does resemble Gillem's mother—not just in coloring or bone structure, but in her very bearing, too. It's like catching a glimpse of Celia Kidd when she was still an unknown schoolgirl. Before she had been scorched, rendered permanently radioactive by the world's eyes.

"Oh good, you found yourselves something to eat," he says.

"Yeah, I hope you don't mind," she replies. "Would you like some omelette?"

"Thanks—I've just had tea." He bends over, curious. "Why are the eggs green?"

"I found some herbs in a pot. Was that all right?"

Gillem picks up a fork and reaches into the pan to take a bite. "Delicious," he pronounces. "Funny—it doesn't taste like that when I make an omelette. Would you like a glass of wine? Oh, I suppose you're a bit too young to drink, aren't you? What age do people start drinking in France?"

He's trying to picture Celia's mother, but he can't. All he remembers is that she looked like Isabelle Huppert and that she was absolutely minute—so tiny he was scared of crushing her. Otherwise, he can only get at it by subtraction, by seeing on this girl what clearly doesn't come from him—the snaggle teeth, the catlike nose.

"Sit down, sit down. Eat. I just came in to make sure you had everything you needed."

He's disrupted their cozy lunch. Even when they go back to eating, they've gone stiff and silent, and he doesn't know how to put them back at their ease. Kate teases him about his ability to cast a convivial gathering into instant paralysis.

What on earth does he have to say to these two children? Nothing. Because this, finally, is what it comes down to: this girl, because of the way she walks and holds her head, may look deceptively familiar to him. But in fact she is utterly alien. They have no more meaningful connection than if she had drawn his name by lottery. It is only some internal adolescent melodrama, a misbegotten quest for "identity," or perhaps her mother's troublemaking, that can have brought her here.

She's already washing up. "Oh, leave that," he says. "Mirjana will do it. Our daily. She's—" He looks at his watch. "She's gone to pick up Artemio from school."

"You don't look the way I was expecting a French girl to look," Artemio says, accusingly.

It is Day Five of Rat and Morgan's stay.

Artemio has finished his homework, and has come into their room, where Rat's lying on the sofa bed, reading, while Morgan sits on the floor, organizing his football cards.

"Haven't you seen French girls before? I thought you had a French nanny."

"She wasn't a girl; she was a hag."

"*C'est quoi,* hag?"

Artemio mimes something witchy.

"What's he up to?" asks Morgan.

"Dunno. I think he thinks it's Halloween."

Artemio likes to come into their bedroom and hang out. He will install himself on the bed or wander around the room, fiddling with Rat's MP3 or Morgan's Happy Meals mini-skateboard till you're sure they're going to break.

In five days, Rat has already had a chance to get pretty sick of her newfound brother—quite a feat, considering he's only home for about two minutes before it's his bedtime. She hadn't realized what an easy ride she had with Morgan—the kind of kid brother you actually have to beg to come and bother you.

Right now, all Rat wants to do is read her book.

All her initial eagerness to get out and explore London has been succeeded by utter exhaustion. Rat can't remember ever having been so tired. It feels as if all the force required to get her and Morgan away from Mas Cargol and into England has been drained from her, leaving a deep bone-aching weariness she can't seem to shake. No sooner does she get out of bed in the morning than she's ready to crawl right back under the covers. All she feels like doing is reading, eating, sleeping.

In her previous life, Rat never read a book for pleasure. But here, everybody reads, and she, almost by inertia, has followed suit. Her father, Rat's discovered, has a large collection of French books from his student days, the kind of books you see in libraries. She's picked out the thinnest volume in the shelf she could find. It was written by a boy who died when he was twenty. It's called *Le Bal du comte d'Orgel,* and it's about a married woman who falls in love with a young man who's not her husband.

Rat has just reached a particularly engrossing part. She looks up, blinking.

"So what were you expecting me to look like?"

This is the deal: Rat speaks French, Artemio speaks English, and only if she's completely lost, resorts to French. In fact, Artemio's French is fine, thanks to the hag-nanny and summers spent with his cousins in Normandy, but he considers the language fussy and effeminate. At school, he studies Latin, which apparently is more manly. And Morgan he won't talk to at all, having decided, as he's confided to Rat, the boy is "a bit 'dodgy.'"

"Dodgy?"

"You know, *street*."

"Oh, I don't know—more like Fleur Delacour."

"Like who?"

"Haven't you seen the Harry Potter films? You know, the head girl of that French sorcery school."

"Oh yeah, it's just that you say the name a little strange."

"That's what I thought you would look like. Blonde, dazzlingly beautiful."

Rat puts down her book, a surreptitious smile twitching the corners of her mouth. "Am I not beautiful?"

She's succeeded in momentarily discomfiting Artemio. He snorts, but doesn't know what to say.

"And you, Artemio? Are you beautiful?"

"Men aren't supposed to be beautiful."

"I think they are. Morgan is beautiful."

Artemio snorts again.

"What did you say? I don't understand," she persists, slyly.

"Morgan is not beautiful—he looks like a . . . well, I won't say what he looks like because it's not very polite. Anyway, you don't talk about men being beautiful; you talk about their being handsome."

"Maybe you don't know what girls consider handsome. Girls think Morgan is very, very handsome. All the girls in his class are in love with him; they fight over who gets to sit next to him at lunch." She has guessed right: this eight-year-old has a precocious interest in females. Artemio looks put out, and concludes by muttering that he doesn't think any girls he knows—certainly not any English girls—would think Morgan was handsome.

Morgan hasn't even looked up from his cards.

"What's he babbling about?" he asks, finally.

"He says he's better-looking than you."

Morgan casts a look of frank amazement at Artemio. *"T'es pédé, ou quoi?"*

"What did he say?" Artemio demands. "What's *Té pédé?*"

Rat hesitates, not wanting to say Morgan's inquiring about his sexual preferences. "He wants to know if you collect football cards."

"Football cards? You must be joking. Nobody plays with football cards anymore; they're totally naff. Ask him which team he supports. Is he for Paris Saint-Germain? I bet he is."

Rat translates, watching Artemio get ready to sully the honor of whichever team Morgan favors.

Once again, Morgan doesn't bother to look up from sorting his cards. "I don't 'support' a football team," he says. "I run one. I'm captain."

Artemio is momentarily stumped, but soon comes back. "How can you run a football team, when you're here in England? I don't suppose you run an English team, do you?" He laughs, triumphantly.

Rat feels a tiny glint of sympathy for this boy who can't stop making such an idiot of himself. She sighs, stows the book under her pillow, stretches, and goes out into the kitchen, where Kate is slicing bread.

"Can I help you with tea?"

"Tea" is what the British call children's supper. In Kate and Gillem's house, the children eat tea at six and go to bed at seven-thirty, and the adults eat later. Rat is in some amphibious state between adult and child, which means she can choose either the six o'clock sitting or the nine. Normally she would prefer to eat with the grown-ups, but her evenings with Gillem and Kate are getting to be a strain.

They are definitely the most courteous human beings she has ever met. Over dinner—usually consisting of dishes which Kate has discovered Rat to be partial to—they will draw her out, asking her about the kind of music she and her friends listen to, or what films she enjoys; they in turn tell her about English fashions, as gleaned from Kate's nieces and nephews.

Even when the two of them are talking between themselves—Kate wanting to know from Gillem if the plumber's been by, or if he remembered to give Mirjana her grocery money—they insist on speaking French, so Rat won't feel left out. She has never in her life felt more solicitously catered to. In all matters except the essential.

But as for the reason Rat is here, the McKanes are as evasive as minnows. It's not that they don't acknowledge, at least tacitly, that Rat is some kind of kin to them. It's more that nothing that Rat had expected to follow from this kinship—the family anecdotes, the bringing out of photograph albums and old letters, the Oh, you've obviously inherited your great-uncle Hector's taste for raw beef—above all, the being looked in the eye and told, finally, This is where you come from and who you are—has been forthcoming. She might as well be a foreign student come to London on an exchange program.

And so inhibiting does Rat find their reserve that she can no longer even conceive of asking Gillem any of the million things she needs to know. All she can do, in fact, is look at him. Look at him, and try to figure out from his gestures, his face, who he is and what it means.

Gillem, Kate has intimated, is under enormous stress working night and day on a commission. Maybe when he's got it well under way, he will be more relaxed and approachable.

Kate turns around. "I thought I'd give them soldiers—that's soft-boiled eggs and buttered toast. Is that all right?"

"Oh yeah, sounds great. I might add a green salad, if you don't mind. Morgan likes his vegetables." She yawns and stretches again.

"Would you like to eat with the Littlies tonight?" Kate smiles.

"Yeah, maybe."

"What are the boys up to? Are they getting along all right?"

"They're fine. They're playing with Morgan's football cards."

"Oh good, I'm so glad. Artie can be a bit . . . overbearing, sometimes." Kate pauses. "I need to have a word with you."

Rat's heart sinks. Already? Are they going to have to leave so soon? Before she's managed to have one real conversation with her father? Before she's managed even to get news of her grandmother?

Kate pours out two cups of tea. "Milk? Sugar? Do you mind sitting in the kitchen? Gillem hates sitting in here. He thinks it's squalid. I think in his heart he longs for a proper old-fashioned house, with a dining room and drawing room and backstairs servants' quarters, and Artemio safely tucked away in the nursery."

"Oh." Rat doesn't understand what she's talking about. "You wanted to ask me . . ."

"Oh right." Kate looks as if she doesn't much want to, but she launches in. "You know, I don't know anything about your home situation. And I don't like to pry. But you have to admit it's a bit unusual for two children to be hitchhiking around the world by themselves."

"I'm fifteen; I'm not a child."

"I'm not talking emotionally, my darling," says Kate, reaching out to take Rat's hand with unexpected tenderness. "Goodness— for a fifteen-year-old, you are . . . alarmingly grown-up. I'm talking . . . well, legally. Does your mother know where you are?"

"Yes, of course."

"And it's all right with her, you two just taking off?"

"Yes."

"Are you sure? I admit, manners are different everywhere, but most parents, if you're sending your child abroad, you call up, you ask, Is it all right if so-and-so comes to stay from such-and-such a date, you buy a ticket, you put the child on the plane or train or whatever, with a nice sum of money to tide them over in case of emergency, you make sure there's someone meeting them at the other end."

Rat wants to disappear. Not for the first time, Vanessa is being judged as a mother and failing. "We did call. I e-mailed Gillem months ago to ask if it was all right if we came. And he said yes."

Kate smiles. "It's not that we don't want you here—my God, after all these years, it's about time we did get to know each other!—it's just—does your mother really know where you are?"

"She knew we were coming here. She didn't mind." Rat lies, then considers. "We tried first to go to my grandmother in Collioure, but she was in the hospital. I suppose we could go back to my grandmother, I'm sure she's home by now."

But in fact she feels too tired even to think of packing up again and hitting the road. She can't afford this encounter with her father to end in defeat. She thought she was tough, but she's not.

Kate once again takes hold of her hand. "My dear girl, don't look so desperate. You can stay with us as long as you like. Why shouldn't this be your home as well as any other? But I want your mother to know where you and Morgan are. I understand if you've had a quarrel or whatever, and you need to get away. I quite understand. But I don't want her to worry, let alone have the Missing Children Brigade suddenly descend on us. Do you feel able to call her up and tell her you've arrived safely and you're going to stay for a bit? Or would you like me to talk to her?"

Rat, mid her discomfort, appreciates the generosity of the offer. She reflects, then says finally, "I'll let her know we're here, and we're safe. I promise." In her head, she's thinking she'll e-mail Jérôme, ask him to pass on the message. She's not ready yet to talk to Vanessa.

Over the next couple of weeks, the newcomers' life at Hawkridge Road settled into some approximation of routine.

In the mornings, when Artemio was at school and Kate and Gillem were at work, Rat hung out with Mirjana, helping her around the house, while Morgan played on the computer.

Mirjana was thirtyish, but she seemed closer to Rat's age than Kate's. She wore her hair dyed cotton-candy pink and teased into a kind of pagoda buttressed by chopsticks, and she dressed in artfully ripped and sequined jeans cut low to reveal her thong. When she was doing the housework, she liked to blast girly music.

Mirjana came from Yugoslavia, a country that no longer existed. She was a war refugee, but the fact that horrible things had happened to all her friends and relatives during this war that Rat had never heard of, only seemed to make her the more determined to have fun. She was smart: she'd been studying law when the war broke out. In London, she joked, you needed at least a doctorate in civil engineering from your home country to get a job cleaning loos.

Mirjana thought France a far more civilized place than England, and was always trying to get Rat and Morgan to teach her French phrases. What she chiefly wanted to know was fancy ways of telling men to fuck off, an aim which to Rat's mind defeated the purpose of all those jeans cut halfway down her bum.

Mirjana had a boyfriend named Zoran whom she'd met when he was the manager of an after-hours club. Now he was opening his own cybercafé in the East End. Zoran wanted Mirjana to come work for him, but Mirjana was pretty happy working for the McKanes, and didn't know what they would do without her.

Kate and Gillem both worked very hard during the week. But on the weekends or whenever they had a free moment, they made a point of showing Rat and Morgan around London—generous tours that ranged from the changing of the guard at Buckingham Palace to Hamleys, a multistory toy emporium on Regent Street where they treated each child to a present of his own choosing, and afterward bought Rat and Morgan a set of warm clothes and Wellington boots from the Gap next door.

One weekend, when Kate was busy, Gillem took the three children to the Tower of London, which Morgan found so scary they'd had to leave midway and hop in a taxi straight to the ice-cream parlor at Fortnum & Mason, where he was fortified with a Knickerbocker Glory. Rat had pretended to Artemio that it was she who was feeling fainthearted, so he wouldn't tease Morgan for being a sissy.

That night, after Artemio was put to bed, Gillem had apologized to Rat and Morgan for his thoughtlessness. He himself had always regarded the Tower as being an absolutely barbaric hole, he confessed.

"I can't imagine what I was thinking of, dragging you there. It just shows you how debased our culture is, that a place that was basically a Tudor gulag should be touted as a Sunday outing for children. How are you feeling, Morgan? A bit better?"

Morgan said he was fine, and since something more was evidently expected of him, admitted that he thought the Parlour at Fortnum & Mason's was supercool.

"Good boy," said Gillem warmly, squeezing his shoulder. "We'll go back next weekend, shall we?"

Rat didn't understand all the business about Tudor gulags, but she did notice that from then on Gillem treated Morgan with a fellow feeling he'd evidently found it difficult to evince when all he knew about the boy was that he was mad for football.

But apart from this initial tremor, Morgan seemed in fact to be adjusting to London better than Rat. He almost never spoke of Vanessa or of Mas Cargol anymore. It was as if what Thierry did to him had contaminated everything to do with his old life and he was quite happy to start again afresh.

Gillem and Kate's house was not far from a beautiful park, and most afternoons, if it wasn't absolutely pouring, Rat made a habit of taking Morgan there. Morgan grumbled about being torn away from the computer, but he was always glad once they got there.

Their shortcut to Queens Park lay across a housing complex. Often there was a bunch of older kids playing football in a concrete court, and Morgan would stop to watch. Morgan would watch the match, and Rat would watch Morgan watching, relishing the way his entire body seemed to be anticipating and reenacting each play. Morgan seemed to have this innate confidence that every ball game in the world was rightfully his, and he waited patiently for the chance to take his place in this one.

One day, the ball came Morgan's way, he kicked it back, and almost imperceptibly joined in.

Now, every afternoon, Morgan asked if he mightn't go over to the Samuel Bacon Housing Trust to play football. And Rat, when she got bored hanging around the grimy courtyard, nodding and smiling at the West Indian grannies on their way to and from the shops, soon agreed that he might as well make his way there and back on his own. He'd limp home at teatime, dirty, bruised, and glowing. There were a couple of African kids he played with who spoke French; they called him Zidane. The only hitch was that because of the insanely early hour at which he and Artie were required to have their tea, he usually had to leave in the middle of a match.

Couldn't Rat intercede with Kate, point out that it was senseless for him to be home by six, when there were a good two and a half hours of daylight left? He'd much rather cook his own supper, and clean up after himself, too. It wasn't so bad when Kate made tea, but Mirjana cooked like a pig.

Rat raised the subject as diplomatically as she could, only to be forestalled by Kate. She was so relieved Rat had brought it up; she'd been meaning to have a word. She was a bit concerned about Morgan's being in Queens Park by himself, she said. (Rat had been deliberately vague about where exactly it was that Morgan played with his mates.) There were a gang of older boys from the neighboring council estate who hung out in the park, she said. Rat needed to be very careful, because Kate's nephew Tarquin, who lived down the road, had been mugged and had his cell phone stolen by those boys more times than you could count.

Rat didn't know what "council estate" meant; she thought it must mean "prison" or at least "reform school," and when she discovered that what it actually meant was subsidized housing—in fact, the Samuel Bacon Trust itself—she felt as if Kate and Gillem's London were an odd place, and much narrower than any world she herself was accustomed to inhabiting.

"Oh, Morgan'll be fine," she said, reassuringly. "At home, all our friends live on council estates."

Kate made as if to answer sharply, but then she relaxed into laughter. "I suppose I look a total fool giving safety lessons to a couple of children who managed to hitchhike from the South of France to Sussex unscathed. But I'd never forgive myself if anything happened to you on my watch."

Several days later, however, she presented Rat with a pass to the London Underground, a program for free summer events, and an old cell phone of hers. "That way you're a bit freer, and we won't have to worry you're dead in a ditch." She had a way of making her most generous gestures sound scolding.

Now that she had her Underground pass, Rat could take Morgan farther afield. She wanted to learn how the city was put together. She liked wandering along the canal that ran from close to their house to Regent's Park. Even better was the Thames. They'd take the Tube to Embankment and then find one of the secret staircases that led down to the water.

The Thames was wide and bronze-green and swift-moving. At low tide, there was a rocky beach where people walked, picking up shells and odd bits of china and pottery, scavenging with metal detectors, letting their dogs and children loose to play. It cheered Rat to wander along this shore, or to sit and watch the churning curlicues of current. She could dream that if she and Morgan hitched a ride on a barge, eventually they might find themselves back among the marshes and flamingo-haunted lagoons of the Pyrénées-Orientales, with snow-streaked Mount Canigou looming in the distance instead of office towers.

Rat was puzzled by her own homesickness. She had spent much of her life angry or bored, but she'd never before been blue.

Once or twice Kate tried to cheer her up by inviting over friends or relatives who had teenaged children but that made things even worse. Rat tried to stay in her room until the last moment, and excuse herself as soon as was decently possible.

She felt embarrassed by how dull and badly dressed she was compared to these fluent, knowing youngsters—the Parisian kids who spent summers in the Pyrénées-Orientales by comparison seemed like louts—and how little of the dinner conversation she followed. Was she supposed to laugh when they all laughed, even if she didn't understand, or did that make her look even stupider? If she'd grown up among these children, would Gillem like her any better?

Afterwards, she would lie awake, reliving her blunders—how when Tarquin had asked her if she liked Pete Doherty, one of her all-time favorite musicians, she'd replied she didn't know who he was, never having heard his name pronounced in English.

Her ambiguous position—was she officially Gillem's daughter or wasn't she?—which was bad enough when it was just her and the McKanes, became excruciating in front of outsiders.

As for her original purpose in coming to London, that remained elusive. Gillem was unfailingly gentle and courteous, but remote. She felt as if she knew him no better after three weeks in his house than she had the first night. She had no idea whether he was pleased she was there, or indifferent, or desperate to be rid of her.

Rat found herself spending hours on the McKanes' computer, exchanging e-mails with Jérôme and, less frequently, Pauline, who was visiting another squat on her way up to the sheep farm. Once or twice, a message from Vanessa arrived from Jérôme's address. She would open it, quickly skim the first few lines, then press Delete.

"I thought I might see about finding a job," Celia says.

It's Sunday noon, un-Englishly balmy. They are in the garden, Gillem and Celia, setting up the table and chairs for lunch.

Gillem, momentarily defeated by the holder into which the umbrella is supposed to go, sits back on his heels and gazes at his daughter. In the last couple of weeks, it seems to him, she's blossomed into a new self-assurance. But today, for some reason, she's looking rather subdued.

"A job?" he repeats. "Whatever for?"

Gillem, as his wife is fond of pointing out, is a man who's never had a job in his life, unless you count that brief spell of stretching canvases for a famous painter friend of his mother's, when he was twenty-seven.

"I just think it might be a good idea," she persists. "You've both been so kind about giving me 'n' Morgan money, buying us things, but maybe it would be better for me to begin earning my keep. Unless"—she adds hastily—"it seems like time for us to be heading back to France."

Gillem avoids her placatory smile. He finds it appalling, the idea that this child imagines that he and Kate might begrudge her a few weeks' board. Have they really made her feel so unwelcome? It's true that Kate keeps urging him to spend some more time on his own with Celia—if you don't want to take any time off work, just invite her into your studio, show her your pictures, she'd love it, Kate says—but he's honestly believed the girl seemed very happy as she was, reading French novels and giggling with Mirjana and playing football with her little brother.

"Of course not. Don't be absurd. But I can't quite see the point of looking for a job *now*. The first week of August, we'll all be going down to Somerset for the month: there's this lovely house on Exmoor we rent every summer. I was very much hoping you and Morgan would join us. In which case, there wouldn't be much point in starting something now."

"Maybe a summer job," the girl persists. "I've seen signs in café windows advertising . . ."

Gillem frowns. "Well, if it's just a question of pocket money, I suppose we could always see about transferring the child support directly to you. Of course, we'd have to set you up an English bank account, but that shouldn't be a problem. That is, if you're planning to stay a bit, if you've definitively left home. Do you think your mother would be able to get along without that income? You said she had some kind of work, or money coming in?"

"I don't understand," says Celia. "Transfer which money to me?"

"The money I pay your mother every month—it might as well go directly to you, since you're no longer living with her. Although if you're living with us, you might not need so much . . ."

"You pay my mother?" The girl looks shocked.

"Well, child support. It's the law."

"How long have you been—?"

"Oh, I don't know. I'd have to check my files. Since you were about a year old, I suppose?" Since the DNA results came in and the lawyers had finally reached a settlement, is what he doesn't want to say.

"Are you sure Vanessa got the money? Because I never—"

"Oh yes, quite sure."

Celia chews on her lip. "I don't think it's right for you to be giving me money—you're already doing too much for us. I think it would be better if I got a job."

Kate, who has come out into the garden to see how they are getting on, now intervenes. "But, Celia, you can't possibly get a job. Babysitting perhaps, but certainly not a real job. You're not allowed to work until you're sixteen."

"Oh." Celia looks only momentarily daunted. "What if I found something off the books?"

"Well, I think it's extremely unlikely you'd find an employer willing to risk it. If you're at loose ends, you're much better off signing up for a couple weeks of English lessons than—"

"A job would be a good way of learning English," says Celia, stubbornly.

.   .   .

That afternoon—just when Rat had given up hope of ever con-
necting with her father—Gillem asked her if she would like to
come poke around his studio. She said she would.

His studio was one glassed-in room, drafty and chaotic. Yel-
lowing newspapers, caked palettes were strewn across the floor.
Surfaces were crudded in paint thick as pigeon shit. Teacups had
been abandoned in odd corners, their insides clotted in ancient
fungal murk. The walls were plastered in postcards, photographs, newspaper clippings, bills.

On one wall was a blowup from a medieval painting of Hell,
with naked sinners being tortured by devils. By its side, a magazine spread of photographs showing a fat naked man cowering in
front of an attack dog, and naked people stacked in pyramids,
being presided over by soldiers, and again the same attack dogs.
The naked people, like the damned in Hell, were doing their best
to hide their private parts. Rat had never seen humans look quite
so frightened. It looked like pictures from a Nazi concentration
camp, but it couldn't be, because the soldiers were wearing modern camouflage gear and there were women soldiers as well as
men. They were grinning.

"What's that?"

"That's Abu Ghraib."

Rat evidently looked blank.

"You know, the prison where U.S. soldiers were torturing
Iraqis."

"Oh."

"Those are stills from home videos the guards themselves
made. Odd, don't you think, the torturer's desire to record his
crime?"

They both stared at the photographs, until finally Gillem said,
"Oh well, let me show you some of my own work."

He sat her down on a stool with a portfolio of drawings. "These are quite old. I started this series one summer on Exmoor, before Artemio was born."

The first set of drawings were pastels of horsemen and dogs. They seemed deliberately rough and out-of-scale, with the men bigger than the horses, and the dogs the same size as the men, but the colors were flamboyant—dogs rust red, horses aquamarine or marigold yellow—and they were drawn with an energy Rat enjoyed. When Gillem drew a dog or a hare, you could see it was running flat out. There were more intricate sketches of oak trees, too, that showed you he could draw properly when he chose.

His artwork was bolder, less crabbed than anything Rat would have expected him to produce and she felt relieved by how much she liked it.

The next section of drawings was more sinister. The first set were sketches evidently inspired by the medieval painting of Hell—naked men and women cowering, children curled up hiding. As the drawings continued, these figures were now placed in the same lovely lush green English landscape of hedges and oak trees. There were naked men and women running, and children up a tree. These were hunting scenes, Rat realized, but what the merry horsemen, the lolloping dogs were chasing was humans.

"These were all sketches for a painting," Gillem explained.

"Can I see the painting?" Rat asked.

"It's in a warehouse. I don't have room to keep any of my larger work here. I'm not sure the painting worked out very well. It was for a group exhibition I had a few years ago at a friend's gallery in Somerset. It was the height of the campaign against blood sports, and everybody thought it was meant to be anti–fox hunting."

"Was it?"

"No." He paused. "It's more about . . . about the evil humans do to each other. I don't think hunting animals is evil."

"It's funny," she said, looking through the drawings again. "Classical art's all about naked bodies, isn't it? But peaceful nakedness, not frightened."

"You haven't seen late Titian, have you? His *Flaying of Marsyas?*"

"No." She doesn't know who "Titian" is. "So this is . . . older work. What have you been doing more recently?"

"I haven't painted for a while," he said. "In the last few years, I've been working with embroidery."

"Embroidery?"

"Yes. Do you know what I mean by the Bayeux Tapestry?"

Rat must have looked a little foggy.

"It's this eleventh-century tapestry that was done to commemorate the Norman Conquest—you know, when William the Conqueror invaded England," Gillem explained. "It's a marvelous object—I have a book of it I can show you. It's like a room-length embroidered comic strip. There are little panels of the king on his throne conferring with his ministers, and of the ships landing, and of battlefields with archers and horses getting speared. The whole thing is full of an unbelievable energy and charm, and at the same time it's also this piece of propaganda: a justification for an extremely ruthless invasion. I'm using it as the inspiration for this new piece I'm doing for a museum in Holland."

"You're going to do something about the Norman Conquest?" Rat sounded dubious.

"No, I'm making a piece about the invasion of Iraq. It's for an exhibition called East and West. A group exhibition, twenty-five artists from all over the world. My piece is going to be called *Freedom Is Untidy.* I don't know how to say 'untidy' in French. *C'est bordelique, la liberté?* That sounds a bit jollier than the original. I like the idea of using embroidery, this art form that nowadays we think of as being very female and antiquated—elderly maiden aunts by the fireside—to portray war and bloodshed and military might, and using it to make a strong argument *against* war."

"How far have you got?"

"I've plotted out most of the scenes I want."

"May I see?"

"Would you like to?"

He opened up for her another portfolio of drawings.

They were colored ink on white paper, simple, almost childish.

It began with an ink drawing of two airplanes shearing through two burning towers. "I was very struck by medieval mosaics of the Tower of Babel—you know, the original Tower of Babel was in modern-day Iraq," he explained.

Then there was an American council of war, with a caption saying, "Let's start a new Crusade. A war against oil-rich Islam!"

There was a big ship sailing across the sea, full of tiny men and fighter planes, and American and British flags entwined, and in the ocean below, octopus and starfish and seahorses all gaping.

There was a mosque, with a long-bearded preacher on the minaret, fist in the air, and written underneath, "Infidels in our Holy Places!"

"It's a bit cartoonish," Gillem said. "But I'm trying to find a newer, more immediate way of drawing. I can't decide if the words work or not. Perhaps one doesn't need them."

There was a drawing of a palace, with giant soldiers posted on either side. The palace had lots of steps. Coming down the steps were an ant's trail of people. Each of them was carrying an object disproportionately larger than himself—a vase, a statue of a dog-headed man.

There was a picture of more soldiers toppling a statue of a mustachioed general.

There was an entire series of drawings based on the magazine clippings of the naked prisoners being tortured. In Gillem's version, the guard dogs were giant wolves, with bared teeth and

great lolling tongues, and the prisoners looked even more notice-
ably like the damned in Hell.

But the strangest picture of all, Rat's favorite, was of a deep
hole, an underground tunnel, from which a man was being
dragged. The man looked like a crazy hermit, with waist-length
black hair and beard, and wild rolling eyes. That was the Iraqi
dictator Saddam Hussein being captured, Gillem explained.

All these ink drawings, he explained, were to be embroidered
in rich colors on a long cream linen panel.

"There's going to be lots of plants and animals—strange birds
and date palms—floating over the space, too," Gillem said. "You
know the Garden of Eden was in Iraq. That's the part I still have
to do."

"How long is it going to be?"

"About a third of the length of the original, I reckon. Fifty
feet?"

"And you know how to embroider? Won't it take you years to
finish?"

"No, I wish I did. The actual embroidery part I'm getting done
by some women I found in northern India, who do very beautiful
work in the most outlandish colors. I draw it, and they copy."

"It's a nice idea. How did you get the idea?" Rat asked.

Gillem smiled. "From my grandmother—indirectly. My grandmother was an extraordinary needlewoman. I don't know if
you've noticed the sofa cushions in the sitting room? When I was
a boy, of course I had no interest whatsoever. It was only after she
died, and my aunt asked if I would like to have some of her
embroidery—my mother couldn't bear the sight of it—that I
thought, This is so beautiful and graceful and understated, it
really is a kind of testament to an immensely civilized culture.
And then much later, when I started in on the Hell and War
series, I wondered if I couldn't do something along those lines
myself. If instead of using a craft to depict beautiful things that

are part of that civilization one loves—birds and flowers and butterflies—one might depict everything one hates."

Rat went back to examining the drawings Gillem had laid out for her—the naked prisoners with the guard dogs, the mosque and the preacher, the bearded man being dragged from his underground burrow like a fox from its hole.

"It's strange," she said. "What you are picturing is so horrible, but you're treating it in a kind of funny, cartoonish way."

"Does that bother you?"

"A bit."

"I suppose it's the same way you sometimes have a song that has a merry tune but sad or sinister words, and the tune somehow makes it even more disturbing."

The phone rang, and Gillem answered. The person he was talking to seemed to be someone who handled his work. They were talking about how a picture was going to get shipped home from abroad, and about insurance. The person at the other end of the line was evidently quite a joker—all this practical business was interspersed with much laughter and kidding around. Rat had never heard Gillem so animated. He had a good warm laugh he didn't use much in his home life, where he often seemed preoccupied or withdrawn. He had evidently forgotten that Rat was there.

Rat poked around the studio some more, examining the postcards on his wall—reproductions, mostly, of French nineteenth-century paintings of horse races and music halls.

Then she picked up her book, curled up in a corner on the floor, and started reading. When Gillem got off the phone, she said, "You have nice light in here. I can't read very well in our room; it's too dark. The garden's nice, though, when it isn't raining."

"Yes, that spare room is a bit gloomy, isn't it? You're welcome to come here and read, whenever you like."

Thus began a pleasant ritual. In the afternoons, when Morgan was playing football or on the computer, Rat would bring her book out into the garden. If it was too wet to sit outside, she'd come into Gillem's studio. She read, while Gillem worked. Once she overheard him talking on the phone to somebody about his mother. It sounded as if she were ill, but although Rat's English was getting better by the day, she still found it almost impossible to follow English people talking among themselves.

Gillem expressed surprise at how little he minded Rat's being in his studio. He had always needed solitude to work, he explained: even when he was just starting out, he'd found it difficult to share studio space with other artists. But Rat was so still he almost forgot she was there, except that her presence somehow made him less restless than if he were actually alone.

"You're a peaceful girl, aren't you," he said. "Too bad I don't do portraits. You'd make a wonderful sitter."

Rat shrugged.

"I always find it a bit worrying, when someone can manage to keep so still."

"What do you mean?"

"Well, if you think of our biological origins, why does an animal need to stay utterly immobile?" Gillem was smiling, so that she would know he was not too serious.

"So it doesn't get eaten?"

"Exactly."

"Nobody's going to eat me," Rat retorted.

Because she was so quiet, Gillem found himself inclined to talk. And she, in turn, discovered that when the man was absorbed in the purely mechanical aspects of his work, he was much freer, more forthcoming than over a dinner table.

There were two Gillems living at Hawkridge Road—the studio Gillem and the home Gillem—and the former was someone you could almost be friends with.

. . .

"When did you decide to become an artist?" Rat asks Gillem one day. He is retracing pencil drawings in colored ink.

"Astonishingly late. When I was young, I spent most of my time taking drugs in nightclubs—yes, I know it's hard to believe now—and it took me a long time to grow out of that and think of actually *making* something. I'd always loved drawing, but I never thought it was something I might do for a living."

"What happened?"

"It was a friend of my mother's, who was a wonderful painter. The one whose picture's on the wall downstairs. He's dead now. He offered me a job as his assistant. He said, Here you are at loose ends, wasting your money, worrying your friends. Why don't you come work for me, at least you'll be doing something useful. He saved my life, really. Are you ready for a cup of tea?" Gillem goes over to the sink to fill the kettle.

"Nowadays, it's superchic to be a young British artist, you can make loads of money and get incredibly famous, but when I was growing up, it wasn't altogether obvious," he continues, now hunting for the teapot. "There isn't much of a visual tradition in this country—historically, the only halfway decent painters in England were German or Dutch. There isn't one great artist in the entire history of the British Isles until Francis Bacon, and he had the sense to ignore the entire Protestant tradition and look to Spain, instead."

Rat doesn't know where to get a foothold in this cliff of names and judgments. "Why aren't they good painters, the English?"

"Well, I suppose because Protestants are fundamentalists, basically; they're not *really* comfortable with graven images. So being an English artist means—well, starting from scratch. You have no Caravaggio or Tintoretto or El Greco to touch on for luck. You're your own godfather." Gillem balances a teapot and two cups on top of a stool already piled with old newspapers. "I'm out of milk, I'm afraid. You'll have to get some from the kitchen, if you want it."

"So you started working for this painter friend of your mother's, and then you went out on your own . . ."

"Yes. I can't say I've had wild success, but it keeps me out of trouble. And I like the life. Sometimes I think art is just an excuse to be alone all day."

"You like to be alone?" asks Rat.

"I like it *too* much," Gillem admits. "It's my oxygen."

"Because," she says, hesitant to mention this side of him, this thing she knows, "when you were growing up, you weren't alone much, were you? There were always parties and famous people, and photographers taking pictures of you and your mother . . ."

"Yes, that's the worst kind of alone," Gillem interrupts, with unexpected vigor. "Goldfish bowl. Always being conscious of how you look to other people, till you're left with nothing real inside. Deadly for an artist—or for someone who hopes to be one, later on."

He halts abruptly, midthought. Rat is about to follow with another question, when he goes on. "It was certainly very hard on my mother, that fame. Even if she loved it, too. Because oddly enough, she was actually quite a private person. I think she found it a terrible strain, feeling she had to perform, be this strange beautiful object everybody was looking at. Even worse as she got older and people weren't looking anymore."

Rat waits until she's sure he's not going to say anything more, and then she speaks. "What was she like, your mother?" she asks, still more hesitant, not wanting to scare him away, now that they've finally broached the subject she's been waiting for all these weeks.

"Unusual," says Gillem.

They both laugh.

"Wonderfully amoral. If she wanted to do something, she just did it.

"She took me everywhere with her, which I suppose parents didn't do much in those days. We spent some wonderful holidays together, in these lost places. Northern Spain. The Mistra peninsula in Greece, where they have the most amazing Byzantine frescoes. There was one year, when I'd got kicked out of school, when we spent the entire winter up in Scotland, in a house some friends had lent us. She loved the country—the mountains, the sea, the moors. That was something strong she gave me. I'd wanted to be able to give that to Artemio," he says, slowly. "The freedom of living in a wild place, where even a child can walk out the door and go for miles, with nothing around you but earth and sky."

"I miss that, too," Rat confesses. "London can feel kind of like living in a cage, if you're used to being outdoors all your life. Back home, there's this place near Collioure where I used to camp out with my friends—a kind of wildlife preserve, on the beach. Me 'n' Morgan lived there for a while this spring, before we came to you. It's my favorite place in the world. Sometimes I think I'd rather be sleeping there, in the wind and rain, than here in a cozy bed."

She stops, struck by the rudeness of what she's just said, but her father's smiling at her. When he smiles, he smiles with his whole face, his eyes, even his hands seem to smile. A smile that's sweet and sad at the same time. "What's happened to that coastline? It's not too spoiled? And you said you knew the house my mother and I used to rent?"

"Yes. It's beautiful. But not kept up. I don't think anybody lives there: the shutters are closed even in the summer."

"Maybe we should all go live there." They both laugh. "It used to belong to a man called Giraud. It must be a bit bleak and windswept in the winter."

"Yes, but nice storms."

"The British countryside is lovely, too. I think you'll like it up on Exmoor. In my ideal life, I'd live there year-round."

"Why can't you?"

"Oh, really because of Artemio and school. He has the misfortune, poor boy, of having got into one of the top schools in London, and now that he's in, we're stuck. Britain still has this absurdly unfair system, you know, where the school you go to, aged seven, determines whether you're going to be a banker or a bricklayer. Or at least that's what they con middle-class parents into thinking. It's a total fraud. Look at you, you went to state schools, and you're not an absolute savage, are you?"

"Yes, I am," Rat interjects. "An absolute savage."

"Quite. We could use another savage like you in the family. Perhaps we should all move to Collioure, put Artemio in a French village school for a couple of years. I'm sure it would be much healthier for him, being with children whose fathers were fishermen and not Russian mafia bosses."

Rat doesn't want to think about this idea, because it sounds so nice, but she knows it's just a fantasy, like Jérôme's saying he's going to quit lycée and go tend his aunt's goats in Corsica.

"I think you are being too romantic about the French countryside," she says. "My high school, it's in a village, but there are metal detectors, there are drug raids. The kids who graduate, they aren't going to be fishermen, because there aren't any more fish. They're going to be on welfare, like their parents."

"Well, that's the reality, isn't it? You've got to meet it someday," says Gillem, a bit vaguely. Then, with sudden energy, "Look, it's odd, but I find it hard to call you 'Celia.' It's odd, but—it's so much my mother's name. You don't have another name, a middle name or a nickname or something, do you?"

"Vanessa calls me Rat."

"Rat? Dreadful! That's even worse than Celia. I might as well call you Cockroach. Why Rat?"

"When I was a baby, her pet name for me was 'little mouse.' Then one day, I got cross and said, 'I'm not your little mouse; I'm a *big big* mouse.' And Vanessa said, 'A big mouse is a rat.' So I said, 'Okay then, I'm a rat.' I don't like Celia, either."

"Rat has a little more—I don't know, bite?—to it," he says, smiling.

"I'd like to meet your mother one day. I didn't even know for sure she was still alive."

Gillem's smile vanishes. "She's not, really. And I don't think it's fair to let people meet her, in this condition. Although maybe not so ghastly as if you knew her before."

"What's wrong?"

"Didn't you know? She has Alzheimer's."

"Oh." Rat feels all the courage ebb out of her, leaving a terrible bleakness. "I . . . just thought she was sick or something. Isn't she kind of young for Alzheimer's?"

"She's sixty-three."

"Is it bad? I mean, is it full blown."

"Fairly," says Gillem.

Rat ponders. She's missed her chance, she realizes. All that saving up for the day her granny would take her shopping and teach her how to eat with chopsticks, and how to fix her hair, and tell her stories about rock stars—it will never happen. She's come too late. That merry mocking woman in the poncho made of white feathers is as long gone as the racehorses and ballet dancers on Gillem's wall.

"I'm sorry," she says, finally.

Gillem does not answer.

"Does she live in London?"

"She lives in a nursing home—an upmarket sort of nursing home off the Marylebone Road."

Rat is taken aback. "Why do you keep her in a home? Can't she live here with you?"

Gillem snaps back with unexpected violence. "Because she hasn't a fucking clue where she is, so she might as well be somewhere safe."

He gets to his feet, depositing the teapot and cups in the sink, and Rat knows that their session is over.

CHAPTER

4

The last week in June is glorious. Hot, dry, clear. You want to be outside all day. Under a horse-chestnut tree in the park, or strolling along the canal. The evenings are billowy, pink-tinged. It doesn't get dark till ten. People do unaccustomed things in the street, such as kiss.

Rat is suddenly determined to get out and explore. Who knows how much longer she and Morgan will be in London?

She's gone on a boat up the Thames to Hampton Court with Kate, and she's taken Morgan and Artemio on a giant Ferris wheel called the London Eye, an expedition marred by Artemio's being in a fury because Morgan had borrowed his Game Boy without asking and run down the battery. And she's gone on her own to the Tate to see exactly what Gillem meant when he said English people couldn't paint and that all the good English painters were Dutch or German.

One evening, Kate's sister and her family came over for dinner, and they ate out in the garden. This time, when Tarquin asked Rat a direct question, she actually managed to answer without making a complete fool of herself.

On Sunday, she and Morgan met Mirjana and spent all day helping Mirjana's boyfriend, Zoran, varnish the floorboards of his new café. That night, Zoran took them to dinner at an African restaurant, and Rat and Mirjana got drunk on palm wine and embarrassed the boys by trying to sing a Serge Gainsbourg song to which neither could remember the lyrics.

All week, she has steered clear of Gillem. When they meet, he is as courteous as ever, but since their conversation about his mother, something has changed. Their fragile camaraderie has somehow been impaired, and he is closed to her. It is as if they are back to zero.

Then one afternoon, Rat can bear it no longer. She goes out into the garden and knocks on the door of Gillem's studio.

For a long time, there is no answer. When she hears his footsteps, her heart beats painfully fast.

"Ah, there you are," Gillem says. His tone is stiff but pleasant. He glances at his watch. "Are you ready for some tea? Come inside."

He shows her the new drawing he's been working on the last couple of days. He's beginning on the flower section now: he's drawn an oversized water lily that looks wildly obscene. And he's received in the mail a sample of the Indian embroidery, but the color of the woolen threads isn't right.

"Gillem?" She gulps down her tea much too fast, and nearly chokes.

"Yes, Celia?" He's looking at her quizzically.

There is something she needs to know.

She stops, stumbles, starts again. "Gillem . . . It *is* true I'm your kid, isn't it?"

Since she's come to London, everything's gone so murky on her. All the things she was dead-sure would become clear once she finally met her English family. The parts of her Vanessa didn't know, or lied about. Now it turns out her grandmother's been put in a home because she's demented, and her father is like this cabinet where for every drawer you manage to open, a dozen more lock tight.

Gillem looks at her from head to foot, twisting his mouth to one side. "Have you ever looked in a mirror? I'm afraid it is."

Rat laughs, but somewhere deep in her chest the laughter's closer to tears.

"I mean, the family resemblance is . . . appalling." He smiles at her. "Don't worry—you'll probably grow out of it." The smile is very sweet, almost beseeching, as if he's hoping she will just leave it at that.

But she can't. She tries to put it as politely as she can, but she's not letting him off the hook. "Well, what I was wondering was—you've been so kind to me and Morgan, now that we've finally shown up on your doorstep, so it's not like you're a monster—but—why didn't you ever want to see me, if you knew I was your child?"

Gillem suddenly looks much older. He sits down, runs his hands through his hair so it stands on end, then gets up. Paces. "Oh dear, Celia. That's rather a thorny question. Are you sure you want to—"

"Yeah, I do."

Long pause, while he dumps the teacups in the sink, searches for a towel to dry his hands. Loops back and sits down again. And then he speaks. "I met your mother—well, twice. Once in a nightclub, the second time in a bar."

He's right. It's painful, much more painful than she was expecting. But she needs to know. "And?"

Silence. "I didn't feel we had much in common," he says finally.

Rat feels the shame-blood flooding to her face. Heart racing, pins and needles. But her voice when it comes out sounds pugnacious.

"But you slept with her. Even if you didn't like her."

"Yes, I did. Once." They are both silent.

"She was very, very pretty, your mother," he says, finally. He pauses. "Not a bit like you. Or me."

They both laugh, a little shakily. For a moment, she thinks it might be all right and she can forgive him. Then he goes on.

"But—forgive me for being crude—if you meet a strange girl in a nightclub, the last thing you imagine is that she's actually looking to have a baby."

"Oh," says Rat, surprised. "Are you sure she was?"

"Quite sure. That's what she told me on the phone, afterwards. More or less. When she found out she was pregnant."

"And you didn't want to have a baby? You wanted her to have an abortion?"

Gillem looks impatient. "Come now, Celia, what percentage of children alive today do you imagine were actually planned or wanted? Here you are, and now I see what a wonderful girl you are, and what a good thing it was your mother stuck by her guns, but at the time I did feel a bit taken advantage of."

"What do you mean?"

"Well, it seems to me that having a child is a huge commitment that involves both parents. More than both parents, both families, really . . ."

He looks up as if appealing for her agreement, but doesn't get it. He sighs. "Look, basically, I'm a cagey, misanthropic sort of person. I think the world is an ugly place, I'm not taking any chances. For me, to have a child, it's something you do properly, when you've been living with a person you love deeply and are utterly committed to, when the time is right, and this child is going to be the center of this universe you've built together."

Rat is trying hard to take this all in, to understand what he means, through the unbearable hurt of it. "But," she says slowly. "I *am* the center of my mother's universe. She's a really great mother. She's really loving, she'll do anything for me, she's given up her whole life to bring me up the way she thinks is right."

Gillem is nodding, but not as if he believes her, as if he's just humoring her, to get this unpleasant conversation over with, so he can get back to his work and his wonderful family. But Rat struggles on.

"And look at Morgan—Morgan's not even my biological brother—she adopted him because his own mother died of AIDS. That's what my mum is like, it's not like we're superrich, but she's so generous, she's got a big enough heart to love other people's kids, too.

"I'm proud of her, I'm proud she had me all by herself and brought me up the way she did." Her voice has gone loud and pugnacious, as if she's hoping to convince him by sheer volume. "We don't have burglar alarms and big spikey metal bars on our windows. Our home is wide open to anybody who's hungry or sick or in trouble or needs a bed," she charges on, glaring at him. "That seems a good way to be, not, Oh, the time isn't right; I'm not sure if our commitment is total enough."

He says nothing.

She stomps around a bit.

She says, "I think it was mean of you never to make a move, never to want to lay eyes on me, even if you hated my mother."

He presses his lips together. "Perhaps," he says.

"I think it was cowardly," she says.

"I'm sorry you feel that way."

She walks out.

"Hello!" Vanessa's voice at the other end is breezy, provocative. Rat can hear the high excitable chatter of television in the background. Her mother never used to watch television in the daytime.

"Mama, it's me."

No answer. Rat wonders if her mother's hung up on her. She used to hang up on Mémé Catherine.

"Mama?"

Finally, an exhalation of breath. "It's you, Rat?" Vanessa's voice now is very low. There's a hint of suppressed tears in its quaver. "I never thought I was going to hear your voice again. God, I've been desperate. Don't ever do this to me again, Rat. Don't ever leave me again, without a word, without a—"

"Mama, you never told me about the money Gillem was paying us."

"What?"

"The child-support money. You should have told me."

"Of course I told you."

"I don't think so."

"I'm sure I did."

"No."

"Well, it's not very much, anyway."

"You should have told me."

A moment's pause, while her mother mutes the television. Then, "Ratkin, my life is more difficult than you realize. I have no parents, no husband, nobody to help me. Nobody. When I had you, I was very young and naive. I thought I could manage by myself. Promise me that when you are older, you will never have a baby on your own. Because once you have a child, you will never sleep an easy night. You can't believe how scared I've been for you, not knowing where you'd gone."

"Didn't Jérôme tell you I was okay?"

"Rat, I'm going to wring your neck. Jérôme told me three weeks after you'd gone, 'Oh, by the way, Rat's fine, she's gone to see her dad in London.' Great. You told me you were going to fucking Collioure. Do you know what it's like, three weeks of not even knowing if your children are alive? And even now that I know you're safe—"

"I'm sorry if you worried," says Rat.

"Never mind; it's done with. I guess it's hard for a child to put herself in a mother's place. You can't imagine how much I long for you, Rat. I think about when you were a little girl, how we used to sleep in the same bed, and you'd wrap your little arms tight around me, and give me butterly kisses on my eyelids—"

"I miss you, too," says Rat, reluctantly.

"You're my baby, Ratkin. My only love. You shouldn't have walked out on me. Everything's so empty without you. People keep asking when you and Morgan are coming back, they say I look terrible. Why didn't you answer my e-mails?

"I haven't slept a night through since you left; I'm nervous as a cat. Dr. Zakroune came around because I was having palpitations. I told him, Before you prescribe me anything, you have to cure the ache in my heart.

"When you have a daughter, you'll see. I can't bear to go into your bedroom and see both your beds empty. I think about Souad and I think I'd rather be dead, too. You could at least have left me Morgan, if you wanted to get away so badly."

"Mama, it's because of Morgan that we left—what Thierry did to him."

There's a pause. Rat can decipher the sounds of her mother lighting a cigarette, taking a deep drag. "You're a little crazy on the subject of Thierry, you know that," Vanessa's voice says, finally. "You've always been mule-stubborn, and once you get some strange idea in your head—I thought Thierry could make us a family, I thought it would be good for you finally to have a man in the house. You and I, we were *too* close. We needed some air in there. And you liked him, too, remember you said how nice it was having him cooking meals and fixing this and that?"

"That was the first few months. Then he stopped fixing stuff."

"Well, we were both wrong. He's a creep, and I realize my life would probably be better without him, but—"

"It's not just that he's a creep, it's that he molested Morgan."

"No, that I don't believe. Let's not talk about it, I don't want us to fight. I'm going to change the subject now. Okay. Tell me what he's like, your daddy-o. Did I pick a nice one for you?"

"Yeah, he's nice."

"And his wife. Is she beautiful?"

"Yeah, kind of. Not, well——"

"What's 'yes, no, kind of' mean? Is she young?"

"Same as him, I guess."

"Rich?"

"How would I know?"

"What's she got, then?"

"She has big breasts."

They both laugh.

"Well, there I can't compete."

"I think she loves him a lot. She's always fussing over him. She's a good cook."

"Motherly," says Vanessa. "Are you getting fattened up?"

"Mmmmm."

"And have you met your grandmother?" There's a different note in Vanessa's voice, a strangled edge. It's Celia Kidd she really cares about, not Gillem, Rat thinks.

"No, not yet." Rat hesitates. "She has Alzheimer's," she says finally.

A silence. Then, "My God," says Vanessa's voice, sounding shocked. "Alzheimer's . . . what a nightmare! That proud beautiful woman! Is it bad?"

"I guess. She's in a sort of nursing home."

"That's awful," says Vanessa's voice, but Rat can tell she's secretly a tiny bit relieved, that she'd rather Celia Kidd was out of the picture, so nobody could have her. "Why do they let her go to a nursing home? With the money they have, you'd think they could at least keep her in her own home."

"I dunno."

"And Morgan, is he happy, are they being kind to him? He must like the wife's cooking, at least. Or is English food as vile as—"

"They're very kind to him. They have a son Morgan's age."

"Only one child? Is he nice?"

"He's clever. And Morgan's doing well. He's made friends with some older boys he plays football with."

"It sounds great, Ratty. I'm really happy for you, honestly I am. I'm glad you're getting something I couldn't give you. Put me on to my darling little Momo, I want to see if he's forgotten his big bad Vanilla."

When Morgan gets on the phone, he says at once, very cheerful, "Hi, Mama Vanessa," and Rat is surprised, because he never used to call Vanessa "Mama." Even if he'd wanted to, Vanessa wouldn't have let him, she would have considered it disrespectful of Souad.

Rat can hear the little twitter of Vanessa's telephone voice asking, "So you speak English now?"

And Morgan laughs. *"Yes, I speak very well. How are you? I am fine."*

The lump in Rat's throat from missing her mother is so big she can't swallow.

Over dinner, she and Gillem are extra-polite to each other, but they can't look each other in the eye. Something's broken, and he feels worse than a stranger. Kate tries her best to make up the difference, chattering about some outdoor music festival last weekend in August that her sister wants to know if Rat wants to come along to, but all Rat can think is, Why would I still be here in August?

That night, going to sleep, she imagines snuggling up against her mother's narrow feline slinky body, as she used to years ago. Then she banishes the thought.

5

"Why are they staying with us, Mum?"

"They've come to visit." Kate is concentrating on the traffic. She's driving Artemio home from his friend Noah's birthday party. Noah's mother had explained in advance to the other mothers that instead of giving his guests party favors at the end, Noah had chosen to make a small donation in each child's name to the World Wildlife Fund.

When Kate had relayed this latest piece of Nouveau London sanctimoniousness to her sister, Constance had said, "I'd be a bit more impressed if it was Noah's daddy's Christmas bonus they'd decided to give to charity. But no, they have to deprive a few innocent tots of their penny bags of sweets."

"When are they leaving?" Artemio persists.

"Who?"

"Celia and Morgan. Don't you find it a bit odd, for years we never even knew they existed, and suddenly they're, like, living with us, acting like our food's their food and my toys are theirs? How much longer are they staying?"

This is the question Kate herself is trying not to ask.

It's not that she doesn't think Gillem's daughter is absolutely wonderful. But it's wearing, coming home from a hard day's work, and having to make small talk in French all evening with a teenager who would probably much rather be off with kids her own age.

She can see the toll it's taking on Artemio, never having his house or his parents to himself anymore. There's a new grimness in his tone when he comes complaining to her that Morgan won't let him put on the Monty Python DVD because he's watching football or that Morgan's left the top off his best fluorescent Magic Marker.

Celia's mother must be a very strange woman, she reflects, having unloaded her two children on an unknown family, with no apparent concern for how they were getting on and were they ever coming home.

When Kate had tried to let off a little steam to Gillem, he had looked at her in amazement, and said, "What, don't you like Celia?"

That's not the point, she'd said.

What is the point, Kate wonders. Is she just a tiny bit jealous of this girl, who with no apparent effort seems to have taken up residence in a corner of Gillem's being that to her has always seemed off-limits?

In the past, Kate could blame Gillem's emotional inaccessibility on his mother: Celia Kidd's narcissism, her semi-incestuous manipulations had left Gillem too scarred to let anybody into his heart. You're too angry at your mother to love anybody else, she'd once told him. And he'd been shocked. Because he did love Kate and Artemio: deeply. He just wasn't very expressive.

But suddenly this long-lost child has appeared, and it's as if she's opened Gillem to everything wonderful about his mother and the magical things she and Gillem used to do together. Now all he wants to do is reminisce about ravishing Collioure, and when Artemio asks, "Why didn't you ever take us there, Dad, if you loved it so much?" Gillem goes completely blank, because, of course, the reason he never went back was because this self-same daughter was there. Scene of the crime.

And as if Gillem and Celia's love-in hadn't been irritating enough for those excluded, now they seem to have had some kind of quarrel, which Gillem refuses to talk about or to do anything to repair, but which is obviously making the poor girl speechless with misery. You can be positively autistic at times, Gillem, even though you think of yourself as so sensitive.

"Well, not for a long time, I hope. She is your sister." Kate can say such things with a kind of no-backtalk firmness, which is why Artemio has gone to her, and not to his father.

"Yeah, but Morgan isn't my brother, is he? He's, like, a totally different color from me."

"No, he's not your brother. He's not exactly your stepbrother, either. There's no name for it. Oh, bloody hell!"

A man in an Audi won't let her cut into his lane, so she misses the turnoff onto Warwick Road. "What a bloody creep. These—"

"Do you think he's Muslim?" persists Artemio.

"Artie, I'm trying to concentrate on the—all right? Just be quiet for a—Are we still talking about Morgan? I have no idea."

"Why don't you have any idea? He looks Muslim."

"What does 'looking Muslim' mean, for heaven's sake?" Kate is hoping if she sounds sufficiently exasperated, her son will shut up and let her navigate the Saturday afternoon traffic.

"You know, Mum. He has brown skin."

Kate relaxes. She's found her way back on to the right road. "Don't be silly, Art. That's not 'looking Muslim,' any more than it's 'looking Christian.' It's a worldwide religion, Islam. You can be a blonde Muslim in a miniskirt, though there are bigots who say you can't."

Artemio, who isn't listening, now perks up. "I know, let's test him!" he bellows. "'Hello, Morgan, here's a good boy, have some pork. Bacon—num num.' He eats bacon, doesn't he? Let's try giving him some chipolatas!"

Kate does not permit herself a smile. "Listen to me, Artemio." She catches his eye for a moment in the rearview mirror. "For us, religion's private, right?"

"Maybe his dad's a suicide bomber!" Artemio shouts, gleeful now. "Don't they have loads of terrorists in France? Maybe that's why nobody knows who his dad is. Maybe his dad's Osama bin Laden! He looks a bit like Osama bin Laden, doesn't he?"

"Enough!" warns Kate.

"Maybe they've come here on a suicide mission, him and Celia. Maybe that's why they're always wanting to see places like Buckingham Palace and Big Ben! *Boom!* Wouldn't that be cool?"

"Depends what you mean by cool."

"We could foil their plans! I could, like, take my X-ray missile launcher and zap them with it!" Artemio's making a rocket with his forefinger, firework noises with his mouth.

Miraculously, there's a parking place on their street. Kate pulls in. "Artie, bring that bag that's in the backseat, all right, darling? I've got a ton of shopping in the boot."

Artemio, as usual, climbs out of the car and starts towards the house, without either bringing the bag or closing his door. "Do those men really believe if you blow up a building or a plane or lots of innocent people you go to heaven? Mum? Do they really?"

"Artie, come back here. I told you to bring my handbag. And please don't leave the car door just—"

She ends up piling the bag on top of her two armfuls of groceries. Fumbles with the front-door keys.

"Mumma?"

"Yes, darling?"

"Why do you and Daddy have to talk French to them all the time? It sounds so silly."

The house is empty. Kate casts a quick eye around the kitchen, peeks into the spare room. Their guests must be out for the afternoon. She wonders where they manage to go for so long. They can't just be hanging out in Queens Park all day. Should she be worried?

Having as yet no teenage child of her own, Kate has little sense of the correct boundaries, what a fifteen-year-old girl should and should not be allowed to do in London. Was it rash to have given Celia an Oyster card? The mobile's proved less than useless, as every time Kate actually tries calling to find out where they are, it turns out Celia's left it at home, or has it switched off in her pocket.

"What did you say, my darling?"

"Why do you have to speak French to them all the time? It sounds ridiculous. They're the ones who chose to come to England; they should bloody well learn to speak English. How do you expect them to *integrate*?"

"I imagine they'll learn."

"Yeah, like, if they stay here the next fifty years," Artemio says, sarcastically. He goes over to the television, picks up the remote control.

"No television till you've finished your homework."

"But Mumma, it's the weekend!"

"You know the rules."

He zaps the remote control absentmindedly at his mother. "Why didn't we ever meet them before?" he persists. "Like, all these years, we never even knew they existed and suddenly they're *living* with us."

Gillem, coming in from his studio, pauses at this last sentence. Kisses Artemio, who is now plopped on the sofa, flipping through the pages of the television guide, and then Kate, who is unloading the groceries into the kitchen cupboard.

"Did you have a good time at the party, Artemio? Who was there?"

"Nobody of interest," says Artemio, quickly. "Is Morgan going to go to English school next year?" he pursues. "He can't even say 'Hello' properly—he's, like, 'Allo!' If he stays, I should think they'd have to put him in nursery school."

Kate restrains herself from pointing out that Morgan may not be able to say "Hello," but he's already succeeded in making friends with those Queens Park hoodlums who are the terror of every middle-class mother and the awe of those mothers' sons.

"Are Celia and Morgan out?" she asks her husband.

"I suppose they must be."

"Do you have any idea where they are?"

Gillem looks vague. "Aren't they supposed to be helping out at Mirjana's boyfriend's café?"

"Really?"

"Yes. I think that's where Celia said they were going."

"Nobody said anything to me about it."

"Didn't Celia tell us that Zoran had said he could give her some work at the café?"

"This is the first I've heard about it," Kate repeats.

"Oh, I don't think it's anything very serious—just serving tea to the customers. But she seemed excited about it."

"That's very odd. I do remember her raising the subject of finding some kind of summer job, but my understanding was that we had told her we didn't think it was a very good idea, among other things because we're all about to head off for the country. I do think it's a bit naughty of her to go ahead without asking."

Kate suddenly finds herself unreasonably angry. And she knows, once she's started, it will be impossible to back down, because Gillem has this passive resister's way of going all opaque and withdrawn that only makes her the more indignant.

Already, she can tell that she's going to get more and more worked up, and that afterwards she will feel thoroughly ashamed of herself.

"And what about Morgan?" she continues. "What's supposed to happen to Morgan while Celia's at work?"

Gillem won't meet her gaze. "Well, Morgan's fairly self-sufficient, isn't he?"

Kate heaves a massive sigh of exasperation at her husband's willful obliviousness. "That's not the point, Gil. The point is that for whatever reason, we suddenly find ourselves responsible for these two children's welfare. And I don't think it very clever of you to have told Celia she can go off and—where is Zoran's café, anyway? Isn't it somewhere like . . . ?"

"Dalston, I think."

"Dalston is bloody *miles* away—it's not even on the Tube, it's National Rail. I do think Mirjana might have asked me about it first. How's she supposed to get there and back?"

"Well, I think they were only talking about her working there a few afternoons a week. I don't know, I didn't think it was such a bad thing, her wanting to earn some pocket money."

"Gillem, she's a *baby*. She doesn't speak English, and she doesn't have any kind of city smarts whatsoever. I'm not sure I trust Mirjana on this sort of thing; Zoran's always seemed to me a bit of an unsavory character. Aside from anything else, it's completely illegal to hire a fifteen-year-old. Do you really want the child to be working in a cybercafé in Dalston? I mean, it's probably a front for some kind of Balkan—"

Gillem casts a warning look towards Artemio, and Kate swiftly changes tack. "I suppose what really bothers me," she says, "is that you all seem to have gone off and arranged this thing—"

"Who?"

"You and Celia and Mirjana. Without consulting me, or thinking through the consequences."

"But nothing's arranged," Gillem protests. "If you don't like the idea, we can say no."

"I thought we already did," says Kate hotly.

Already in her mind she can see the expression that will come over Celia's face when Kate tells her that she can't work at Zoran's cybercafé: an expression of deliberately blank inwardness. The same look that's now on her husband's face.

The High Life Café is on Dalston Lane.

Its walls are covered in comic strips, and they serve coffee and cake. Just walking through the door, you feel jolted into a glucose-caffeine euphoria.

Dalston is a working-class immigrant neighborhood that is just beginning to get a kind of arty mix. Zoran is hoping to capitalize on the fact that most people who live there are still too poor to have their own Internet access. Once the neighborhood gets trendy enough, he'll unload the computers—which he got supercheap from a guy who was planning to donate them to charity—and turn it into a proper café with real food.

Rat had hoped to improve her English working at the High Life. But in fact, everybody at the High Life comes from somewhere else. Mirko, the manager who runs the computers and fixes the espresso machine when it backs up, is a Bosnian Serb; Sophie, Rat's fellow server, is Dutch. The customers are mostly mustachioed Kurds who come to read the Kurdish newspapers online, Ghanaians searching the Internet for a secondhand car or a room to rent. But since the only language they have in common is English, they do all speak it, in some weird variant. When she tells the McKanes about the kind of English spoken at the High Life, Kate says sociologists call it "Globish." It's the language of the future, she says.

Rat's never had much sense of the future—certainly not in the demographic sense. All her life, she's lived in some kind of fairy-tale time—a blend of her mother's stories of the past and her own projections of those stories onto an equally improbable future—so now it's quite bracing for a change to be part of some collective reality that's about to happen.

Zoran is rarely at the High Life, which is just as well, since he's actually kind of a megalomaniac. But Rat's coworkers are jolly, and the clientele easygoing.

Sometimes Rat brings along Morgan and lets him play on one of the older computers. And if business is slow, Mirko will play war games with him. On their way home, they'll stop for a kebab by the train station. Although she works daytimes, it's usually evening before they get back to Hawkridge Road.

Rat likes her new life. She likes kidding around with Sophie and Mirko; she likes getting to know the regular customers. She likes having money in her pocket, even though Zoran's paying her less—and less regularly—than he'd promised. It makes her feel on a more equal footing with the McKanes, coming home in the evenings from her own job, however part-time and illegal. It almost makes her able to overlook how angry she still is at Gillem.

With her first paycheck, she buys Artemio a Pokémon game for his Game Boy, after which his relations with Morgan are considerably calmer.

One day, in an accessories shop near the train station, she spots a pair of fuzzy pink rabbit ears on a kind of hair band that light up. She thinks Vanessa would get a kick out of them.

"They're all the fashion," the salesgirl maintains. "You wear them to nightclubs and pop concerts."

Rat wonders when she will see her mother next. She remembers how Vanessa always reached to the back of the supermarket shelf to find the milk with the longest sell-by date. Maybe Rat should pick something that hasn't yet come into fashion, but will next year. "Excuse me, do you think they will be in fashion for a long time?"

The salesgirl looks at her as if she's demented, and Rat's so embarrassed she goes ahead and forks out five pounds for the flashing rabbit ears.

6

When Rat opens a sleepy eye, there's a boy sitting on the bottom of her bed. She lunges to grab him, only to find it isn't Morgan, but Artemio. Remembering she's naked except for her under-pants, she slinks back under the covers, but not before his big brown eyes goggle.

"What do you want, Artemio?"

"Mumma said I was to wake you, and ask you if you wanted any breakfast before you go. She said you need to leave in plenty of time, the whole city's snarled up because of the G8 conference—don't even think of taking a bus."

"Oh. Thanks." She hasn't really followed all that: Artemio's got a lisp, on top of his gargly English accent. "Isn't it time for you to have left for school by now?"

"I'm ill."

"Shouldn't you be in bed, then?"

"I'm not that ill." He still doesn't move. "I am here to offer you my official condolences."

"What's condolences?"

"Condolences are, Ha-ha, you lost."

"I lost what?" It seems to her sometimes she's lost everything.

"You lost the Olympics."

"I lost the Olympics?"

"*Ja. Jawohl, das is richtig.* Paris lost, London won. There's going to be the Olympics in London in 2012 and Jacques Chirac is in a snit about it. Ha-ha."

"Oh, yeah, I heard at work already. What is a snit?"

"When you're angry."

Snit. Nice word, snit. They could use it in French. *Franche-ment, Morgan, tu me snites.*

"Paris is a mausoleum. London's young and dynamic," Artemio continues. "London's up, Paris is down." Bouncing on her bed.

"I've never been to Paris," says Rat, meditatively.

"You haven't? I have. There was an underground strike—we had to walk everywhere. Is it true that French people are always on strike because they're lazy bastards?"

"What do you think?"

"I'm asking you."

"How many French people do you know?"

"You. And Morgan. And Corinne, my old nanny."

"Is Morgan lazier than you? Morgan makes his own bed every day, he helps Mirjana with the washing up. When Morgan takes a shower, he cleans the bathroom afterwards, he doesn't throw his clothes and towel on the floor for someone else to pick up."

"Yeah, but he can barely read. All he reads is comic books."

"That's lazy? That's on strike?"

"Is your mother French, too?"

"Yes."

"What's she do for a living?"

"She's a *brocanteuse.*"

"What's that?"

"She sells things in the market."

"What, she has, like, a vegetable stall or something?" Artemio screws up his eyes.

"No, she sells old things. Old clothes and old magazines. Things people don't want anymore she takes and sells."

"You mean, she's, like . . . a *ragpicker?*" Artemio is utterly appalled. "That's like—that's like something out of *Oliver Twist.* How'd she even meet my dad? Was he, like, throwing out something old, and she asked if she could take it and sell it?" He's spluttering with laughter, but the thought that his father might have had dealings with such a person obviously disturbs him. "My mum works for a film producer."

"I know."

"Her company won an award for a series they made about the Peninsular War."

"The what?"

"The Pen-in-su-lar War. You know, Napoleon. One of the other times we beat you."

"I thought Peninsular was a kind of medicine," Rat mutters to herself.

Artemio roars with triumphant laughter. "I can't *believe* we're related. Don't they teach you *anything* in French schools?"

"Artemio, I'm gonna get dressed now."

Artemio doesn't budge. He looks down at her complacently. "It's a good thing we found out about each other," he remarks. "Otherwise, we might have grown up and got married, without knowing we were brother and sister. I saw a film where that happened: this boy was about to marry a girl, and then at the last minute the priest tells him, Sorry, Jean, you can't marry that girl, I confessed your dad the night before the Gestapo tortured him to death, and he told me he'd had an affair with that girl's mum and that she's actually his illegitimate daughter."

Rat casts an eye at the clock. *"Casse-toi, Artemio, s'il te plaît, je m'habille. En tout cas, je pense pas qu'il y a grand risque que tu te maries avec la fille d'une, quoi, d'une* ragpicker."

Rat catches the train from Westbourne Park.

Kate's made her a dentist's appointment for the exposed nerve on her broken tooth.

Occasion for more shame: the dentist, Kate reported back, had asked could she please get her French dentist to send him her most recent set of X-rays. Rat had been obliged to admit to Kate she couldn't remember ever having been to a dentist, let alone having X-rays.

Kate, as usual, had simply goggled.

Rat was reduced to mumbling, "I thought X-rays gave you cancer."

Kate's assured her that the dentist won't do anything but look at her tooth today. Besides, she says, going to the dentist isn't what it used to be—they've got this whole new generation of technology that means it's about as scary as a trip to the dry cleaner.

Rat's not convinced. Doctors belong to the class of adult she prefers to stay clear of.

Eight forty-five.

The train is full of people on their way to work in offices and shops. This is the world into which Rat is dipping an amateur, part-time toe: the workaday world of people who wake to an alarm clock every morning because there is some job they are paid to perform. Even if it's as menial as bringing customers a cup of coffee, noting down what time they log on to their computer, what time they log out, she wants to be part of that world. She can't imagine going back to school, and being treated as a baby.

The men are reading newspapers whose headlines celebrate

London's winning the Olympics. A news story she reads over her neighbor's shoulder crows at the Gallic inanity of France's president, who's accused the British prime minister of "cheating." The women are reading novels. Rat wonders why women in the Tube don't read newspapers and men don't read novels. That same sort of playground division she's known since preschool—boys play marbles, girls play hopscotch—continues. Does it matter? Would men and women get along better if they shared the same tastes?

If Vanessa were interested in why Protestants are weak in the visual arts instead of being interested in famous people from star magazines, might she and Gillem have stayed together for more than a night? Or is Artemio right, and the bottom line is that nobody from his father's background could ever have anything in common with a southern French ragpicker?

Maybe Rat was misled by Gillem's bare feet, his longing for the moors and the sea, his inveighing against posh school parents and their private jets. Maybe those anarchic puritanical impulses that made Rat feel, despite the obvious differences, that she and her father might have something in common were simply part of a more complicated form of snobbery than she could get her head around.

Or maybe there's some screw loose in Rat's head, some permanent disgruntledness which means she's never going to be able to settle down, never be able to fit into anybody else's home life.

Which is too bad. Because even if her life at Hawkridge Road is increasingly untenable, work is fun. She feels comfortable with those other outsiders—Mirko who's a war refugee, like Mirjana and Zoran; Sophie who left Amsterdam because her boyfriend was abusive. She feels a kinship, too, with the customers glued to their screens like fish in an aquarium, people leading double lives, their waking selves in a dismal rainy high street in East London, their dream selves back with their families and friends and neighbors in a village in central Anatolia, a shantytown outside Accra.

One more stop to Baker Street, where Rat can either get out and walk a few blocks, or stay on till Great Portland. As the train pulls out of the Edgware Road, there's a big boom. So loud the whole car shakes. Like an explosion. People's eyes flicker round, gauging each other's reactions.

"Crikey," mutters the older man next to Rat. A fat lady, who's grabbed hold of her neighbor's arm in alarm, now releases the stranger, giggling apologetically.

The train limps on, half-speed, to Baker Street. Stops, but the doors don't open. The lights go out. As soon as they go out, the passengers, like canaries, are silenced. There's a crackle of a service announcement over the loudspeaker, but no voice. More crackle.

They wait. Now the lights come on and an official voice blares over the sound system. Rat can't understand a word. For all she knows, he might be saying France has invaded England in revenge for losing the battle for the Olympics.

She leans towards her neighbor.

"What he say?"

"They're saying there are difficulties on the line, and everybody has to get out at this stop. Power outage, I reckon."

The platform is already so crowded you can hardly get out of the carriage. All you can do is sway, try to keep your balance and not fall, except there's no room to fall. She feels like a stalk of corn in an overfull cornfield. People are stumbling, trying not to shove. It occurs to Rat that she's never been in so crowded a place in her life. It's hot and airless and no fun being underground. All her early apprehensions about taking the Tube—descending into hot stinking hell—resurge. She looks at the station clock. It's ten past nine. She's already ten minutes late, and she doesn't know how long it will take her to walk to Harley Street.

An airless eternity before Rat even gets up into the daylight. At the station entrance kiosk, people are being turned away.

"There are no Circle Line trains running, no Circle Line," an Underground worker is announcing. Would-be passengers crowd around the officials, asking for information.

"What happen?" Rat asks a woman.

"There's been an accident. A train's been derailed."

"Oh, so that was the big noise? It sound like a bomb."

"No, rest assured: it's not a bomb," says an official, who nonetheless looks worried.

Rat studies the map of the neighborhood posted at the Tube entrance, and heads off in what she hopes is the right direction.

The streets, too, are jammed. That government conference Artemio was talking about, or more overflow from the Tube?

Rat pauses at a bus stop to see if she can spot another map, but there are so many people waiting for a bus that she can't get anywhere close. And the traffic is barely moving. Policemen all over the place.

When she finally passes the Baker Street station, the officer is telling people that not only the Circle Line but the whole Underground system is being evacuated and shut down, and that if passengers will be patient, they are going to be providing special bus service.

"What happen?" Rat asks a man.

He shrugs, frowning, as he moves away. "Some sort of series of power failures. They're saying it was a power surge in the grid."

It's almost ten when she rings the bell at the front door of the dentist's surgery. When she's buzzed in, the receptionist looks at her in surprise.

"My goodness," she says. "You are . . . ?"

"Celia Bonnet. Sorry I'm late, there was—"

"My goodness, I'm amazed you even got here. Were you in the Tube? Mr. Williamson! Your nine o'clock has just arrived."

Mr. Williamson, a large ruddy-faced young man in a white

coat, appears in the doorway. "Heavens," he says. "A survivor! I think it's fairly safe to assume you are going to be my last patient of the day."

When Rat leaves the surgery, the receptionist asks if she would like her to call a minicab.

Rat pauses. "No thanks," she says. "I prefer to walk."

But truth to tell, it's not like a normal walk. Everywhere the streets are jammed with people walking, walking, not like an ordinary city crowd, but like sleepwalkers, all dazed, all in the same direction, and police everywhere, standing at every inter- section, herding pedestrians along. Streets cordoned off. Heli- copters hovering overhead. Worse than Perpignan in the riots. A power surge is no joke. If it derailed a train, there must have been lots of injuries. She stops at a newsagent to hear if there's any more news. The newspaper seller is hunched over his radio.

"What happen?" she asks, for what feels like the zillionth time that morning.

"A bus has been blown up."

"Where?"

"Bloomsbury."

"No, it's not a bus—it's the Tube," she says.

He looks at Rat as if she's simple. "It's the Tube and a bus they've blown up."

They?

Rat dodges her way through the crowd milling along the Marylebone Road. Now all she wants to do is get home quick. She knows the right direction—west, northwest. She only has to follow her nose, wiggle her way around major obstacles such as Paddington Station and the A40 and any strategic infrastructure and amenities "They" might also have decided to blow up.

When she walks through the door of Hawkridge Road, the first sound she hears is the superagitated patter of the television news in the sitting room.

Then Kate's voice, high, panicked. "Celia? Celia?"

Gillem rushes to meet her, followed by Kate. They both stare at her. Gillem is ghostly white. "Are you all right?"

Kate hugs Rat so tight she feels like a child trapped by an exploded air bag. "Thank God you're safe. Were you in the Tube when it all happened?" She's crying, wiping her eyes. Crying! "Thank God!" she repeats, laughing at her own tears, and hugs her, if anything, still tighter.

Mirjana's joined them. "Is she all right?"

"Yeah, I'm fine. Really." She doesn't feel fine. She feels shaky, and their white ghastly faces, Kate's tears, aren't helping. "What—I still can't figure out—what happened. Somebody blew up a bus? Or was it a train?"

Gillem now speaks, and his voice is trembling with fury. "Why the hell didn't you have your mobile on?"

She slips the phone out of her back pocket and checks. "Sorry," she says. "I was in the dentist's and . . ."

"Why do you think we gave you the fucking phone?" he persists. "Precisely so we'd know you were all right, if some idiot decides to blow up the Underground. It's past noon. Didn't you even think to call home once in three hours?"

"Gillem," chides Kate. "There's no point getting cross with her—half the mobiles in London aren't working anyway."

"It's noon," he insists. "She should have thought to call us from the dentist's."

"I'm very sorry," Rat mumbles again. It's the first time she's ever heard him raise his voice. When she tries to figure out afterwards what shocked her so much, she realizes it was because he was scolding her in the raw, unmediated way a father scolds his daughter.

"Gillem, will you please let the poor girl talk?" Kate still has her arm around Rat. She gives her another brief, almost absentminded squeeze, then lets her go. Holds her at arm's length and examines her. "Were you in the Tube when the bombs went off? What happened?"

Rat recounts her story. "Who did it?" she asks. "Are they saying it was terrorist bombs?"

"Yes," says Gillem. "Apparently there were six bombs that went off in different trains simultaneously. Plus the bus. You know, which exploded just when all the people who'd been evacuated from the Tube were being rerouted onto buses. Christ. Absolute carnage. They have no idea yet how many people have been killed." He is talking much too quickly. "They can't tell yet whether it was suicide bombers or bombs that got detonated by remote control, like the train bombings in Madrid."

"Ghastly. Well, thank God you're home safe," says Kate. "We tried calling Mr. Williamson's office as soon as we heard, but it was just the answering service."

"Sorry," says Rat, once again. She follows her stepmother into the living room, where Artemio and Morgan are still huddled on the floor in front of the television set. Rat sits down on the floor beside Morgan, who leans his body against hers. She takes his hand.

"So you didn't die," he says to her, softly.

"Not today."

"I knew you didn't. If you were ever hurt, I would feel it here." He thumps his heart with her hand, the hand that's holding his. "When you die, I'm coming with you."

She snuggles him up against her. "Yeah, I wouldn't want to live without you, either."

On the television screen are slow grainy gray images that have been sent in from people's cell phones, interspersed with aerial photos of a London street, and a bus whose top's been blown off, its insides gutted. Is that what she missed, so barely?

"God, makes you nostalgic for the IRA, doesn't it?" Kate says, wonderingly. "Such sweet bumbling amateurs. And sporting— they always gave one a little warning."

"Yeah, I'm so glad I moved to London from war-torn Balkans where crazy people are always blowing each other up for no reason," Mirjana rejoins.

Artemio swings around. He is still wearing his pajamas, which makes him look even younger. His face has gone bright red. "Will you two please shut up so we can hear!" he shouts.

"Artemio," Kate reproves him. "Do we really have to watch it over and over again on television when your sister's just been through it? I want to hear more about what happened to her."

"JUST SHUT UUUUP!" bellows Artemio, jamming the volume button on the television's remote control until the sound is as loud as that morning's boom, but continuous.

"Artie . . ." Gillem takes the control from him and mutes the sound. "It's all right, darling, it's all right."

But Artemio has just flung himself at his father and burst into big shuddering sobs. "IT'S NOT, IT'S NOT, IT'S NOT. It's never going to be all right again!"

Arms and legs wrapped around his father, baby-gorilla style, Artemio sobs. When his tears have finally subsided into the occasional gulp and snuffle, Gillem picks him up and carries him upstairs to bed. Just before he disappears, Gillem looks back over his shoulder and gives Rat a look that is half frown, half smile, equal mixtures worry and tenderness.

"Celia, your mum called just before you got back to see if you were all right," Kate says, as if that's something absolutely normal. "I told her we'd phone as soon as we heard from you."

Rat is soaking in a bath scented with honey-ginger essence. She feels as if her body and hair still stink of the London Underground, of poisoned tunnels, policemen, mass fear.

The others are still watching television, glued to the same tarot deck of reshuffled images: burning bus, hovering helicopter, derailed train, ashen crowds. Face cards: the man from the Ministry of Defense; the man who knows about Middle Eastern terrorism, the expert on explosives.

Her cell phone is ringing. She's left it out on the kitchen counter, but she can recognize its little bleat.

She jumps out of the bath, wraps herself in a towel, grabs the phone just before it goes on to message service.

"How come all the calls are for Celia, how come nobody wants to know if I'm all right?" she can hear Artemio complain to his mother, but his tone is jokey. Gillem's got him calmed down somewhat.

"You still alive?" It's Jérôme. "I'm with Florian," he says. "We just heard."

Rat describes to Jérôme what it was like to move in that silent obedient crowd being herded by Underground officials up to the surface, and down the London streets. "It felt like zombies in a science-fiction movie, everybody was so obedient. You just know, if it was France, they'd be bitching their heads off."

"I think it's time you came home," says Jérôme's voice, firmly. "Are you coming back soon? If you aren't, me 'n' Flo are coming to London to get you."

"I dunno know, Jérôme. It's kind of interesting here. I wouldn't want to leave just because of some bomb. And I've just started working, it's really fun. I mean, can you believe it, I'm this kid who can't even speak English, and immediately I find a job? In France, you can have six advanced degrees and you still can't find work."

Jérôme snorts his disapproval. "What do they have you doing, clearing mines? Well, don't take the Tube anymore. Or the bus."

"Yeah, we're all talking about getting bikes. What's going on at home? How are things?"

"Well, I have interesting news for you. I didn't want to say anything till it looked a hundred percent sure, but—"

"What?"

Dramatic pause. "Thierry and your mom have broken up. He's moved out."

"YES!" shouts Rat, whooping so loud the others look over at her in surprise.

"Yeah, this weekend some friend of his came by, and helped him load up all his stuff."

"I didn't think he had any friends. I didn't know he had any stuff of his own, either. It's probably all stuff he's ripped off from me and Vanessa. So he's really gone? Just like that?"

"Oh, I think it's been a long time in the making. He'd got fired by Jens for real—I don't think your mom was too happy about that, and then she found out that Thierry'd forged this big check in her name, so that her bank account's, like, frozen. And I think that did it.

"Your apartment has definitely been . . . lively for the past few weeks. Every now and then, my mom would look at my dad and say, Don't you think it's time you knocked on the door and made sure they're still alive in there? And Dad would be, like, No, actually, I think it's your turn."

"And how's Vanessa?"

"She's a little sad. She was over for dinner last night. She told us"—Jérôme's voice goes dry with embarrassment—"she'd wanted to have a baby with him. She said she'd figured he was her last chance of having a baby, and that makes her sad."

"Well, that was a near miss. So he's really gone."

"Looks like. I mean, an asshole like that doesn't give up easy, especially when she's supporting him. But she seemed pretty convinced it's over. Anyway, she was talking about putting out an injunction on him. Forging checks is the kind of thing that gets you in serious trouble."

"Is she admitting now he really was a child molester?"

"You know what? It didn't come up."

"Yeah, that's so Vanessa. Molest my son, fine, but steal my money and you're outta here."

"So your dad's nice?"

Rat checks to be sure Gillem's out of earshot. "He's all right. Doesn't like the city. He likes to wander around barefoot, just like me. And his artwork's really cool. I wrote you about how he's making this great big quilt against the invasion of Iraq, right?"

"Barefoot? I thought he was driving around in a red Ferrari."

"Fuck off."

"And so you have a little brother."

"Half brother."

"Is he nice?"

"Aw, he's a pain like all the little brothers in the world except for Morgan."

"You're not gonna stay, are you?"

"If Thierry's gone?" It's true, Thierry's departure puts a different complexion on things. "I don't know. I like it here, London's, I mean, it's superexpensive, but it's cool—"

"Long as you manage not to get blown up by suicide bombers," Jérôme's voice intervenes.

"You know, I was planning to work till the middle of August, and then my dad wants us to come down to the country with them for a couple of weeks. But I dunno, maybe I'll come home after that . . ."

Rat feels the excitement mounting as she says these words.

She starts thinking how nice it would be to return to Mas Cargol with some money in her pocket. If they get back the end of August, that's still a month of swimming in the sea. If she manages to save enough money, maybe she could even take her mother and the Cabreras to dinner one night at Chez Ernest. Only thing that's certain, she's not going back to Victor Hugo in September. Soon as she gets Morgan settled in school, then she's heading up to the Ariège to Pauline's sheep farm.

Next, Florian wants to speak to Rat. She hears his familiar dope-soaked rasp.

"Girl, you are all over the news, you've definitely hit the big-time. The Pyrénées-Orientales are so beat. We had a bunch of shop windows broke, cars burnt, and we thought it was Armageddon. You Londoners, it's not enough you get the Olympics, you also get the entire metro system getting blown sky-high by multiple, totally synchronized suicide bombers. What a happening place!"

As soon as Rat hangs up from Florian, the phone rings again.

Rat knows who it's going to be.

At first there's silence at the other end of the line, and then a great sob, and then all Vanessa can say is "Rat, Rat, Rat, my darling Ratkin" over and over.

"I'm fine, Mama, we both are, me and Morgan," Rat reassures her.

"But you could have been blown to smithereens! God, I was so worried. When I heard on the television, I almost died. And then Gillem's wife said they hadn't heard from you yet . . ."

"I'm fine, Mama." Rat clears her throat. "How about you? How are you doing?"

"Don't ask," says her mother's voice with a big gulp in which tears and laughter are mixed. "God, girl, I am such a mess."

"What's wrong?" asks Rat. Although she knows.

"What's wrong? I guess I'm just someone who lets people take advantage of me. I never learn, do I? Some pitiful creep comes up to me and says he's lost his job, his girlfriend's left him for another man, his father used to abuse him when he was a little boy, and I'm like, Oh, here're my car keys, here's my credit card, come move in with me, make yourself at home. Well, Rat, I finally did it. You would have been proud of me. I threw out

Thierry. God, what a worm he was. I mean, he was so sweet at first, no one's ever made me feel so beautiful and sexy, I really thought we had something going those first couple of years. It's funny—I always thought if I could only get him out of my life, I'd feel liberated, but I just feel sad. And then I hear about the London bombings and I think, Oh great, I bet Rat and Morgan were on that bus, God's punishing me . . ."

"Don't worry, Mama," says Rat. "You did the right thing; I know it's hard, but I'm proud of you."

"But I feel like shit!" wails Vanessa. "I'm tired of being Mother Teresa; I want someone to take care of *me,* for a change!"

When you're little, you worship your mother. You want to be just like her. You want to melt into her flesh so you two will never be separated. Then you start to grow apart. Suddenly you can see through her tricks and betrayals, and you harden yourself against them. You try to make yourself so cold inside that nothing she says or does will ever touch you. It's only much later, when you think you're permanently numb and that you couldn't possibly feel anything genuine for your mother even if you tried, that you realize you've come to love her in a new way, amused, wary, but still infinitely tender.

"I'll be back soon," Rat promises. "You hang in there, Mama; Morgan and I will be home in no time."

Rat is ready to go back to Mas Cargol. People will think it's because of the bombing and it's a good excuse, but it isn't. She can see that her father and Kate have grown fond of her, even to accept her as a kind of adjunct daughter. But all that means is that it's okay to leave, because she'll be able to come back to them again.

Gillem is dreaming. He is dreaming, as he often does, about Celia Kidd.

Everybody else in London, after the second set of terrorist

bombs which exploded two weeks after the first, is dreaming about burning buses, crashing airplanes; Gillem McKane is dreaming about his mother.

In his dream, he is sitting in a hotel dining room in a foreign country with his mother, who still has Alzheimer's, but not as badly as she does in real life.

She's dressed in a very smart tweed suit with a purple velvet collar. He thinks, I haven't seen that Vivienne Westwood suit in years, not since we went together to have it fitted, although in fact, there was no such suit. They are waiting for Rat to join them and Gillem is trying to explain to his mother who Rat is.

"She's my daughter. Not by Kate, by a Frenchwoman." He keeps repeating this in a placatory sort of way, appealing to his mother's Francophilia. Emphasizing that the girl's mother isn't Kate, whom he knows his mother considers infradig—"rather hot and sweaty," as she once put it.

And finally, Celia Kidd seems to understand, and a big salacious grin spreads across her face.

"By another woman? A Frenchwoman?" she repeats. She cackles with satisfaction. "Well done, darling. You used to pretend to be so pious. But I always knew you were one of us!"

And Gillem feels himself maddeningly checkmated, because to protest, That's not true, I *am* pious, I'm *not* one of you, would sound worse than ridiculous. Of course she's right, he thinks, all that struggle has been in vain: I am one of Them.

In the dream, what being "one of Them" means is quite specific: to be one of the libertines, to whom nothing is of any weight.

When he wakes in the morning, Artemio is in the bed between him and Kate, hugging his mother tight.

"What's this little tree frog doing in my bed?" Gillem asks, mock gruff.

"Artemio's having a bit of a rough time, aren't you, darling? He needed a cuddle."

"Artemio havin' bad dweams," says the boy, in a baby voice.

"A lot of confusing things happening at once," his mother sympathizes.

"Pwomise Artemio Mumma no take public twansport," whispers Artemio.

"I promise you, darling. I've got my lovely new bike. But don't worry. All the terrorists are gone. Everybody's safe now. No more bombs, nothing scary. Didn't you hear what they said on the telly last night? The government has it utterly under control."

Gillem rolls over onto his side, and tries to block out the sound of his wife's telling his son nonsense. But of course, the child would rather hear such totalitarian certainties than his father's waffle about how the suicide bombers are men with understandable grievances against Western policy in the Muslim world, but a very distorted view of Islam, and that unfortunately there's very little way of stopping people who are willing to blow themselves up, without turning yourself into a state in which Brazilian electricians get mowed down by policemen in a crowded Underground carriage because their skin is the wrong color.

When he gets out of bed, he realizes that's what he's going to do: bring Celia to meet her namesake.

The woman is propped up in a chintz armchair. She is leaning
back against a nurse, who is trying to brush her hair. Suspended
from the opposite wall is a television set, sound almost mute, on
which an energetic young man is demonstrating how to prepare a
summer pudding.

The woman is so emaciated that her face looks all teeth. Her
teeth are enormous and yellow. The only thing left that's beautiful about the woman are her eyes, which are huge and icy green.
Expressionless as a camel's.

She's wrapped in a mohair shawl the color of her eyes, and
under it, she's wearing a white linen dress.

The nurse is brushing out her mahogany-red hair. Every time
the nurse draws a brushstroke, the woman emits an unearthly
scream like a seagull's. It's a sound devoid of meaning, unless its
meaning is simply malicious, to hurt one's ears.

"Re-lax, Celia. I'm not hurting you; I'm being careful-careful.
You be nice to Mandy, now. I'm gonna make your hair soft as
silk."

"You are *too* hurting me," the woman whimpers. "How would you like it if I pulled *your* hair?"

Suddenly she whips round and yanks hard on the nurse's hair, so that the young woman cries out in pain. You wouldn't have thought there was strength enough in those sticklike arms to inflict such pain.

"You are a devil today, Celia," complains the nurse. And then, catching sight of Gillem, who has just come through the door, "Wait until I tell your son how you be acting."

"What son?" demands the woman, with weary disgust. "I have no son. No son."

"And who's this? Who's this good-looking young man come to visit you?" The nurse beckons to Gillem and propels him to his mother's side. "Look at the beautiful flowers he bring! Do you know the name of these flowers?"

"No."

"They are lilies, aren't they?"

"No."

"Your favorite, lilies."

"No."

"Hello, Mummy," says Gillem, and he bends over to kiss the woman. She screws her face away and tries to repel him with her matchstick arms. "Mummy, I've brought someone to meet you."

He beckons to Rat, who is still standing in the doorway.

Celia Kidd's eyes skate across her and back to the cooking program.

"A visitor," intercedes Mandy, brightly. "Isn't she pretty? Is that your niece?"

Gillem clears his throat. "No, this is my daughter." He sits on the chair beside his mother and leans close to her, speaking in a low clear voice. "Mummy, I'd like you to meet my daughter. Her name is Celia, too. She's named after you."

Rat moves closer to the lady. "Hello, Mrs. Kidd," she says.

Takes her grandmother's hand a little gingerly. Soaking up the smell of scented lotions, talcum powder, the sickly sweetness of the woman's breath.

Celia Kidd looks down at her own hand, being held by a stranger's. Then returns her attention to the cooking lesson.

"This is your daughter, Gillem?" Mandy sucks in her breath, eyes mock-wide. "I never knew you had a daughter. Celia, you never tell me about your granddaughter."

"She lives in France," says Gillem. And to his mother, "Near Collioure. Remember when we used to spend summers in Collioure, Mummy? Celia comes from Collioure."

"She's *tall*. How old are you, love? Does she speak English?"

"A little," says Rat.

"Goodness. She look just like her gran, doesn't she? Same big beautiful eyes."

"Yes, she does," Gillem agrees, with a wan smile. He glances at Rat with a kind of barely mastered desperation, as if pleading that she will get them out of there.

"Take a seat, love. Here on the sofa near your gran. Can I get you something to drink? Cuppa tea? Some coffee?"

"How is she today, Mandy?" Gillem asks. He sits down on the sofa beside Rat, but immediately gets up again and wanders over to the window. Outside, a curdled gray sky, office blocks, a highway overpass.

"Pretty good. She sleep well, she eat a good breakfast."

"They don't feed me here," says the woman, sadly. "They pretend to bring me trays, but then when I try to eat, they snatch it away."

Mandy laughs. "Yesterday, you bit me. Do you remember that, Celia? I was giving you a spoonful of carrots and instead you bite my finger?"

Celia's gaze returns to the television screen.

"She has all kinds of little tricks. She likes to hide food away, don't you, Celia? She'll take the cheese and biscuits and she'll hide them under the pillow. Once she even tried to put the custard under her pillow! Didn't you, Celia? We have to watch out for all your little tricks, don't we, Celia?"

"No."

"Do you remember your son's name, now, Celia? You tell me his name. Do you know his name?" To Rat, Mandy explains in a loud whisper, "I like to keep her mind working. We have all kinds of lessons we run through every day; I show her pictures from a magazine, pictures of her family. Who's this one, who's that. This is your son, Celia, isn't it, now? What's his name, again?"

"Yes." The woman stares at Gillem, pensively. "That's . . . that's . . . a . . . that's a . . . person who worked for . . ." She's thinking hard. She presses her fingers to her temples. "For my father?" she ventures, at last. "I think he's somebody my father sacked for . . . for . . ." She gestures vaguely. "I never knew his name. Perhaps . . . Barry? He worked for my father, before I was born. My father was a greengrocer, you know."

"And you, Celia, isn't it true you was a top model?"

"No."

"Now, Celia, I seen all your pictures when you were a famous model." Mandy gestures to the dresser, which is covered in framed photographs. "Celia and I, we like to look over the photographs, she like to tell me about the beautiful clothes she wore. Gillem, maybe you can fill me in on this. Somebody told me it was your mum who invented the miniskirt. Is that true?"

"No," the woman says, very definitely. "That's not true. I . . . I helped my parents in their shop. I knew the . . . I was very good at the . . . at working the cash . . . the cash register. I was very good . . . I was very good at giving people, giving customers *the correct change*. I can't . . ." She shakes her head in sudden distress. "I can't . . ." Her eyes return to the television screen, and she is silent.

"Celia, don't you think your granddaughter looks just like you?" Mandy demands, loudly. "How come you never tell me about your granddaughter named after you, living in France? We got to get a picture of her, up on your dresser. Where do you live, darling? You live in Paris?"

"No," says Rat. "I live in the South of France, by the sea."

"You hear that, Celia? Your granddaughter lives by the seaside in France. Don't you think it's about time you and I took a little trip to the South of France together to visit her? Wouldn't that be nice?"

The woman mutters something under her breath.

"What's that, Celia? You better speak up so your visitors can hear."

The woman makes an effort to speak. Her tone expresses an almost bottomless disgust and weariness. *"I don't know who they are.* I don't know who *any* of you are. I don't know why they keep bringing them around. She's less hideous than the last one they brought, but I can't bear the way they dress and their shrill voices." She addresses Rat directly, for the first time. "You might as well just go back into your box and leave me be. All of you."

"What box?" asks Rat, curious.

"THAT box!" shouts the woman, suddenly furious, pointing a finger at the television set. "Go on, now, scoot! Back in your box! SCOOOOT!"

She waves her arms at them, making pushing motions, till Gillem and Rat finally make their good-byes and leave her.

Mandy follows them down the corridor to the elevator. By the elevator is a group of old ladies in wheelchairs, their expressions running from vacant to peculiarly malignant. Rat tries not to look. She tries not to breathe in the canned institutional odor. From open doors, you hear the contrasting clamor of a half-dozen televisions.

"Don't mind your gran," Mandy says to Rat, while they are

waiting for the elevator to arrive. "It's nothing personal. She doesn't have her head right, and it make her angry, sometimes."

"How has she been this week?" Gillem asks.

"Oh, today is a *good* day. Yesterday, you couldn't get a word out of her. Wouldn't eat, wouldn't move, just lying there, head flopped down on her chest like she was asleep, only her eyes are wide-open staring. I gave her a little sponge bath, I did her nails, usually she like that—this time, nothing."

Gillem gives a sigh that's more of a groan. "I don't know what we'd do without you, Mandy."

"I love your mum. Sometimes she can be a riot. You just have to get used to her little ways."

Gillem and Rat are both silent on the elevator ride down to the lobby. Rat has never seen her father looking quite so grim. When they're back out on the street, however, he gives Rat a pale smile. And suddenly, they are both laughing. It's the semihysterical laughter of people who are shamefacedly relieved because they are alive and well, and have safely escaped prison or the hospital or the madhouse or the grave.

"Come on, young lady," Gillem says, taking her by the arm. "Let's . . . *scoot!*"

They break into a run. His legs are longer, but she's more in practice. Passersby stare, because these are days when people are very jittery, when someone running suggests a new civil emergency, cause for collective panic. Gillem and Rat are still laughing when they reach the Euston Road.

"Whew," he says, stopping to draw a deep breath. "What do you need, to get that out of your system? Me, afterwards, it's either a long hard ramble or a double whisky. Both at the same time, and I end up in a ditch, very happy."

"Ramble?" suggests Rat.

"Let's start with the ramble, then we can move on to the whisky."

He hails a black cab. "Hampstead Heath, please."

. . .

"So that's the story," says Gillem. "This is where it's ended. When she first started losing the threads of her mind—when I'd cleaned up my own life and was feeling immensely self-righteous—I thought it was some kind of judgment on her life of excess. It took me a long time to accept that what's so terrifying about disease is its impartiality.

"Now I come away from visiting her and I think, if only I had the decency to put a pillow over her head. Because what you see today is nothing. People with Alzheimer's, they spend much of their lives in a state of . . . abject terror. She is going to be robbed of everything human slowly, implacably, drop by drop. She's sixty-three years old and she's strong as an ox. The women in her family live forever. She could go on for another thirty years."

He lets out another deep groaning sigh. "I don't know why I think Hell's in Baghdad. I should be drawing the residents of Blythevale House."

They are sitting over coffee and cakes at an old-fashioned pastry shop in Hampstead. Rat reaches out and takes his hand and he grips it tight for a moment before letting go.

"I feel I gave you a rather unfair impression of my mother the other day, calling her amoral," he continues. "She was one of the most extraordinary people I've ever met. Utterly allergic to cant. Quite strict in her own way, too. There were things she loved, and she wanted me to know about them, too. She didn't mind bad behavior, but she couldn't stand ignorance. I'm sorry you didn't meet her when she was still there, mentally. You would have enjoyed each other. You've got some of the same freedom."

Rat nods. That moment's joy at escaping from the nursing home has been succeeded by monumental depression. She feels too depressed even to hold up her head. It takes a tremendous effort to force out the words. "What sort of things was it she loved?"

"She loved continental Europe. She wanted me to speak other languages—not to be a British philistine. She loved the sea. She swam even when it was very cold. She was a beautiful swimmer. To watch her dive off the rocks . . . I have very strong memories of her in those inlets south of Collioure. Where you told me your dynamite factory was.

"She loved paintings, certain periods of painting. Nineteenth-century French painting, Daumier, Toulouse-Lautrec, Degas: the satirists. She thought the French very shrewd and witty. Certain poets. We used to read Shakespeare plays together. She liked *Antony and Cleopatra,* she said, because they were such shameless old fools.

"She loved food. You wouldn't think it because she was so thin, but she ate like a horse. Couldn't cook, but she loved to eat. The last trip I took with her, just after Artemio was born, we went to San Sebastián, to the film festival. It was autumn, we'd walk on the beach. There was a tea shop she loved where you got the best hot chocolate in the world.

"She was already getting a bit Alzheimerish, although I thought at the time it was her liver that was shot—you had to hang on to everything for her, her passport, her wallet, she was always hiding cash in odd places in the hotel room and forgetting it, she couldn't follow the plots to films anymore. I'd take her to a film in the afternoon and afterwards I'd have to explain it all to her, and by dinner, she'd be saying, Weren't we going to a film today. And she'd stopped eating real food, you'd take her to these wonderful Basque restaurants, and either she couldn't take a bite, or she'd suddenly start trying to shovel up the soup with her fingers. But she still had a sweet tooth."

"What's a 'greengrasser'?"

"A what? Oh. A *marchand de légumes.*"

"Was that what her parents did? My mama always said her family were aristocrats or something."

"No. Her father was a stockbroker. Neither aristocrat nor greengrocer. There was another family called Kidd, she didn't exactly discourage the idea we might be related, but I don't think they were any relation." He pauses. "It was called the Avenida Veinte-something."

"What was?"

"The hot-chocolate shop in San Sebastián. I think that's the most words I've ever said at one time in my life! Shall I shut up for a bit?"

They both laugh.

"Not yet."

He reflects. "That's what I want for Artemio." He hesitates. "That's what I think about for you, when you talk about dropping out of school."

"What?" She's completely lost now. "Hot chocolate?"

"A cultivated mind."

"*Putain,*" Rat groans.

His eyebrows shoot up, but he smiles and continues, doggedly, "Things you love that are—inside you. Poems you know by heart. Paintings. The sea. You had a brush with death the other day. Imagine you had died—what would you picture as you lay dying? Imagine you were locked up in solitary confinement for years, like those men in the photographs, the prisoners at Abu Ghraib. No MP3, no Internet. No books, even. Torture, humiliation, interrogators trying to destabilize you, make you forget who you are. That's what my mother tried to give me: a kind of imaginative self-sufficiency.

"You know, the world we live in, Artemio's going to this superprestigious school where all the other parents look at education as this kind of brand-name chit you cash in fifteen years later for a job in the City. Why else would you be paying ten thousand pounds a year? For me, it's a way of stocking your mind with things that would keep you from going mad if you were ever sent to Guantánamo Bay. Does that sound very pretentious or self-dramatizing?"

"Yes, it does," says Rat. "Very. Let me get this straight." She looks at him, trying to master her irritation with this lecturing male. "You think a prisoner who has gone to a private school survives better than a prisoner who hasn't?"

He thinks. "No, but perhaps the same person . . ."

"And look at your mother, she loved Shakespeare and paintings, she was so cultured, and—and—now—"

"True. It's all chance. But I want you to have the best chance."

"Right," Rat says, abruptly. All the anger she thought she'd vanquished is flaming up again. "You know, all of a sudden you have all these ideas about the paintings and poetry I should be remembering next time I die in a terrorist bombing. But you know, you didn't exactly have a very hands-on sort of role in my education. In fact, last time we talked, you made it quite clear you wished I hadn't been born."

He groans. "I didn't say anything that idiotic, did I?"

"You did."

He stares down at his plate. Then he answers very slowly, like someone walking across a rope bridge. One word wrongly placed and they might both fall into the abyss. "It's true I wasn't there for you, I didn't want to see you or know about you. Because I was an idiot, and I was frightened. But now that we've met, I realize what a loss that was. For me, for Kate, for Artemio, for all of us. And you can either accept that. Or not."

Rat's lower lip is stuck out, as if she were a small child sulking, and for a moment it makes Gillem want to laugh. His own mouth trembles with the effort of staying serious, and then he's scared she's going to cry, because then he might, too, but no, thank God, she isn't.

"All right," she says. "But no lectures about my education. You've got no right."

"No lectures," he agrees, but they both feel awkward. He

pays the bill quickly, and they ride home in the taxi in a painful silence.

"We're going home?" asks Morgan.

"Yeah, because Thierry's packed up and gone."

"What if he comes back?"

"It's different, now that Mama realizes he's a slimeball, too. We're all on the same side. He's a coward; he's scared of Mama. He's always been scared of Mama. With Mama on our side, there's nothing he can do to us."

Morgan is down on his knees. His eye is at ground level. He is lining up one marble with another larger marble. He tosses it. Crack. The smaller marble skids across the oak floorboards and disappears under the sofa. The sofa that's piled with needlework cushions portraying birds of paradise and dragons and trellised grapevines, embroidered fifty years ago by a stockbroker's wife in Wiltshire.

"Don't you want to go home?"

"I dunno. What time of year is it at home?"

"It's summer, like here. But hotter. Fig time. Peach time. Ice creams on the beach time."

"Is school out?"

"Yeah, school's out."

"Do you think marbles are in fashion back home, too?"

"I dunno. If not, you can always make them the fashion."

Morgan sighs. "I'll miss that Game Boy of Artemio's. How are we gonna get back? Are we gonna have the same trouble getting across the border?"

"Nah, getting back into France is easy. Gillem's gonna put us on a plane to Perpignan."

Morgan looks up. His face is suddenly illuminated. He raises his sinewy golden arms like wings. "We're going to fly?"

"No, stupid. The plane is."

.　　.　　.

Rat is sitting in a deck chair under the umbrella, converting her threadbare corduroys into a pair of shorts.

Once the corduroys were navy blue. Now they've faded to some pigeon shade of pinkish lavender, and there's a rip in the seat. First she cuts them along the latitude she's marked with a Magic Marker and sews a hem, and then she searches through Kate's sewing box for a piece of cloth to cover the rip.

Gillem is sitting on the grass, reading the paper and watching her work. Usually it's she who sits and watches him while he works; today it's the other way around.

Rat chooses a square of pale green for her patch which he recognizes as coming from an old pair of overalls of Kate's. It's pleasant to imagine her wearing this little scrap of Hawkridge Road back in Saint Féliu—a piece of Them.

"You sew like a man," says Gillem.

"What's that mean—messy?" She smiles back at him.

"Big stitches, but you can tell they will hold," he says. "Do you ever wear dresses? I should give you some of my mother's clothes, next time you come to London."

Gillem goes back to his newspaper, but he's finding it hard to concentrate. Tomorrow he will take Rat and Morgan out to the airport. He hates airports almost as much as he hates good-byes. The sadness, the incipient panic of loss is something he can feel in his lungs.

Two months ago, he didn't know this girl. Now he feels as if she's flesh of his flesh, as if she'd caused him pains of childbirth. He wished she had, because he will never be able to recoup the years he missed.

Tomorrow night she will be back in Saint Féliu with that slippery mother of hers. He wishes she weren't going. Beneath Rat's stories of an idyllic childhood roaming the beaches till nightfall with her friends, he can detect an underlying narrative of neglect, of rootless families scourged by alcohol, joblessness, mental illness, violence. He doesn't want to relinquish her to a world in which it is unremarkable for a child to quit school at fifteen.

She will go back to where she comes from, and he will follow her; he will show up in her life again and again, shadowing her with his awkward undeclarative kind of love. She will take him to her secret places, the dynamite factory, the Nazi bunker, she will introduce him to the friends she has just begun to tell him about.

And he too over time will take her to the places he loves—to Rome, to San Sebastián, perhaps even to Ghent to look at the *Mystic Lamb*. And perhaps, if he plays his cards right, she'll come live with them again. Perhaps he can even get her to like school. Perhaps, if he's very patient, very underhand, he can change the way the story goes, so she too doesn't end up a single mother in an out-of-season beach resort.

And perhaps one day, she will be able to speak of Gillem to her friends as other young women speak of their fathers. Not as a glamorous stranger, but as the person who taught you how to drive and who used to nag you to turn your music down, the person you complain to when you can't figure out your taxes or when your mother's gone completely mad. Somebody irritating, interfering, and infinitely familiar.

He thinks he'd like that.

A NOTE ABOUT THE AUTHOR

Fernanda Eberstadt is the author of four novels—*The Furies, When the Sons of Heaven Meet the Daughters of the Earth, Low Tide,* and *Isaac and His Devils*—and one book of nonfiction, *Little Money Street,* an account of Gypsy music in Perpignan. She was born in New York City and graduated from Magdalen College, Oxford. She lives between London and France with her husband and two children.

A NOTE ON THE TYPE

This book was set in Fournier, a typeface named for Pierre Simon Fournier fils (1712–1768), a celebrated French type designer. Fournier's type is considered transitional in that it drew its inspiration from the old style, yet was ingeniously innovational, providing for an elegant, legible appearance. In 1925 his type was revived by the Monotype Corporation of London.

Composed by Creative Graphics, Allentown, Pennsylvania
Printed and bound by RR Donnelley, Harrisonburg, Virginia
Designed by Wesley Gott